MH370 AIRLINER DOWN!

A FLIGHT PLAN GONE WRONG

A.A. ZICARD AND J.E. HOLLING

outskirts press

Dedication

In memory of my dear friend and
book writing accomplice,
the late James E. Holling
Truly a calm and gentle soul

malaysia airlines

Boeing 777-200

Interior Arrangement

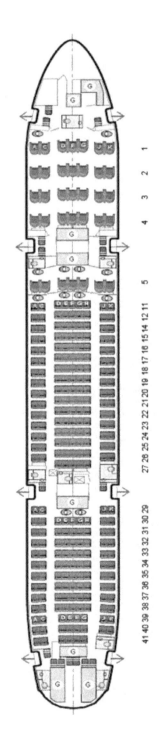

Cabin

 Business class

Economy class

 Lavatory

→ Emergency exits

G Galleys

Bassinets

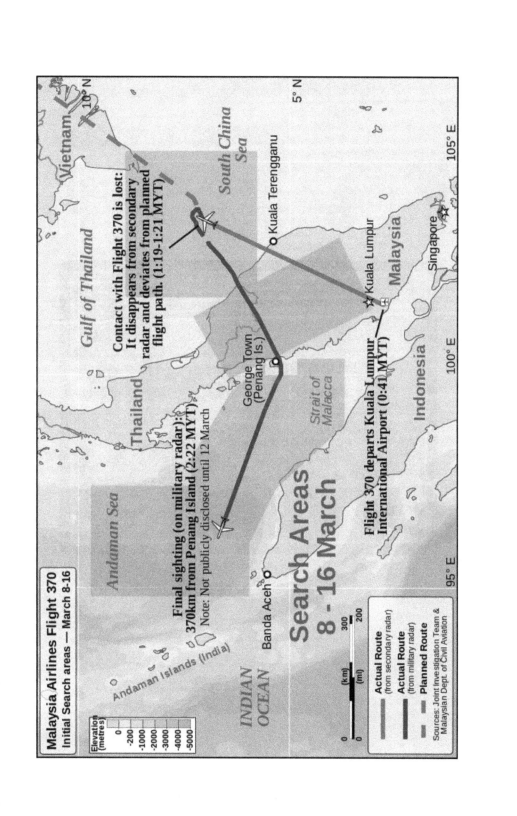

Malaysia Airlines Flight 370
Initial Search areas — March 8-16

Elevation
(metres)

0
-200
-1000
-2000
-3000
-4000
-5000

Vietnam

10° N

South China
Sea

Gulf of Thailand

○ Kuala Terengganu

5° N

Contact with Flight 370 is lost:
It disappears from secondary
radar and deviates from planned
flight path. (1:19-1:21 MYT)

Thailand

Andaman Sea

George Town
(Penang Is.)

Strait of
Malacca

☆ Kuala Lumpur

Malaysia

⌂

☆ Singapore

Final sighting (on military radar):
370km from Penang Island (2:22 MYT)
Note: Not publicly disclosed until 12 March

Indonesia

Flight 370 departs Kuala Lumpur
International Airport (0:41 MYT)

Andaman Islands (India)

INDIAN
OCEAN

Banda Aceh ○

Search Areas
8 - 16 March

100° E

105° E

95° E

0   300
(km)
0   200
(mi)

Actual Route
(from secondary radar)

Actual Route
(from military radar)

Planned Route

Sources: Joint Investigation Team &
Malaysian Dept. of Civil Aviation

Advanced home flight simulator

LIST OF CHARACTERS

Zara Ahmari (senior captain, Malaysia Airlines)
Nurul (Zara's estranged wife), Jamal (Zara's son), Misha (Zara's daughter)
Haziq Syed (senior captain, Zara's best friend)
Aishah (Zara's girlfriend)
Hashim Merican (Malaysia Airlines, first officer)
Jack Walker (agent, Central Intelligence Agency); John Wilson (Jack Walker's alias)
Josh Edwards (director of Operations, CIA)
Addison Stark (agent, Australian Secret Intelligence Service); Susan Villa (Addison Stark's alias)
Adam Cussins (Northrop Grumman flight test engineer)
Lieutenant Rob Barry (SEAL platoon leader)
Raheem (Taliban spy)
Amir Sharif Kahn (Taliban warlord)
Rehyan Abed (Iran MOI agent)
Farzad Bahadori (second Iran MOI agent)
Peter Chen (Hang Shen Import-Export Company, China MSIS)
David Lee (Hang Shen Import-Export Company, China, MSIS; CIA agent)
Shen Chow (leader of the Chinese technical team, China MSIS)
Ahmad Osman (Penang freight forwarder, paid informer)
Hope Lee (lawyer, activist daughter of MH370 passenger)
Noah Jacobs (freelance, investigative reporter)
Mike Jacobs (brother of Noah Jacobs)
Ralph Henderson (AP, *Southeast Asia* news editor)
Minh (Royal Malaysian Police detective)
Siti Mawar (MAS Human Resources department)
Ana Miles (Australian Transportation Safety Bureau investigator)
Brian Sloan (National Transportation Safety Board investigator)

PROLOGUE

Malaysia
Early Morning, March 08, 2014

It was a quiet, early Saturday morning in the Kuala Lumpur Area Control Center (KLACC). Air traffic controller Abdul Hoqq sat in front of his two radar scopes. Along with another controller named Singh managing traffic tonight, Hoqq was the younger controller, still not senior enough to get off the night shift. The team also included a junior controller trainee and a data planning administrative controller. It was a sleepy time of night, and air traffic had diminished to less than half of the regular traffic during the daytime hours.

Abdul's air traffic control (ATC) job was to keep the airplanes separated from each other, thus avoiding collisions. Controllers are taught to know the performance capabilities of the various aircraft types. They continuously manage an ever-changing picture with different aircraft types—crisscrossing in all directions—often to differing destinations. In this regard, controllers have accepted a great responsibility for the flying public.

A controller watches his assigned "airspace" (a sector) and keeps the aircraft five miles apart horizontally and one thousand feet vertically. To do that, pilots and controllers must establish and maintain direct radio communication with each other. Pilots must understand and follow the controller's instructions. A severe mistake causing death has driven more than one controller off the job, with even the consideration of suicide.

Malaysian Airlines Flight MH370, whose destination was Beijing, China, was airborne from Kuala Lumpur Airport only a few minutes ago. She was heading northeast on its assigned route, proceeding directly to a navigation fix called IGARI. IGARI was a reporting point high above the South China Sea. MH370 was about to leave Malaysian Airspace at IGARI, where Vietnam airspace began. This sector boundary requires an orchestrated "handoff" of responsibility from KL Control to Ho Chi Minh Control (HCM). To officially take responsibility for MH370's separation and control, HCM would need to see MH370 on its radar and establish radio communications with the flight.

At 1:19 a.m. local time, Malaysian controller Hoqq contacted MH370. "Malaysian three seven zero, this is Lumpur Control. You are approaching IGARI. Radar service terminated. Contact Ho Chi Minh frequency one two zero decimal nine." Four seconds later, the pilot from MH370 acknowledged those instructions with, "Good night. Malaysian Three Seven Zero."

MH370 was leaving Malaysian airspace and was gone for the night. Out of sight and out of mind. Hearing that radio transmission reply from MH370, the KLACC controller Hoqq assumed his responsibility for MH370 was complete—a handoff event like one thousand times before. Little did Hoqq ever understand that this was the last recorded transmission anyone would receive from MH370.

In the cockpit, completing his radio call, the captain of MH370 closed his eyes and took a deep breath. Opening his eyes again, he stared blankly at his instruments for a moment. Then he began to shake his head to gain focus. The pain he suffered was too great to endure. He thought, *It's time to start; no turning back now*.

The HCM air traffic controller saw MH370 approaching Vietnamese airspace at the IGARI intersection. In a few minutes, HCM expected the flight to "check in" with a radio call initiating contact, a handoff event like one thousand times before. But distracted for a time by another controller's question, he did not see the MH370 symbols disappear off his screen. Then, suddenly, the HCM controller remembered, *Did MH370 call in? Oh no! Where did MH370 go? I don't see him now*. There was no radar "blip" on his screen for MH370, nor any ident tag showing a call sign "MH370," nor the assigned altitude.

It had already been several minutes since MH370 should have reported by radio to HCM. The controller immediately broadcasted several calls to the plane. "Malaysian 370, this is Ho Chi Minh. Are you on frequency?" Silence. He called MH370 a second time. Again, no radio contact. The controller was growing increasingly concerned. He had not established communications with MH370; he had no way to control the aircraft, nor could he verify its where-abouts. This had never happened to him before. The HCM control-ler switched to another strategy, calling a nearby unrelated plane, asking him to call MH370 independently on the universal air-to-air frequencies. Still, there was no response. The silence grew louder!

Highly agitated now, the HCM controller picked up a direct phone line connected to KLACC. At 0138 a.m., he called his coun-terpart, controller Hoqq, at KLACC and, speaking a little too fast, asked, "Where is MH370? He never reported on frequency, and I no longer show him in radar contact."

Abdul was startled; his stomach dropped. *"What the—What happened? Why is HCM calling me?"* Although he had not been watching continuously in the last eighteen minutes after instruct-ing three-seventy to contact HCM, the Malaysia Airlines' flight to Beijing disappeared off his radar screen for no apparent reason.

Hoqq responded to the Vietnamese controller on the direct line, "I don't see MH370 either. We said goodbye twenty minutes ago, and he has never called back on this frequency. Why didn't you call me sooner?"

HCM simply responded, "I have no contact with MH370."

Hoqq, looking around for another answer, thought, *Maybe some-thing went wrong with my display.* He called out to his fellow con-troller sitting nearby, "Singh, do you have MH370 on your display?"

"No, I have negative contact with three-seventy. Haven't seen him for a while."

A feeling of dread welled inside Hoqq. *What happened to MH370? Even though he should be in Vietnam airspace, I usually see the traffic for a period after they leave the Malaysian border. Have I done something wrong? It's been over eighteen minutes since we talked last.*

Hoqq was very worried. MH370 was gone! *This just doesn't happen!* He kept looking at the radar screen, unconsciously hoping it would now appear. *Was there an explosion? Did it come apart in the air? Was the airliner in the water below? And why didn't the pilots of MH370 call if they had troubles?* His mind quickly played the events of the last minutes over again, and the sector handoff to HCM seemed perfectly normal—until HCM called back!

Hoqq keyed his microphone to talk on the last frequency used by him and MH370. With his voice shaking and the volume of his voice almost screaming into the microphone, he started, "Lumpur Control calling MH370. Lumpur Control calling MH370. Do you read me? Acknowledge! Acknowledge!" Nobody answered. MH370 had vanished! The silence almost made his heart stop.

Singh, sitting next to Hoqq while managing his assigned sector, leaned over to one side and suggested, "I wonder if the air force controllers at Butterworth Air Base have any info on MH370. Their radars are more powerful than ours."

Hoqq's mind had only partially processed what Singh was suggesting. "I don't know. I've never talked to them before." He never realized that the air force was watching this same event unravel before their eyes.

Butterworth, a Royal Malaysian Air Force Base, was situated five miles from the town of Butterworth in Penang province. This base was built to respond to aerial threats to Malaysian national security. The station used powerful military radar units and a squadron of U.S.-supplied F-18 fighter aircraft to accomplish its mission.

Tonight, an RMAF air traffic controller sat at his console and monitored air traffic in the country's northern sector, surveying the neighboring borders of Vietnam, Cambodia, Thailand, and Indonesia to the west.

The north sector controller called out, "Sir? I think we have a problem." His supervisor, who stood a few feet behind him, turned and replied, "What's wrong, Sergeant?"

"Sir, a few seconds ago, I had a commercial aircraft—MH370—displaying tracking information as it approached the IGARI intersection, and now, it's gone. I mean—I still see a primary 'blip,' but its ID, altitude, and heading information are gone—like someone turned off the transponder. I assume it is a civilian transport aircraft—it's big enough—but it is flying suspiciously parallel along the Vietnam, Thai, and the Malaysian border."

"Or maybe he had a communication systems failure? Did he squawk 7500 or 7600 or transmit a distress call on the Guard frequency?"

"No, sir. No distress calls and no distress transponder codes. It looks like he made a left turn westbound, coming in from the South China Sea, and is now heading right at us. Should we scramble the F-18s and check him out?" Scrambling fighters for an unusual, noncommunicating aircraft had almost become an international protocol since the 9/11 attack in New York City years earlier.

"Hmm, I'd have to run that up the chain of command, and it's the middle of the night. If I wake the general, and this turns out to be nothing important, I may as well kiss my career goodbye."

"Yes, sir, but what if the plane is not friendly, or it's been hijacked? What if it turns toward Kuala Lumpur? You know, those Petronas Towers—"

"Not likely, Sergeant. If it were a hijacking, he would have squawked the emergency code 7500. If he lost all communication capability, he would have squawked 7600. No, just stand by and keep him in sight. You just keep doing your job, Sergeant, and I'll do mine."

The sergeant returned his attention to the radar screen. He thought about calling his counterpart in Lumpur Air Traffic Control via their direct telephone line to ask questions about MH370 but decided to "follow orders" after his supervisor's rebuke. He had a bad taste in his mouth. Something was very wrong with his unannounced radar intruder.

PART 1

The Pilot . . . the Package

CHAPTER ONE

Kuala Lumpur, Malaysia
EARLY JANUARY 2014

Captain Zara Ahmari watches his copilot put the Boeing 777 into a descent for the Kuala Lumpur Airport. It has been a smooth and uneventful return flight from Bali, Indonesia. He knew his inattention in the cockpit could be fatal, and he forced himself to pay attention, but his mind began to wander again . . .

I'm so tired, he thought, *but my mind races. What's going to happen to me now?* In less than two hours, he will be home—alone again, in the empty rooms and hallways of his beautiful suburban home. Nurul, his estranged wife, had left him eight months ago. His mind kept going back to their last argument. *Nurul stood in the open front door of their home and screamed, "I'm not going to put up with your womanizing any longer! I'm tired of the sideways glances our friends give me and their whispering behind my back. Go back to your airline whores—I'm leaving."* She slammed the door behind her, and the couple had not talked since she left. His wife discovered his numerous flirtations and indiscretions with various airline flight attendants. She confronted him, and he had no answers. She now spent most of her time in their original hometown, Penang, a four-hour drive north of Kuala Lumpur, while Zara remained in KL. After experiencing thirty-plus years of married life, he felt confused, sad, and alone.

He had some success learning to compartmentalize his unwanted dark thoughts in more recent months when he entered the cockpit. Lately, however, he found himself distracted and forget-ful. As a Malaysia Airlines (MAS) senior captain, he could easily control and lighten his cockpit workload with the careful delega-tion of cockpit procedures. He would assign pilot flying (PF) duties to his copilot. At the same time, he would take the responsibility of pilot monitoring (PM) duties—observing the instruments, ongo-ing cockpit procedures, reading checklists, and responding to radio calls. That arrangement worked to his advantage and helped him mask his temporary sad outlook on life. Piloting an aircraft—any aircraft—required the pilot's undivided attention, but he found him-self preoccupied more and more about past and recent misfortunes. Today's trip to Bali was suddenly unsettling when it triggered one very traumatic memory.

Nurul had become pregnant immediately after their arranged teenage marriage in 1981. About the same time, Zara tested for pos-sible selection as an air cadet for Malaysian Airlines, the country's flag carrier. That job would be an excellent social and economic opportunity for his new family. Just twenty years old and with no flying experience, the airline selected Zara to become a new copi-lot. As part of the commitment, Zara would spend eighteen months at school in the Philippines for initial pilot training. That same month, his son, Jamal, was born. Nurul would not accompany Zara to Manila, remaining in Penang, living with her family during his absence. Every three months, he would return home for a week to be with his family.

Upon his graduation and return to Malaysia, they resumed their family life together, now residing in Kuala Lumpur, the headquar-ters for Malaysia Airlines. The family developed friendships with other airline employees who had small children, and they social-ized at private parties and company gatherings as Zara's airline ca-reer progressed. They joined the local Muslim mosque and enjoyed quality local schools for the children. Nurul had one more child, a daughter, Misha.

Zara and Nurul were happy and looking forward to a long life together when tragedy struck. Their daughter drowned while on a family vacation in Bali. Walking on the beach with the children, Nurul talked to Jamal, their oldest child, adjacent to the resort hotel. She turned her back for what she thought was only an instant while Misha played in a tidal pool. When Zara returned to the beach with food for the family picnic, he saw his two-year-old daughter floating face down. "Oh no. Misha!"

Zara dropped the food tray, ran to her small, limp body, and lifted her out of water. "Misha! Misha!" he screamed.

Nurul, alerted by the commotion, rushed to her husband's side. "Oh, my baby," Nurul panicked.

Zara lay her on the sand, placed his ear next to Misha's mouth, and realized she wasn't breathing. He had CPR training and began chest compressions while he said a silent prayer. *Please, Allah, help me save my child's life.* Other beachgoers started to congregate around Zara and Misha. Zara yelled to anyone who would listen, "Someone, please, call for help! My baby is not breathing."

Through her sobs, Nurul pleaded with her husband to keep trying to save their baby girl. Paramedics arrived in ten minutes and took over the resuscitation efforts. Nurul clung to Zara's arm, hopefully optimistic that the paramedics would be successful. A shockwave of fear and desperation coursed through her body when one paramedic stood and approached the couple.

"I'm sorry. We tried our best, but—"

"NO!" Nurul screamed. "NO! NOT my baby girl!" Zara steadied her as her legs buckled, and she sank into his arms, sobbing. Zara was speechless. *This can't be happening.*

Captain Zara sat motionless in the cockpit and stared straight ahead. A tear formed in the corner of his eye as his mind replayed the events of that tragic day. Since that time, a simple knowing glance between Zara and Nurul would remind the couple of their lost child, with unspoken recriminations and a pang of consuming guilt. Zara's marriage and relationship with Nurul had changed forever on that tragic day. The trauma of Misha's death resulted in less communication, more silence, and less interaction with the remaining child: the entire young family was ripped apart.

His copilot glanced across the cockpit at him, waited a couple of seconds, then glanced again. Zara's expressionless face maintained a straight-ahead stare.

"Sir? Sir, is everything all right? You didn't acknowledge Lumpur Tower's last call." Without acknowledging the copilot's question, Zara picked up his microphone and returned the tower's call verifying their position on the approach.

Coming back to the present from his brief daydream, Zara refocused as the speedy B777 intercepted the final approach course to Kuala Lumpur. Zara let his copilot continue to manipulate the large jet's movements, intercepting the final glide path to landing. They were minutes away from touchdown and putting the finishing touches on yet another uneventful daily roundtrip flight to Bali and back. Zara read the Before-Landing checklist while his copilot verified the required task and then responded with a "Check."

"Captain, we just passed the outer marker. Do you want the controls and land her?"

"No, you're doing fine. It's your turn to land."

Zara's copilot, happy to get the landing practice, nonetheless sensed something was wrong, as if he were flying alone. The copilot landed smoothly straight ahead, and they taxied the aircraft to the gate as instructed by ATC. After deplaning the craft, they both said goodbye and left the airport to return home for the evening. The copilot had flown with Captain Zara numerous times, but now, the captain's behavior signaled something had changed. He shrugged. *I'll let it go*, he thought. *Everyone has a bad day once in a while.*

CIA Headquarters, Langley, Virginia
DECEMBER 2013

Jack Walker sat in a metal chair with insufficient seat padding that caused him to distort his lean, six-foot-two-inch frame while trying to find a comfortable position. He had a two o'clock appointment with his boss, Josh Edwards, assistant director of operations, and a glance at the black-and-white plastic wall clock confirmed what he already knew—his boss was late.

Damn these government-issued chairs, he thought. *I think one of the spec requirements written into the purchase contract for these things is, "must be uncomfortable."* "Come on, Josh—where the hell are you?"

Loud footsteps outside the closed office door brought Jack's attention back to the matter at hand, and before he could twist all the way around in his seat, the door opened.

Edwards stepped into the room and apologized. "Sorry for being late. The director had my ear, and I couldn't tell him I was late for an important meeting. Well, I could have said that, but I like my job." Walker smirked when he heard Edwards's comment because he knew from firsthand experience that Director Chase was a bureaucratic hard ass.

"All right, let's get down to business. We have a job for you. I know you've been chomping at the bit to get back in the field, and I think you'll like this assignment. First, let me give you some background. You've probably heard about the Northrop Grumman contract we've partnered on with DARPA—Defense Advanced Research Projects Agency. They—"

"Hold on a second," Walker interrupted. "I've heard some general information, but can we take a deeper dive into the details here, so I feel like a partner in this and not just an onlooker?"

"Fair enough—I'll tell you as much as I know, which is limited to the contract requirements and some general technical stuff. The technical experts are at Northrop Grumman, and you will be traveling to Afghanistan with one of them." Edwards's comment piqued Walker's interest.

"Yes, Sir, go on. I'm listening."

"N.G.'s engineers developed a multi-mission drone that learns as it performs its missions. In other words, it gets smarter the more it flies because the data it acquires, such as observed patterns of behavior and changes in geographical features, is constantly updated and uploaded into the artificial intelligence database. It's designed to operate on its own or in a swarm. When they swarm, they also learn from each other. The development has reached the point of maturity where the DOD is ready for a field eval—that's DOD-speak for field combat evaluation."

Walker smiled a knowing smile because he knew the government, in general, and the DOD, in particular, had an acronym for everything, and it's like learning a new language.

"Did I say something that amused you?"

"No, not at all, boss. It's nothing."

"As I was saying—the drone's been evaluated on the range at White Sands, but the air force program manager wants a real-world operational evaluation, and that's where we come in. You'll deploy, with an N.G. engineer, to a forward-operating base in Afghanistan. He has the test plan, and he'll be responsible for conducting the test. Your part in this is to make sure everything and everyone gets back here in one piece."

"Let me stop you there for a minute. I get the AI part. Robots that learn are the new up-and-coming thing, but why do we need autonomous, swarming drones on the battlefield? It seems to me that our boots on the ground and our eyes in the sky are a better combination than trusting robots to get the job done, right?"

"Yes, to a point, but the foreign policy has changed. The old approach to nation-building is changing. The administration doesn't want to engage in endless wars, but they recognize the danger of creating a vacuum by leaving the battlefield. That vacuum will suck in undesirable elements like the Taliban or a reconstituted ISIS if unchecked. These intelligent, armed, and swarming drones are intended to fill that vacuum and provide a previously unimagined level of security.

"The software architecture of the drones and the hardware supporting it are top secret. The information must be processed so fast—in about ten milliseconds—that it required a new processing chip, and it didn't stop there. The computer engineers then integrated that chip in a network pathway they developed that mimicked the neural networks in the human brain. Instead of using an extremely fine wire to connect the artificial neurons in the AI network, they used optic fibers a tenth the size of a human hair. This made their 'package' impervious to electronic jamming. The aero-engineers then developed a small, stealthy airframe to carry the package, and the final product is an intelligent drone the size of an old VW Beetle that is both invisible to radar and able to learn."

Walker sat in silence for a moment with his chin resting on the palm of his hand. Then he took a deep breath and let out a slow swoosh of air. "Wow, that sounds impressive. So, besides being a babysitter, do I have any other role to play in this futuristic-fantasy-battlefield mission?" he said with a touch of sarcasm in his voice.

"Don't be cute, Walker—this is your chance to redeem yourself with the director after that close call in Venezuela—"

"Hey Boss, that wasn't my fault. How was I supposed to know that stranger at the bar was a Chinese spy, and we were both after the same gold shipment?"

"Well, you were supposed to know, and besides, it was your wandering eye that distracted you long enough for him to spike your drink."

One year ago, the event in Venezuela haunted Walker because he made a simple mistake. Then he got sucker punched!

He recalled the details of that evening in Caracas. It caused him to squirm a bit in his seat. He shadowed a Venezuelan treasury official who had tried to smuggle one hundred million dollars of gold bullion out of the country. Walker followed the official to a strip club, and while sitting at the bar, he was distracted by a partially clad dancer. The dancer smiled at him as she passed—Walker automatically smiled back—and he followed her with his eyes as she took the stage. That brief moment of inattention gave someone enough time to drop a rufie in Walker's drink. Walker realized soon after that he was drugged but took immediate action to blunt the drug effects and recovered quickly enough the following day to gain final possession of the gold.

"Listen, Walker, what's past is past. You are my best agent, so that is why you get this priority assignment. Please understand, though—Under no circumstances can any of this equipment fall into enemy hands. That includes the laptop computer, the backpack controller, the flight computer on board the drone, and that N.G. engineer. That said, we also want your opinion of the evaluation results. Not that we don't trust the DOD—which we don't—but the director wants assurance that this thing works as advertised, especially if the U.S., the United Kingdom, Australia, and certain other allies are going to pony up fifty million bucks this year to fund this damn thing."

"On a lighter note—the drone is being flown on a C-17 from Long Beach, California, to Dover Air Force Base. It arrives there tomorrow morning. The N.G. engineer—Adam Cussins—is flying commercial and arrives at Dulles Airport tomorrow at nine in the morning. Make your plans to meet his flight, and then the two of you can drive together to Dover. The drive will give you guys a couple of hours to get to know each other. Any questions?"

Walker shook his head. "Nope. I guess I better get home and start packing."

Kuala Lumpur International Airport
January 2014

After landing in Kuala Lumpur, his flying day complete, Zara made his way to the employee parking lot. Settling in for the thirty-minute drive home, he began to reminisce about happier times. He had always loved aviation, and flying was his passion. With his failed marriage, flying became his fifty-three years' lone, single satisfaction.

Zara recalled a fond moment from the past: Malaysia Airlines selecting him and a man named Haziq Sayed and twenty-six others to receive the eighteen-month cadet training. Air cadets Zara and Haziq boarded the Malaysian Airlines flight from Kuala Lumpur as strangers; they would get off the plane in Manila as friends. Both twenty years old, they were off on an adventure of epic proportions. Sitting on that plane and chatting away—even they did not realize the profound significance of the opportunity that they had been given.

They sat together again on the charter bus to Clark International Airport, a two-hour drive north of Manila, in Pampanga, Central Luzon. Clark Airport, or Clark Field as it was called in WWII, was also the home of the Philippine Air Force and an S.E. Asia base for the United States Air Force. As the bus neared Clark Field, jet airplane traffic appeared, flying low overhead. Haziq's eyes widened as he commented, "Wow, look how big those planes are! Can you believe that we will be flying those big jets someday soon?"

They stopped on the airport's perimeter and the bus parked at the Malay Flying Academy's cadet dormitory. Loosely assembled, both staff and teachers were happy to greet all twenty-eight new cadets. The dean of the academy gathered the new cadets inside the dorm's student lounge to address them.

"Welcome to the Malay Flying Academy. And special congratulations to each of you on your appointment to our unique and prestigious school. For the next eighteen months, this will be your new home for the hard work, toil, fun, and accomplishments that will lie ahead. You are on the path to becoming a professional airman, joining a cadre of airline pilots the world over, and joining the elite pilots of Malaysian Airlines. It's a great life you have chosen to begin. Welcome aboard!"

The dean offered all the resources and assistance required to make their next months of effort a resounding success. He failed to say that approximately 25 percent of this cadet class would not survive to the scheduled completion of the eighteen-month training, dropping out voluntarily or being asked to leave.

The school staff had paired students with two cadets to a room. They informed them to get their luggage to their rooms and regroup in the student lounge in thirty minutes. After a short orientation tour of the campus facilities—administration building, library, classrooms, and cafeteria—the cadets walked through a large Quonset hut out to a flight line to see several small but intimidating aircraft they would learn to fly in the coming months. They saw a line of five Cessna 172s, a popular four-seat light aircraft for their primary flight training. Also on the flight line were several Piper Arrows and a twin-engine Piper Seminole for advanced training. The students would use each plane type in succession in the months ahead to provide new lessons, using faster aircraft with increasingly complex flight systems. As he began to picture future events, Zara nudged Haziq and quipped, "What have we gotten ourselves into?"

———— ◉ ————

Zara, his drive from the KL airport to his suburban home now ending, pulled into the driveway. *Boy, that was a quick trip! I don't remember the last twenty minutes. Another daydream! But how long can I continue like this—distracted and preoccupied, with my heart in pain? What will I do with myself? My next flight is not for a week.* Shutting off the engine and getting out of the car, he walked to the doorway . . . his empty house of dread . . . his prison on earth.

CHAPTER TWO

Jack Walker, thirty-nine years old, lived alone in a two-bedroom home not far from CIA headquarters in Langley, Virginia. Born and raised in Bucks County near Philadelphia, he consistently applied maximum effort to excel in sports and the classroom. His parents encouraged him to go to college, but Jack felt he needed a break from school and decided to pursue something he had been interested in from an early age—the Navy SEALs. One month after graduation, he enlisted in the navy. Later, he was accepted into the SEAL training program. After completing the gut-wrenching twenty-four-week introductory course and the twenty-eight-week qualification program, Walker became part of the 1 percent who graduated and received the SEAL Trident Insignia.

While in the navy, he also took college courses and, upon his discharge, had most of the credits needed for a bachelor's degree in business administration. After being discharged from the navy, Walker started his career with the CIA sixteen years ago as a technical analyst.

At that time, the Chinese aerospace industry had begun its technological rise by negotiating technology transfer agreements with Boeing and Airbus, for example, and others. In exchange, the Chinese government allowed the companies to build manufacturing facilities in China, and the government opened some Chinese markets to Western products. Many second-and third-tier suppliers to the giant Western aerospace conglomerates followed suit. They shifted much of their manufacturing to China, globalization they call it, and transferred manufacturing and management technologies to gain an economic advantage through lower labor costs.

Walker's primary job function would be to scrutinize the scope of the technology transfer agreements between the Chinese companies and Western corporations and determine the business and military implications of those agreements. He believed he could use that experience as a stepping-stone to secure a management position at a large aerospace company. All that changed when he applied for a position in the field operations directorate. He was offered and took a new job in the field. He soon loved his new assignment, which included international travel opportunities and lots of intrigue. He never looked back.

However, in the months ahead, his private life stood in stark contrast to the excitement and satisfaction he derived working as an agent. He did not have immediate family nearby. Over the years, he had several romantic relationships, but they never survived the personal battle he fought when forced to choose between a girlfriend's needs and the job's requirement. The job would always win that battle, and it did not take long before the girl caught on and moved on. *Maybe someday I'll find someone who means more to me than the job*, he would often think, but so far, nothing on the horizon.

Like that girl in Australia—Addison something, whom he could not seem to forget, while her last name, he could not remember—but his picture of her remained imprinted in his brain. Years before, Jack was asked to observe an Australian Secret Intelligence Service agent's orientation and training in underwater operations, including hands-on weapons. His previous Navy SEAL experience came to mind when his boss, Josh Edwards, was asked to provide the liaison/ observer from the CIA.

The Aussies were asking for another set of eyes to help review this new one-week training course used in the curriculum for new agents. Josh thought it would be a nice reward for Jack after returning successfully from an extended mission in the Middle East. Jack thought, *Well, it can't hurt. Never been Down Under before.*

The weeklong course was a mix of classroom lectures from ASIS instructors, reading assignments, speakers, practical hands-on experiences in the training center pool, a weapons lab, a firing range, an outing to a local lake, and beach surfside action along the Australian coast. The seven new agents, both men and women, had been with ASIS less than a year, and it made Jack think back on his SEAL and CIA training. It was a challenging presentation, taken seriously by these new agents, all trying to keep their heads above water. And as always, it contained an occasional dose of Australian humor. And there was a girl named Addison, twenty-six years old, both very curvy and athletic, with beautiful blue eyes.

By the end of the week, with satisfactory completion of coursework achieved by all, it was time to relax and let down one's hair. It started at the local ASIS "designated" watering hole, the nearby Bridge Bar, with agents, instructors, and Jack as a welcome guest.

Jack had quietly watched Addison all week in class and was quickly attracted to her. Now, he was looking for an opportunity to chat her up at the bar. As she stood nearby, he leaned over and shouted in her ear, "Boy, you guys sure do know how to drink."

Addison smiled, nodding her head in the affirmative. "We have our priorities. It is said that Australian men's first recreational priority is 'drinking'—second is 'sports'—and third is 'girls,' and in that order much to an Aussie girl's dismay."

Jack chuckled and looked directly into her eyes as he softened his voice. "American men have been trained to put 'girls' first, 'drinking' second, and 'sports' comes third. *That* is the correct order!" Addison smiled again, thinking, *Is that why American men can be so attractive?*

After a straightforward conversation about the week's events, they drifted sideways and mingled with their compatriots. After another round, Jack felt his first wave of tipsy and decided maybe it was time to get something to eat. Subconsciously, he sought out Addison. He found her nearby and touched her arm to get her attention. "I'm getting a little tipsy, and I think it's time to get something to eat. Would you care to join me?"

Her mouth curved up into a slight smile, and she said, "Yes, I was thinking the same thing." Pausing momentarily, she continued,

"There's a small seafood restaurant a few blocks away that I can recommend if you like some lighter fare. Ever had green-lipped mussels or barramundi, Australia's best whitefish? And NO! They don't serve the infamous 'shrimp on the barbie' there."

With his evening beginning to take a new direction, Jack made the rounds to say goodbye, thanking all the agents and instructors for their heartfelt hospitality and making a sincere invitation for them to visit the USA.

Addison was on his arm as they stepped out to the sidewalk. Jack looked left and stepped into the street to hail a taxi. Addison quickly pulled him back, out of the way of a car coming from the right. Australians, like the U.K., drive on the wrong side of the street, compared to the U.S. protocol. Quickly realizing the situation, he spoke genuinely, "Thank you for saving my life. I'll do the same for you one day."

At dinner, the conversation flowed freely, and so did the wine. Jack and Addison could not take their eyes off each other. He asked, "How did you ever become an agent in the ASIS?"

Addison paused momentarily and began, "Okay, I'll give you the short version. Even from a young age, I have always been interested in flying. After university, I applied and was selected as a Royal Australian Air Force pilot. After basic pilot training, I was offered a slot as an intelligence officer flying in a reconnaissance squadron, flying an E7A radar plane—really, a converted Boeing 737 twin-engine jet. It was designed for radar surveillance and command and control of battlefields from above. Six months ago, while leaving the RAAF, I was offered a job as an intelligence agent with the ASIS. So here I am in another basic training for them."

"Wow, what a nice résumé you have."

Addison said, "Thank you. Hey, you've been around awhile. Do you think I'm going to like this job? The lifestyle?"

Jack, in that moment, saw his whole adult life flash before his eyes. He began recounting his history after the Navy SEALs' tour of duty ended and detailing his advancement in the CIA. "There are pros and cons to this life—plenty of excitement, traveling, and independence. Sometimes, boredom and lots of aloneness. It's not fertile ground for a traditional romantic relationship. At some point, that may become a concern. Will it be family and kids? Or will it be this professional lifestyle and national service? I'm still trying to figure it out."

"I'm just beginning to see what you mean, Jack. I do see choices to be made in the future, but for now, it's still looking to be a pretty exciting and rewarding future."

Addison heard all the words and tried to take mental career notes but couldn't take her blue eyes off his gorgeous green eyes and handsome face. And he was smiling back at her like a schoolboy. The attraction experienced by both of them for each other was beginning to boil over.

As dinner was ending, Jack said, "What shall we do next?"

Addison surprised even herself with her quick response. "Let us finish this conversation at my apartment."

Her apartment was lovely, and what happened there that night in that apartment was more than beautiful. Much to their disappointment, Jack was booked on a flight back to the U.S. the next day.

Southern California

Adam Cussins loved working for Northrop Grumman. Upon graduating from Cal Tech with a dual degree in mechanical engineering and computation and neural systems, Northrop Grumman Aerospace Systems in Pasadena, California, offered him an engineering position in their unmanned aerial vehicle development division. He liked the testing phase of development the best. N.G. staffed a test engineering department at Edwards Air Force Base in California's western Mojave Desert, and Cussins would split his time between there and Pasadena.

He looked forward to the Afghanistan operational evaluation of the new drone with both enthusiasm and trepidation. He developed the new autonomous drone for two years, and a successful OPEVAL was the last step before the DOD would authorize N.G. to begin full-scale production. On the other hand, he would be going to a combat zone to conduct the evaluation. They assured him security would be tight. He thought, *I pray to God they're right.*

Cussins had taken the red-eye flight from Los Angeles to Dulles International Airport outside Washington, D.C. It arrived at nine in the morning, and the sleep Cussins hoped to get during the six-hour flight never materialized. The cabin noise and his anxiety about his mission conspired against him, and he barely slept. He felt like a zombie when he deplaned and half-walked, half-shuffled his way to the baggage claim area. *I hope that the Walker guy is waiting for me. Maybe I can get some shut-eye on our ride to Dover.*

Walker was not thrilled about being some wet-behind-the-ears engineer's chauffeur, but orders were orders. To make matters worse, Edwards told Walker to hold a small sign with Cussins's name to expedite the process. Walker's eyes surveyed the increasing number of passengers arriving at the baggage-claim carousel. He tried to ID a person who fit his mental image of what a nerdy, whiz kid-engineer looked like. As he looked to his right, he heard a voice on his left say, "Mr. Walker? Are you my driver? I'm Adam Cussins." Walker swiveled his head in the direction of the voice and saw a young, thinly built man wearing dark-rimmed glasses— almost a head shorter than himself—who stood there holding the handle of a carry-on bag.

Walker took a moment and dressed him down with his eyes before he answered. "Yeah. Hi, I'm Jack Walker, and no, I'm not your driver; I'm your babysitter. Come on, let's go."

━━◉━━

Years Earlier
CLARK FIELD, PHILIPPINES

After the initial weeks of classroom ground school were now over, Zara and Haziq found themselves strapped into a Cessna 172 aircraft on the ramp of Clark Field. Haziq proclaimed, "Before-Start checklist complete!" Haziq, sitting in the left front seat, methodically engaged in the cockpit preparation, "setting up," as pilots called it, for his training flight today. In the right front seat sat Captain Tom, a likable, full-time instructor pilot for the Malay Flying Academy. In the back right seat behind Captain Tom was Zara, attentively watching the activity up front. Today, Haziq would be flying. Yesterday, Zara flew the two-hour lesson, and today, he observed. They all wore headsets to hear each other as they talked amongst themselves on the intercom while listening to any radio transmissions made on the tuned radio frequencies.

Captain Tom's eyes follow Haziq's actions closely, but he kept silent today, taking an occasional written note. He wanted to confirm that Haziq can complete all his procedures and control efforts, done independently with no instructor input. It will soon be time to take the bird out of the nest and let Haziq fly by himself. Today could be an especially happy milestone for the cadets and him as well. In today's briefing before flight, he had advised both Haziq and Zara that one day—soon—he would allow them to solo the aircraft around the airport traffic pattern by themselves. Last week, however, a fellow Malay air cadet was asked to leave school and return to Malaysia, as his ability to make crosswind landings became a recurring problem. After many attempts to correct the problem, school authorities gave up on him, washing him out of flight school. The tension around the campus went up one notch.

Ready for taxi instructions, Haziq tuned the VHF radio to frequency 124.3 for Clark ground control, took a deep breath, and called for "taxi clearance." Zara remarked silently that Haziq's use of English sounded pretty good to him. *Amazing*, he thought, *a Malay pilot in the Philippines, speaking required English to the third country's air traffic control.* Since day one of training, all instruction had been in English—aviation manuals, regulations, ground school lectures, oral tests, and now, flight instruction in the aircraft. After World War II, the United Nations established the International Civilian Aviation Organization (ICAO), which selected English as the language to be used worldwide. This created the uniformity needed for safe flight between all agreeing countries.

Having been tested for rudimentary English skills as prospective cadets, with Zara and Haziq scoring very high, they quickly learned their new aviation language. It seemed that English was all around them. Thank goodness for the Far East Network (FEN), a twenty-four-hour American AM radio and broadcast TV station, easily accessible for all U.S. personnel in the vicinity of Clark Air Base. The AM radio station, famous as a pop music station, could often be heard while walking down the cadets' dormitory hallway. Months from now, after attaining their commercial pilots' license, cadets would take the ICAO aviation language proficiency test, allowing pilots to operate their aircraft worldwide.

Clark ground control issued taxi instructions. Haziq responded with a full read back of instructions, released the parking brake, and began his taxi. He took another deep breath. Today would be a busy day, trying to perfect takeoffs and landings. *Zara did well yesterday, and today will be my turn.* A look of determination came on Haziq's face while thinking, *I'm getting better every landing.*

Lined up on runway 02 left, Cessna 56R began its takeoff roll. Haziq executed the takeoff, maneuvered around the traffic pattern with left turns, returned to the same runway, and made a full-stop landing. He repeated this sequence flawlessly for the following three circuits.

While taxiing back for takeoff, Captain Tom told Haziq, "Stop the aircraft here and set the parking brake. Time for you to take this airplane around the traffic pattern by yourself. Make three more circuits with a full stop landing and then return to the school's ramp. We'll meet you back at the hanger." Turning his head around to look at Zara, Captain Tom added, "Zara, we'll get out here and let Haziq show us how to fly this plane alone!"

Haziq taxied on, realizing that he was not scared but confident that he could do the job. He made three new circuits and made three good landings!

As he taxied into the ramp area, Captain Tom signaled where he should park. Zara walked up and greeted Haziq with a big smile and congratulatory handshake. Zara was very happy for Haziq and realized that he had a new best friend. All of them appreciated the significance of this solo event in the life of a pilot.

Captain Tom had his camera ready, and numerous pictures recorded this happy day. He reached into his backpack and pulled out a pair of scissors, ordered Haziq to turn around, and promptly cut out the back of his slightly sweaty polo shirt. Inside the building nearby, he proudly printed Haziq's full name, date of solo, and aircraft number, then pinned it on the wall for all to see. The next day, Zara soloed.

Months later, Graduation Day

Today, Zara and Haziq presented themselves for graduation after these many months in training. Now, all the studying was complete, all the written exams passed, a three-hour oral exam endured, and a final flight check flying skill demonstration completed satisfactorily. With a big smile on Zara's face, he commented to Haziq and a couple of friends, "Hey, let's go into town tonight and properly say 'goodbye' to this place. You know, we leave in two days back to Kuala Lumpur, and this will be our last chance to celebrate our accomplishments together and have some fun." The others agreed, and in an hour, they were in a taxi whirling into the nearby town of the City of Angeles.

The City of Angeles was famous for a bar district—Field Street—with bright lights, karaoke, girlie bars, sex shows, and more, frequented by Westerners and military personnel from Subic Bay and Clark AFB. Notably, there was also a great selection of street food for the partyers, much like the food courts of their home country of Malaysia. Haziq, not used to this level of fun and freedom, quickly had too much to drink. Zara was careful to bring him home safely at the end of the night.

The following day, Zara looked across his dorm room and saw a bleary-eyed Haziq struggling to wake up. Haziq pulled a pillow over his eyes because of the light flooding in from the window. Zara moved close to give him a friendly shake and address him. "Just like they said, Haziq, it's eighteen months later, and here we are, graduating from the academy. Time for you to wake up!"

Zara continued, "Haziq, you've been a great friend and so helpful to me these past months. We studied together, worked well together, and you got me up in the morning! Tomorrow, it's back to Kuala Lumpur for our first MAS airline assignment. I can't wait to introduce you to my wife, Nurul. Here's hoping we can find each other in KL."

Haziq, relaxed and smiling broadly, nodded in agreement, happy that the "cadet" adventure was now behind them, and a professional pilot life was beginning. "B737 first officer sounds great to me, and I'm looking forward to seeing you and Nurul in KL. My wife will love you guys!"

The next day, the graduating cadets boarded their flight returning to Malaysia. In Kuala Lumpur, Zara's young family—wife Nurul, son Jamal, and now little Misha—were there to meet the flight. Nurul was thrilled that their time apart was over and greeted Zara with a big hug, an unusual public display of affection. Three years old, their son Jamal looked at his dad with a questioning stare but allowed himself to be picked up and kissed by Zara. Zara saw his son's questioning look and thought, *I've been away too long.*

CHAPTER THREE

Alpha Base, Spin Ghar Mountains, Afghanistan
January 2014

His office consisted of an eight-by-ten-foot room in one of three shacks perched high on a mountaintop in the Spin Ghar Mountains between Afghanistan and Pakistan. Navy Lieutenant Robert Barry, who commanded the SEAL platoon at Alpha Base, dumped his tired six-foot-four-inch frame in a chair behind a large, empty, wooden cable spool that served as a makeshift desk. After sitting for thirty minutes, his butt hurt, and his back ached. He pushed the chair back from the desk and bent at the waist to stretch out his aching muscles.

Ahh, that feels better, he said to himself. After returning upright, he again slumped over the desk to complete the mundane required paperwork when he heard two loud raps on the door. "Come in," he responded without looking up.

The door swung open, and Senior Chief Robinson stuck his head through the opening and said, "Sir, that special package is inbound. Should be here in about ten minutes."

"Thanks, Chief. I'll join you at the landing pad when I hear the Osprey in-bound." After the door closed, Barry stared into space for a couple of minutes and recalled the details of a secure phone conversation he had yesterday with Headquarters in Kabul. He and his platoon of SEALs had spent the last thirty days at Alpha Base and covertly observed the Taliban's comings and goings, but it had been mostly quiet and boring. The contents of the phone call gave him hope that things were about to change.

Barry's commanding officer instructed him to expect an airborne delivery of two civilian visitors and a sensitive piece of equipment this afternoon. The technical details were way over Barry's head, but he understood his mission was to provide security for the civilians and the "package" while they performed an operational evaluation. He also understood the assessment consisted of autonomously flying a new drone controlled with third-generation artificial intelligence software. The new AI software allowed the drone to decide the best way to perform its mission.

Barry's briefing only included his part in the mission and did not include the evaluation's full scope. He and his team had the appropriate security clearance level. Still, this mission had the additional classification of "NEED-TO-KNOW." The decision-makers in Washington decided, for security reasons, the fewer people who knew the full scope of the mission, the better.

Alpha Base was one of six locations simultaneously evaluating the same type of drone. As it flew the mission profile, the information acquired by each drone was transmitted to the other five. The new AI software would allow the computers to "talk" among themselves and learn from their acquired information individually and collectively. The first phase of the evaluation would validate the AI software's ability to receive and share information while performing a benign reconnaissance mission. The second phase would be to arm the drones and have them destroy high-value targets autonomously, using artificial intelligence-based decision-making. The top-secret joint Defense Advanced Research Projects Agency (DARPA)/CIA program had the ultimate goal of developing and unleashing a swarm of autonomous, hunter-killer drones on the battlefield instead of using "boots on the ground." This policy change resulted in a phased withdrawal of American forces from Afghanistan and the Middle East. The lessons of history were not lost on the decision-makers. In the past, when American troops left the battlefield, terrorist groups such as the Taliban or ISIS filled the vacuum. This time, armed drones, supercharged with artificial intelligence, would remain on patrol and ready to strike. The evaluation at Alpha Base would set that ball in motion.

Bagram AFB. Kabul, Afghanistan

Raheem, a man in his early sixties, had many talents and few loyalties. He presented an unassuming appearance as he busied himself sweeping the dirt and dust from the lobby of the American officers' quarters in a compound adjacent to the Bagram Airbase, outside the Afghan capital of Kabul. He owned a truck during the Soviet occupation and leased it to the Soviets when they needed additional capacity to resupply their bases around the country. For a fee, he would then inform the mujahedeen about the shipments. He would tell his friends, "I am loyal to only two masters, Allah and myself." Above all else, Raheem was a survivor, and he now played the Americans against the Taliban. His official job description of custodian helped mask his unofficial duties as a Taliban spy. He kept his eyes on the floor as he swept but inched closer to the two American officers conversing near the reception desk. With his head still lowered, he could now hear their discussion. The two U.S. Marine Corps aviators had finished a grueling five-hour flight to Bagram Airbase in their MV-22 Osprey from an amphibious assault ship in the Indian Ocean. As they waited for the receptionist to check them into their rooms, they engaged in idle conversation to pass the time.

"Man, I'm beat. I can't wait to get out of this flight suit, take off these boots, and relax. What's taking so long?"

"Relax, George. Oh, by the way, did you make arrangements to secure our cargo?"

"Nah, those two civilians said they'd take care of making the security arrangements with that marine detail that met us on the ramp. That's a pretty neat little package, that small drone and its control station. I wonder what's so special about it that it took a priority C-17 lift from the States to get it here and all the security and stuff." *That* comment caught Raheem's attention. He inched closer to the two men.

"Your guess is as good as mine, but I caught part of a conversation our two civilian passengers had. One mentioned artificial intelligence and a swarm of hunter-killer drones. It sounds like some serious Buck Rodgers shit! All I know is we're supposed to deliver it, and them, to a mountain base somewhere tomorrow. I guess we'll get the coordinates at tomorrow morning's briefing. All I wanna do now is get out of these clothes, take a shower, and relax."

The receptionist gave each man his room key and directed them to their rooms.

"Hey, Bill, I'll meet you here at eighteen hundred, and we'll get some chow, okay?" George gave his copilot a thumbs-up, and then both men, carrying their small overnight bags, slogged off in the direction of their respective rooms.

Raheem finished his tidying up, returned his broom and pan to the custodian's closet, and left the building. Once outside and out of earshot of any would-be eavesdropper, he removed his encrypted satellite cell phone and placed a call.

Amir Sharif Kahn, a Taliban warlord, listened to Raheem intently for five minutes as he relayed the details of the conversation that he had overheard between the two American officers. "Thank you, Raheem. This information is beneficial. Please keep me informed of any additional information you may hear."

"Yes, my Amir. The Americans will receive a mission briefing that will include the drop-off location for their special package tomorrow morning. I will call you again tomorrow with that information. Go with Allah."

The mission briefing took place in the flight operations building at 0700 hours the next day. Raheem also had custodial responsibility for the flight operations building, and he busied himself cleaning the restroom when the meeting began. He made sure the bathroom was empty, stopped cleaning, and locked the door. He pressed his ear to the wall, and thanks to the building's substandard construction, he could make out portions of the conversations taking place in the adjacent room. He heard two crucial pieces of information: Spin Ghar

Mountains and Alpha Base. After the briefing ended, Raheem made a second call to Amir Sharif Kahn.

"Thank you, my brother. That's all I need to know." Kahn pressed the end-call button and placed the cell phone inside his tunic.

Kahn led a small, military-style unit comprised of fifty Taliban fighters who operated in a small village fifty kilometers east of Kabul. Raheem's call intrigued him. *If this cargo is so important to the Americans that it warrants such high security, then it might be important to others, as well,* he thought. *In fact, like our brothers, the Iranians, or the Chinese, others might also be willing to pay a high price for it.* Thoughts continued to swirl in Kahn's brain until they settled on a plan of action. Then he summoned his second in command.

"Kahlil, come here, please. I have something to ask you."

"Yes, my Amir, what is it?"

"We will soon have an opportunity to acquire an important piece of military equipment from the infidels. If we are successful, I'm sure our Iranian and Chinese friends will be interested. This mission is an opportunity to sell it to the highest bidder. Use our courier network to contact our friends and arrange a meeting in one week. Tell them that this has to do with new drone technology and artificial intelligence software. In one week, we should have those items in our possession." Kahn's lips parted into an evil smile as he relished the thought of a bidding war. His grin turned to a frown when Kahlil reminded him of an unfortunate reality.

"Excellency, I'm sorry to bring this up, but I don't think we should waste our time and talk to the Iranians. The American economic sanctions are squeezing our brothers' economy and have created a severe shortage of hard currency. Besides, developing artificial intelligence for military and commercial use is a high priority for the Chinese government. I'm sure they will be more than willing to pay a high price to acquire this technology."

Amir, with his eyes fixed in a straight-ahead stare, nodded. "So be it, my brother. Send a courier and make contact. Praise Allah."

Kuala Lumpur

Zara often reminisced about his luck in coming to Malaysia Airlines years ago, and living the good life in Kuala Lumpur. In those early years, Zara and Nurul were indeed happy before their family tragedy struck—daughter Misha dying in Bali. It was a hurt that they could never overcome.

Zara, suffering from this damaged marital relationship, compensated by plunging himself into his professional life. After numerous years of flying as a first officer, Malaysia Airlines awarded Zara his first captaincy. This meant he was assigned to fly smaller planes to regional destinations while refining his command and management skills. In 1997, he was awarded a captain seat on jumbo jets flying Boeing's latest commercial airliner, the B777, on many international routes from Kuala Lumpur. His superiors also assigned him flight instructor and check-pilot duties because of his steady airmanship and flying abilities. Those collateral duties allowed Zara to mentor younger pilots and share his flying experiences and passion for flying.

From the outside looking in, Zara's friends and colleagues saw a healthy, happy man with many professional achievements who was living a remarkable life. His personal life, on the other hand, stood in stark contrast to his external accomplishments. His broken family and marriage caused him sleepless nights and a deepening sadness.

Tonight, walking along the dimly lit hall of his home, Zara thought, *I do not feel like a success story*! He stopped at his study, glanced at his computer sitting on his desk across the room, and thought about checking his emails or Facebook accounts. He moved to his desk and sat motionless for a moment, then decided he was too tired to make any postings tonight on Facebook.

Social media had begun to take its toll on him. Two months ago, he had fallen "in love" with two Chinese twins, a gorgeous pair of porcelain dolls he met on the internet. To his dismay, they never responded to his posts, flirting, and offers of attention, some seventy crafted messages trying to get them to engage. He finally realized this internet boondoggle had become a surrogate experience, filling up his empty shell of a life with virtual friends and fantasy romantic interests. Looking through the fog of his sad reality, he knew he was spending too much time slogging through countless pages of internet distractions. He thought about Nurul and his son in the months and years leading up to Nurul's decision to leave him and live in Penang. During that time, with his marriage crumbling around him, he also sought distractions in the form of companionship from numerous female cabin crew members. One such opportunity presented itself just over a year ago. A delightful vision of beauty flooded his mind.

One day, while other crew members read or chatted in the company crew lounge, Zara read a newspaper quietly waiting to board his London-bound flight. The lounge door opened, and in walked a thirty-something flight attendant who looked stunning in her uniform and high heels. She stopped, looked around the room with a smile on her face, and walked in the direction of the other flight attendants. Zara did not know this woman, but he intended to remedy that situation. Unbeknownst to him, she was the chief purser on his flight today. Her name was Aishah. Meeting her that day was fortuitous. They soon became friends and, later, lovers.

At that time, Malaysia Airlines flew two nonstop flights a day from Kuala Lumpur to London—one with a quick one-and-a-half-day layover in downtown London and one with a three-day layover. Zara had achieved senior captain status based on his thirty years of airline service, and that seniority allowed him to have his pick of flights. He preferred the London flight with the three-day layover. Zara looked forward to flying to London and other European cities with eager enthusiasm. In the months ahead, Zara and Aishah would share each other's monthly schedules, leaving notes in their respective company mailboxes at the airport describing what days and nights he or she would be in London the next month. Depending on the flying schedule they were awarded, they could meet or work the same trip together, either outbound or returning to KL.

Zara and Aishah arrived in London early that morning after a thirteen-plus-hour flight, and they sat side by side on the crew bus into town, making plans for their day together. Aishah suggested, "Let's take a nap first, and I'll meet you in the lobby, say 3:00 p.m. Then we can take the Tube to Leicester Square and peruse the many half-price ticket vendors for a show that evening at one of the near-by theaters. We'll have time for a drink and a bite to eat before the show. I think I'm in the mood for a musical."

Zara, watching her eyes light up with this idea, said, "Yes, my beautiful new friend, that all sounds lovely. It's a great plan for the evening."

Zara was waiting in the hotel lobby when the elevator door opened, and Aishah stepped out, looking marvelous in her tailored slacks, cashmere sweater, and tasteful leather waistcoat. She looked spectacular. To Zara's big surprise, behind her walking into the lob-by was his good friend Haziq in full uniform with two copilots trail-ing. Zara realized that Haziq and his crew were assembling to leave the hotel in a few minutes to proceed to the airport and fly back to KL this evening.

Haziq had never met Aishah before but was aware of her exis-tence, given a few short comments from Zara in the past. Seeing them together and so comfortable with each other, Haziq immedi-ately knew that this couple was more than just friends. Zara spoke first, "Haziq, let me introduce you to Aishah. Aishah, this is Captain Haziq, my very dear friend." They greeted each other with a friend-ly exchange, speaking primarily about life in KL and not having flown together before. Sensing a delicate situation, Aishah quickly excused herself, crossing the lobby to talk to a friend she recognized in the outbound cabin crew.

Professionally, Zara shifted gears, changing the conversation to describe the pertinent details of his arriving trip to London this morning and the weather Haziq might have to navigate on his way home.

It was soon time for Haziq and his crew to board the crew bus to the airport, and he and Zara said goodbye. As Haziq took a seat on the bus, he realized the potential ramifications of this romantic entanglement and that he should be careful not to mention any of this to his wife back home. She had become good friends with Nurul over the years. *I hope none of this story ever slips out of my mouth.*

Minutes later, Zara and Aishah were outside, walking to the Underground tube station. They proceeded to Leicester Square station. Then they went aboveground and suddenly were surrounded by hawkers and ticket kiosks, touting the shows available at nearby theaters for tonight's purchase. The idea of a musical remained their first choice, and after considering *Mamma Mia! Wicked*, and *Phantom of the Opera*, they chose a wonderful classic, *Lion King*, starting at 7:30 p.m.

Walking in the West End with time to kill, they came upon a pub with a vacant outside table beckoning them. They grabbed the seats and settled in. Zara said, "Aishah, have you ever had a Pimm's Cup? It's a delightfully fruity, herbaceous gin drink. I think you would like it." She nodded approval as a hostess came up to serve them. He ordered, "We'll have two Pimm's Cups, please."

After a moment, Aishah spoke. "I feel like a new person after my nap at the hotel, considering being up all night working. Zara, how are you feeling?"

"Yes, I needed that nap. I feel good now, but I will probably crash later after the show and the evening's excitement wears off. Funny, you look so different now compared to seeing you a few hours ago in your full-length uniform and your hair up, a beautiful Asian flight attendant. Now, you're a beautiful, modern, sophisticated woman—very alluring with your hair down—and eyes to die for. Aishah, how do you manage this life so well?"

Aishah thought for a moment about how to answer the question. For her, she knew that she lived two lives, having two personas: One was dominant in Malaysia, as a generally conservative Muslim woman, knowing her place in society and keeping a low profile. And that was okay with her. But flying around the world also made her feel free to try new things and enjoy all that humankind could offer—wherever she should find it. The world was her oyster!

"Zara, I do like my life and my flying job. Flying makes me feel free, and the world is my playground today. And you, Zara . . . You always make me feel wanted and fulfilled at the same time! In Kuala Lumpur, of course, I do not have the same free space. Yes, it's a little quieter, a little more introspective, but fully satisfying. By the way, I've heard some rumors that your wife is now living in Penang. So, if you would like to get together in KL—quietly—discreetly—that would be okay with me."

Zara remained quiet for a moment. He couldn't help comparing her life with his . . . her blissful, upbeat freedom compared with his pictures of mental dilemmas; her life's satisfactions compared to his life of suffocating pain.

———◦———

CHAPTER FOUR

Zara denied that he had a mental health issue but rather surmised his problem was a deep, sometimes dark, sadness. One minute, he felt "normal," and the next minute, he would crash into lethargy and pessimism. He refused to seek professional medical help because of the negative impact he perceived it would have on his flying career. Instead, Zara turned to his internet research and self-diagnosed his problem as an anxiety disorder, fatigue, with a dose of insomnia. Based on an internet-directed scheme and the sheer strength of his will, he decided to self-medicate and take the anti-anxiety drug, Xanax, to help him get things under control or at least stabilize his health.

Zara had a friend in nearby Singapore who worked for a pharmaceutical drug distributor. He knew his friend had connections, and, for a fee, he could arrange for a few bottles of Xanax to disappear from their inventory list. Two months ago, a private courier delivered four bottles of pills to Zara's residence. Zara considered his supply problem solved, but he ignored an essential piece of advice in his rush for relief, listed on every medical website he visited. The websites advised, "a patient should be under a doctor's care when taking Xanax because the amount of Xanax in a person's body should be carefully controlled and monitored." The websites warned about side effects and possible toxicity if too much Xanax accumulated in the body or was mixed with other drugs or alcohol. Zara believed if he took the standard adult dose, he would be fine, but in his case, side effects began immediately after he started using the drug. These side effects manifested as physical discomfort from headaches, an upset stomach, and intense nervousness. Zara denied that his behavior was spiraling out of control. He also forgot to read the possible side effects section on suicidal ideation.

Zara thought he was in control of his situation. *I'll get better*, he would think. Maybe he believed in his heart that he committed a sin of not being there for his daughter, or not being there for his wife, or not trying hard enough to save the child. But to seek help would require that Zara recognize his continuing mental instability. His denial continued as a series of internal deceits that he would tell himself, making his questionable behavior appear okay.

Tonight, he found himself in a gloomy episode that caused his thoughts to race and his body to fill with nervous energy. Zara tried to calm his racing mind on past nights by flying familiar routes on his in-home flight simulator. Through trial and error, he found by forcing himself to concentrate on following stringent airline procedures while engaging in a physical activity requiring active hand-eye co-ordination, he could get his mind to reset and relax. Unfortunately, he learned the hard way that depressive episodes took longer to sub-side—instead of minutes, they would last for hours—or even days.

While still sitting in his study, Zara took a final look at the desk-top computer and decided to shut it down for the night. Then he sat there staring into nowhere. Suddenly, fully awake again, Zara lowered his head, covered his eyes with his hands, and began sob-bing. He was experiencing those memories and emotions again, a rehashing of events that caused his marriage to fail and his son to desert him. He knew where his mind was going, and he could not stop it. He reached for the pill bottle next to the computer keyboard and popped two more Xanax tablets into his mouth. He swallowed hard, let out a loud sigh, and let his thoughts drift, unconsciously seeking escape.

He recently recalled a fatal accident report of an event sixteen years earlier. An Indonesian SilkAir Boeing 737-300, Flight 185, from Jakarta to Singapore, crashed in the Musi River in south-ern Sumatra, killing all one hundred four people onboard. Two independent agencies, the Indonesian National Transportation Safety Committee (NTSC) and the United States National Transportation Safety Board (NTSB), investigated the cause of the crash. The NTSB was invited to confer because the aircraft was manufactured in the U.S. The NTSB's report concluded the crash resulted from deliberate flight control inputs—nose-down inputs, diving the airplane into the ground—most likely caused by the captain. There were no system failures in the 737 found by the investigators. The Indonesian report declined to speculate without concrete proof of pilot malfeasance and finally reported the accident results were "inconclusive."

The captain of SilkAir 185 seemed a troubled soul. In the weeks and months before this flight, he had arguments with his fellow pilots about his leadership and decision-making skills in the cockpit. The captain had lost one million dollars on a stock trade two weeks before this flight. One week before the flight, he bought a six-hundred-thousand-dollar life insurance policy. Eighteen years before this crash, the captain, a previous Singaporean fighter pilot, lost four squadron mates on the exact date of the SilkAir crash. With no system failures discovered, investigators postulated that a recovery of the airplane was possible but was not attempted. The two black boxes on the plane, recording cockpit voices and positions of the controls, went "inoperative" just ten minutes before the dive into the ground.

Zara dismissed all these surrounding events and even the lives lost in the crash. He only saw the escape from mental anguish. He talked to himself. "I hate my life. I think the SilkAir pilot had the right idea. End it all with a forward push on the control yoke—nose it into the ground at six hundred miles per hour—no one would feel a thing." At that moment, he made up his mind and set himself on a course of no return.

He raised his tired body from the computer desk, walked out of the study, and proceeded to the guest bedroom doorway. Two years ago, he repurposed the guest bedroom into his personal flight simulation center. Zara installed his "electronic baby"—a Microsoft FSX home simulator—that duplicated his assigned airliner, the Boeing 777. His setup, a control yoke and rudder pedals with three giant LED television screens, including overhead and center control panels and realistic flight instrument displays, rivaled most professional simulation-based training facilities. The computer's memory capacity and speed enabled him to program flights to most of the world's large airports, using the most common airline routings. Looking out the "front cockpit window"—a TV display screen above his instrument panel—he could see the unmistakable landmarks of the arrival city and the actual airport layout of the runways and taxiways. The Microsoft simulator's fidelity amazed other professional pilots with B777 experience, with its precise replication of the aircraft's data entry keypad, aircraft performance calculations, and displayed results. Zara had put together an impressive flight simulator for his professional practice and personal pleasure.

Tonight, physically tired but mentally anxious, fueled by melancholy and the escape offered by the SilkAir type plan, Zara decided to fly a route he had crafted in the last month, one he soon called "his final solution." Seated at his simulator's controls, Zara loaded the file and positioned the simulated aircraft at thirty-five thousand feet in cruise flight above his hometown of Penang. Out the window of his fantasy cockpit, he could see the outline of the Malaysian coast, Penang Island, some major roads, and the rural countryside. *I used to live down there*, he thought, *when life was simple.* Next, he programmed the aircraft to fly to the northwest, along the Indonesian/ Thai airspace boundary, and over the Andaman Sea. After many years of airline service, he knew this territory well. He recalled that aircraft passing westbound into the Indian Ocean from here would disappear from land-based radar screens and would only come alive again on display screens later as they approached landfall somewhere else.

By inputting both latitude and longitude coordinates with keystrokes on the simulator's entry pad, Zara programmed the simulator's final flight phase, repositioning the aircraft to one last waypoint. The plane banked hard to the left and flew south, deep into southern Indian Ocean airspace. After one last adjustment to a simulator, setting zero fuel remaining in the wing tanks, both engines quit three seconds later. He allowed the aircraft's nose to drop as he set up a smooth glide to nowhere . . . into the oblivion of the dark ocean below.

Karachi, Pakistan

Peter Chen, CEO of the Hang Shen Import-Export Company in Karachi, Pakistan, stood by his office window, his hands on his hips, and stared at the hustle and bustle in the vast shipyard below him but saw nothing. Thoughts entered and left his head as he tried to concentrate on the last two days' events. "So much to do . . . so much to figure out," he mumbled to himself as he rubbed his forehead.

Chen's company operated as a front for China's Ministry of State Security. Headquartered in Beijing, that government agency was the intelligence, security, and secret police agency of the People's Republic of China, responsible for counterintelligence, foreign intelligence, and political security. The ministry delegated to Chen the responsibility for pursuing leads and taking actions in South Asia that pertained to anything civil or military that might help China achieve technological superiority over the West, particularly the evil United States. A Taliban warlord contacted Chen a week earlier and made him a proposition. He offered to deliver to Chen a new piece of American technology for the "modest sum," as he put it, of twenty million U.S. dollars.

Chen turned from the window, picked up the receiver of his desk phone, and punched the intercom button. "Yes, please send in Mr. Lee." During his fifteen-minute stare out the window, Chen formulated a plan in his mind, and he thought it the opportune time to share that plan with his chief of operations, David Lee.

Chen and Lee were born into privilege. Since their fathers were members of China's National People Congress, they went to the best schools and enjoyed a higher standard of living than most fellow citizens. Their background and education made them well suited for their assigned tasks. Both received their undergraduate degrees in engineering—Chen in electrical and Lee in aerospace—from American universities and advanced degrees in computer science. They spoke fluent English, and Lee also spoke fluent Thai and the Malaysian standardized dialect of Bahasa. Lee knocked on Chen's office door and opened it without waiting for a reply. "Yes, sir, you wanted to see me?"

"Yes, please, have a seat," Chen said as he gestured toward a plush leather armchair in front of his desk. "Our Taliban friends came to me with an offer. It appears the Americans will soon test a new drone with their latest version of AI software in Afghanistan. The operational evaluation is intended to validate the software and record the drone's performance in a tactical environment. The Americans will conduct the evaluation from one of their mountain bases in the Spin Ghar Mountains. A Taliban warlord, Amir Sharif Kahn, intends to attack the base and 'liberate' as much equipment as he and his men can carry. The Amir knows about our interest in this technology and has offered to sell it to us. I accepted his offer. If all goes well, he said he can deliver it to us here in Karachi in the next ten days."

"That all sounds excellent," Lee commented. "I'm sure our superiors in Beijing will be pleased, but how do you propose we get it from here to Beijing? Overland would be a long and difficult journey through regions where the local peoples have questionable loyalties. Do you have a plan in mind?"

"Yes, I do, but many details still have to be worked out—and that means I'll be relying on your logistical genius. I took care of the business side of the deal with the Taliban. We agreed to an initial 50-percent payment upon our receipt of the material, followed by the final payment after our technical people inspect the material and make their assessment. The most secure route may not be the quickest, but the lack of speed is balanced by using a route we control, for the most part, or we can bribe people we either control or who sympathize with us.

"Once in our possession, I think we'll transport the package on one of our ships from Karachi to Penang, Malaysia. That should take about a week. As you know, we have a special relationship with a freight forwarder in Penang, Mr. Ahmad Osman. He has helped us transport certain materials to Beijing before. For a price, I'm sure he can help us again.

"In Penang, the drone equipment can be hidden within the packaging of his regular electronic shipments and will be delivered to Malaysia Airlines in Penang, then trucked by the airline to Kuala Lumpur, where it will be put on one of Malaysia Airlines' daily, nonstop flights to Beijing."

Chen continued, "The timing of the package's arrival in Penang will correspond with a climate change conference in Singapore. Our superiors will include several experts on drone technology and artificial intelligence in our environmental delegation. As you know, American spies monitor our activities in this part of the world. It would be easier to create a cover story that justifies our experts traveling to nearby Malaysia instead of coming here to Pakistan. Part of your job will be to arrange a time and place for our experts to examine the package. That's a simple overview. What do you think? Does the plan make sense?"

Lee nodded and continued the conversation. "Yes, I think it's very doable. The best opportunity for our people to inspect the package is in Penang, especially if we intend to air-ship it to Beijing. I will ask Osman, our freight forwarder friend, to accommodate our inspection requirements in his warehouse at Penang Airport. After the inspection, he'll then help us get the shipment through Malaysian customs."

Chen thought about Lee's remarks and nodded. "How much time do you think you'll need to work out the details?"

Lee rubbed his chin a couple of times before answering. "I should have it all worked out by the time the package comes here to Karachi."

CHAPTER FIVE

Alpha Base

Members of the U.S. Naval Mobile Construction Force, better known as the Seabees, had used hundreds of pounds of explosives to level a section of a mountain peak to create a landing pad adjacent to Alpha Base. They also blasted rock to form slit trenches around the base for perimeter defense. Other than climbing a steep two-thousand-foot mountain on foot, the only way to reach Alpha Base was by air. Lieutenant Barry heard a faint sound and knew his "package" would soon arrive. As the sound grew louder, Barry left his command shack and circumvented a couple of knee-high boulders on his way to the landing zone, where he met his senior chief.

"Sir, there she is," Robinson said as he pointed due west. The sun had begun its westerly descent that caused Barry to shield his eyes with his right hand. An experienced ear could hear the unique sound of an MV-22, neither a pure helicopter nor an airplane but a combination of the two, before it became visible to the naked eye. As the two men looked toward the direction of the sound, a tiny speck mushroomed into the unmistakable outline of the plane. As it decelerated and began its near-vertical descent toward the ground, the two men turned their backs to protect themselves from its hurricane-force downwash and its accompanying flying debris. The plane touched down, and after a one-minute cool down, the pilot shut off the engines. Barry and Robinson turned, faced the aircraft, and observed the rear ramp descending. A crew member left the plane and approached them.

"Sir, we have a delivery for you. Can you provide a four-person detail to help remove the cargo?" Barry glanced at the senior chief, and Robinson replied, "I'll get right on it, sir."

Barry returned his eyes to the Osprey crew member and said, "Staff Sergeant, please ask your two civilian passengers to join me in my office when they finish their business with you. My office is that wooden building over there," he said, pointing over his left shoulder.

"Yes, sir, will do," he responded as he turned and jogged toward the aircraft.

When Adam Cussins descended the MV-22's rear ramp and stepped onto the rocky surface adjacent to the landing zone, a shudder moved through his body. *So, this is where the rubber meets the road*, he thought. Nothing about this place, the least little bit, resembles Southern California. Cussins had no military experience, and this was his first trip to a combat zone. His apprehension stood in stark contrast to the demeanor of his fellow passenger, Jack Walker, who felt right at home. The former Navy SEAL, Walker, pumped both hands onto his chest and inhaled a deep breath of cool mountain air as he stepped off the MV-22's ramp. He turned his head and looked at the worried Cussins, who stood stoop-shouldered next to the ramp.

"Don't worry, son; everything will be just fine."

The crew chief relayed Lieutenant Barry's desire to meet the two men in his office when they completed securing their cargo. Walker nodded and grabbed Cussins by the arm.

"Come on; let's help this detail get our stuff off this bird, and then we'll pay our respects to the old man."

Cussins cast a worried, sideward glance at Walker and thought, *Oh my God, what did I get /*

Cussins and Walker each had a specific role in the drone's operational evaluation and its AI software. DARPA awarded the engineering and manufacturing development contract to Northrop

Grumman, Cussins's employer. He would perform the assessment by interfacing with the drone and monitoring the performance of its systems. On the other hand, Walker represented the CIA's interest, which included the tactical effectiveness of stealthy, swarming drones to perform covert missions. Walker did not have any technical responsibility for the project; that was Cussins's role, but the drone's design and performance impressed him. As he carried a box of spare parts down the ramp, he could not help but wonder. *I'm not easily impressed, but N.G. sure packed a lot of capability in a small package. That thing is small, stealthy, smart, and has three hardpoints under each wing for weapons!*

An hour after arriving at Alpha Base, the MV-22 fired up its engines and prepared to depart. Walker and Cussins watched it leave toward the west until it disappeared from view. Then Walker turned to Cussins and said, "Come on, kid. Let's go see what the old man wants."

Cussins frowned and replied, "Will you please do me a favor and don't keep calling me 'kid' or 'son'? My name is Adam."

Walker shot him a sideward glance, smiled, and said, "Sure, kid—I mean Adam—whatever you say."

When Lieutenant Barry heard the Osprey's engines start, he stepped outside his makeshift office and watched it depart. He saw the two civilians walking toward him, and he decided to wait for them outside. When they were three feet in front of him, he extended his hand in greeting. "Afternoon, gentlemen. My name is Lieutenant Robert Barry. Come on in and have a seat. Sorry about the spartan accommodations."

The three men spent half an hour in Barry's office. At the same time, he explained the base routine, the sleeping and working accommodations for Cussins and Walker, and emergency procedures in the unlikely case of an attack. As Barry explained the purpose and locations of the slit trenches, Walker glanced at Cussins and noticed him fidgeting with his glasses and tiny beads of sweat glistening on his forehead. Walker leaned toward Cussins when Barry finished and said, "Don't worry, son; you're in good hands." Cussins's face reddened, but before he could respond, Walker added, "Only kidding, Adam—relax."

Barry noticed the tense interaction between the two but continued without saying anything. "OK, gentlemen, that's what we do here. Now, what exactly are *you* going to do while you're here?"

Cussins decided that was his cue to explain their test plan to the lieutenant, but Walker had a way of getting to him, and Cussins did not know why. He glanced at Walker, who nodded and smiled, further agitating Cussins. *Damn, asshole*, he thought.

"Ah, yes, sir, our test plan calls for two test periods per day for seven days, weather and other factors permitting. We'll start the first period tomorrow at 0700 until 1100 hours. The second period will start at 1300 and end at 1700 hours. We'll launch the drone from the LZ, and I'll control it with my laptop computer and the ground control station in my backpack. At the same time, five other drones from various locations will become airborne. When all are airborne and in stable flight, I'll switch it to autonomous operation and just monitor it. The drone's onboard radar will show me when it rendezvouses with the swarm, and GPS will track their flight path. The mission is programmed initially with a flight path, but I expect that path to change as the swarm collects and shares information and learns how to optimize the mission based on the swarm's collective intelligence."

The men exchanged glances, and Barry nodded. "Sounds like an interesting program. If I can clear up my paperwork here, would you mind if I look over your shoulder when you fly that thing?"

"No, sir, not at all—my pleasure."

"Well, I guess we're finished here. Good luck with your test program tomorrow morning."

Cussins and Walker spent the rest of the day inventorying their equipment and inspecting everything for any apparent damage. After completing their inspections and finding the drone and its supporting equipment in perfect condition, they performed a series of power-up checks. As the sun settled behind the western mountain peak, the two men decided to call it a day.

"Man, I'm impressed," Walker commented. "Considering how far this equipment has traveled, and all the manhandling it's gone through, it's come through in great shape. You guys make some pretty durable stuff that a bunch of jarheads can't mess up."

"Thanks, Walker. I'll take that as a compliment."

"Come on; we've done enough for today. Let's grab some MREs and call it a day."

Exhausted by the day's activities that began well before dawn, Cussins nodded and followed Walker to the mess tent. As they walked, Cussins asked, "What exactly is an MRE?"

Walker flashed a knowing smile but did not immediately answer his question. Instead, he saw two open cardboard boxes resting on a six-foot-long table upon entering the mess tent. He grabbed two plastic pouches from the box nearest him and handed one to Cussins. He then plopped his tired, aching body on a wooden stool, and Cussins sat next to him on a metal chair. Cussins looked at the pouch, turned it over in his hand, and asked, "What the hell am I supposed to do with this?"

"You're supposed to eat what's inside. MRE stands for Meal Ready to Eat. Here, let me show you." Walker unsheathed his Ka-Bar combat survival knife and slit open the plastic pouch. He looked at the contents and remarked, "Hmm, looks like you got spaghetti with meat sauce." Cussins grimaced at the thought of eating cold spaghetti, and even without a word, Walker knew what he was thinking by the look on his face. He removed another item from the pouch and handed it to Cussins. "Here you go, kid—use this ration heater to heat it. It tastes pretty good when it's warmed up."

After finishing the MREs, the only thing left to do was relax and get ready to turn in for the night. They made themselves comfortable in a large tent located alongside a vertical rock face on the compound's west side. Rows of padded cots provided adequate comfort, and propane heaters kept the cold night air at bay. Walker settled in as if he were staying in a friend's guest bedroom. He lay on one of the cots, pulled his cap over his eyes, and said, "See ya at 0530—night."

Cussins wondered if he would be able to sleep. All sorts of thoughts raced through his mind, and the sound of Walker's deep breathing did not help.

———◦◦◦———

As the men at Alpha Base prepared for the night, Amir Sharif Kahn's men prepared for their assault. The SEALs protected their mountaintop location by using a two-person roving patrol throughout the night. Relieved every two hours, each two-person patrol, equipped with night vision devices, walked the base's perimeter. As a defense strategy, the base's location was no accident. Below the SEALs' flat surface area was a three-hundred-and-sixty-degree circle of jagged rock formations and steep drop-offs. Mother Nature provided 99 percent of the base's security, and the SEAL night patrols provided the remaining 1 percent—or at least that was what they thought.

Amir Sharif Kahn studied the writings of Sun Tzu, the ancient Chinese military strategist. His teachings stressed the importance of the surprise attack where and when it was least expected. To this end, Kahn led his twenty fighters along a concealed and treacherous path, known only to the local tribe members, to position them slightly above and behind the SEAL defenders. Then he instructed one of his men to move forward and place himself where he could observe the base and direct the mortar fire using his encrypted satellite phone. An hour before dawn, Kahn's men were in position, and as they huddled against the predawn cold, Kahn thought, *In a few hours, praise Allah—we will have a grand prize.*

———◦◦◦———

Cussins felt as if he had closed his eyes for only a minute when Walker began shaking him. "Come on, buddy. Time to get up." A glance at his watch confirmed it was 0530 hours. Cussins groaned, rubbing the sleep out of his eyes as he ducked inside his insulated sleeping bag for a few more seconds. Walker finished dressing, picked up his government-issued GORTEX jacket, and slid his arms into the sleeves.

"OK, buddy, let's grab some breakfast and get to work."

Cussins sat up, unzipped the sleeping bag, and swung his legs over the side of the cot. When his bare feet hit the ground, he knew it was cold outside. *I need socks and boots on, NOW! Thank God for those propane heaters*, he thought. Cussins's body confirmed what his feet already knew when he stepped outside the tent. The temperature dropped below freezing overnight but was forecast to rise in the midforties by early afternoon. He jogged to catch up with Walker, who had already approached the mess tent.

After a quick beef taco-MRE breakfast, the two men got to work. They and three SEALs removed the tarps covering the drone and positioned it in the LZ. Cussins performed a preflight inspection. After finishing the static assessment, he started the engine. His computer screen danced with numbers and symbols as he advanced the throttle to the idle position. He next performed the prelaunch checks, which confirmed flight control freedom of movement. Satisfied, Cussins advanced the throttle control, and with an increasing decibel level, the drone began a vertical ascent to a fixed position hover fifty feet above the ground. Cussins moved the flight control joystick attached to his laptop—forward. The drone's nose dropped slightly, the jet engine vectoring nozzle rotating aft, and the drone began to fly forward in a northeasterly direction. It soon attained one hundred fifty knots. Walker used his right hand to shield his eyes from the rising sun as he watched the drone become a faint speck in the sky. After five minutes of flight, Cussins was satisfied with the drone's performance, and he pressed Ctrl-8 on his keyboard.

"OK, now we watch and wait."

"Whadya mean by that?" Walker inquired.

"I mean, the drone is now flying itself. Come here and look at the display." Walker stood ten feet behind Cussins, but he now walked to Cussins's right side and looked at the display. "See that red dot?" Walker nodded. "That's our drone. See these five green dots over here?" Walker's eyes followed the tip of Cussins's finger. "That's the swarm, the drones launched from the other bases. This flight will last an hour, and then we'll recover our drone, fuel it, check it, and do it all over again this afternoon." Cussins glanced at Walker and had a big, boyish grin on his face. Walker nodded and gave him a thumbs-up. He then meandered to the side of the LZ, where he set up a couple of lawn chairs and plopped himself down into one.

Might as well get comfortable while junior plays his video game, he thought.

An hour later, the drone returned, landed, and shut itself down, all without human intervention. "See, Jack, it learned where it started its mission, returned here, and followed the proper shutdown sequence. So far, everything is working as planned."

While the two men enjoyed another MRE meal, Cussins commented, "You know, these aren't half bad. Either that, or I'm starving."

"Probably a little of both. Hey, on a different note, I've got a question for you."

Cussins looked up and, with his mouth full of vegetarian taco pasta, asked, "What?"

"I noticed the three hardpoint mounts under each wing. What are you planning to hang on them? And don't give me any of that need-to-know crap."

Cussins smiled and swallowed the rest of the food in his mouth.

"APKWS, the Advanced Precision Kill Weapon System." Cussins noticed Walker leaning a little forward and felt good that he, at last, had the upper hand in a conversation. "It's a blend of old and new technology," he began. "BAE Systems developed a guidance package that—" Just as Cussins was about to describe the versatile nature of the APKWS regarding its variety of warheads, a mortar shell suddenly exploded in the middle of the compound.

One of the SEALs yelled, "Incoming!" Everyone grabbed their weapons and dove for the protection of the slit trenches—that is, everyone except Cussins.

He froze like a deer in the headlights until Walker grabbed him by the collar and yelled, "Come on. We gotta get under cover."

As the two civilians hurried toward the nearest trench twenty yards away, a mortar round landed twenty feet behind them. The last thing Walker remembered hearing was yelling, followed by excruciating pain in his legs—and then darkness.

PART 2

The Chase

CHAPTER SIX

CIA Headquarters, Langley, Virginia

Josh Edwards did not feel well this morning. A ringing phone woke him at three o'clock in the morning with the news of the attack on Alpha Base. His stomach had been in knots ever since. That phone call this morning from the duty-desk officer informed him Taliban fighters had overrun Alpha Base. Most of the American defenders were either killed or wounded in the ensuing firefight. When two Cobra gunships arrived half an hour later, the Taliban had escaped into the remote mountain wilderness. Exploded mortar shells had pockmarked the base and destroyed many of the structures. The Cobra flight leader called a medivac V-22 while he and his wingman provided air cover. Preliminary information from the ground reported seven SEALs killed, thirteen wounded, and two civilians missing.

Sitting at his desk, Edwards contemplated his meeting with Director Chase, which made him feel even worse. If Walker and Cussins were missing, that meant the Taliban probably captured them. He was frightened and angered to think that their disappearance suggested the Taliban knew about the secret test program and that they also confiscated as much of the equipment as they could carry.

Edwards popped two antacid tablets into his mouth, stood up, grabbed his notepad, and left his office. *Might as well get this over with*, he thought. *Damn, I can't wait to retire.*

Art Zicard and Jim Holling

Alpha Base after the Attack

Walker did not have a weapon, except the Ka-Bar knife he kept in his boot. When the shells began falling, he and Cussins hurried toward the nearest slit trench. Shrapnel from an exploding shell ripped across the back of Walker's legs, and the concussive force slammed him to the ground, which knocked him out. When he came to, he was lying on a rock ledge with Cussins sitting beside him.

"What the—?"

"Relax, Walker, and save your strength. We're on the north side of the mountain about twenty feet below the base. I carried you here after you got knocked out because I figured the bad guys wouldn't look for us here. It sounds like the fight's over, and I haven't heard any gunfire in about ten minutes."

Walker propped himself up on one arm, looked at Cussins, and realized he misjudged his companion. When he moved his legs as he tried to sit up, he winced in pain. "Aww, what the hell? What happened to my legs?"

"You got hit by shrapnel. After carrying you here, I ripped my T-shirt into strips and bandaged you the best I could. A couple of helicopters have been flying around, so I imagine help is on the way."

"You carried me here? Boy, did I ever underestimate you!" Walker's comment caused a small smile to part Cussins's lips. "Maybe now you'll stop calling me son or kid." Walker forced a smile and replied, "Yes, sir, Mr. Cussins. Roger that."

Fifteen minutes later, as two AH-1Z Cobra gunships provided air cover, a medivac-equipped V-22 Osprey landed at Alpha Base and began evacuating the dead and wounded. Cussins helped Walker to his feet, but Walker could only put partial weight on his left leg.

"Here, put your arm around my neck and lean on me," Cussins said as he hoisted the back of Walker's belt. Then as the two men struggled toward the noises above them, Walker asked, "Where'd you learn all that first aid shit? I didn't think they taught any of that in engineering school."

"I was an Eagle Scout and a volunteer EMT. Save your breath. We're almost there." Walker gave Cussins a sideward glance and muttered, "No shit." When they reached level ground, the Osprey's crew chief spotted them and yelled to two corpsmen while pointing in their direction. The two corpsmen, carrying a litter between them, ran across the LZ and assisted Cussins, trying to get Walker to lie down.

"No, no, I can walk," Walker insisted, knowing full well he could not. Moreover, accepting help from anyone would run counter to his macho persona—especially help from a civilian geek.

With a reassuring voice, Cussins encouraged Walker to let the corpsmen do their job while he checked the status of the drone and his test equipment. Walker finally relented, and as the two corpsmen carried him to the V-22, Cussins weaved his way around three shell craters and a couple of dislodged boulders on his way to the drone staging area. What he saw both encouraged and disturbed him. The drone appeared intact, except for some minor damage from a couple of near misses. *It looks like those guys dropped those mortar shells in here and tried to hit people and not the equipment.*

The tents and wooden shacks were destroyed, and even the protective slit trenches took several direct hits. When the attack began, Cussins and Walker were standing near the drone, and Cussins had removed his backpack controller and had laid it on the ground with his laptop computer. His eyes darted from one spot to the next, and his heart sank when he realized both pieces of equipment were gone. *Could I have put them somewhere else? No, they were right here,* he thought. The sinking feeling in his chest deepened, and desperation welled inside him when he saw the three access panels were removed from the left side of the drone's fuselage. He ran closer, looked inside, and his eyes grew wide in disbelief. The flight computer and the neural processor were missing. He stepped back and, despite the cool mountain air, wiped a few beads of sweat from his forehead. *This attack was a hit job. Those guys came here to steal our equipment.*

Lost in thought about the consequences of losing all their AI-related hardware and software, Cussins felt a nervous shudder drive through his body and did not hear the crew chief approach him from behind. "Sir, we're ready to leave—"

Startled, Cussins gasped and replied, "Jeez, you scared the crap out of me." He looked around again and exhaled loudly, "OK, OK. There's nothing left to do here anyway. We lost it!"

Bagram Air Base, Afghanistan
DAYS LATER

Walker and Cussins stood face-to-face in the lobby of the base operations building and shook hands. "Well, I guess this is goodbye, Jack. My ride back to the States is boarding. Thanks for all your help. I'm glad we got through this all in one piece. What are your plans now?"

"I'm going to wait until the end of the week and give these s and my leg muscles a few more days to heal and then head back home myself," he lied. Cussins smiled, turned, and walked out of the building toward the waiting C-17. Halfway to the waiting aircraft, Cussins glanced over his shoulder and saw his new friend hobble toward a base taxi and could not help but think, *Good luck, buddy. I think you're going to need it.* Cussins had no way of knowing how prophetic that thought would be. The day before yesterday, Walker received a message from the office of the CIA station chief at the U.S. Embassy in Islamabad, Pakistan which ordered him to report as soon as possible.

American Embassy,
ISLAMABAD, PAKISTAN

Jack Walker showed his identification to the marine guard at the American Embassy in Islamabad, Pakistan. Still holding Walker's ID, the guard lifted his phone and made a call. Walker turned his head and gazed at his surroundings and was impressed by the modern appearance of the embassy's lobby. When the guard finished the call, he handed Walker his ID.

"Here, sir, Mr. Simon is expecting you. Go through those double doors to your right, and his office is the second door on your left."

The guard's voice startled Walker, who snapped his head around, smiled, and said, "Oh, thank you; have a nice day." As he walk towards the doors, one would hardly notice a slight limp, due to his sore muscles. He body would soon be back to one hundred percent.

Bill Simon felt energized this morning as he sat behind his desk and reflected on the past week's activities. He relished his job as CIA station chief because every day brought a new challenge. One week ago, Simon received a phone call from the assistant director of operations, Josh Edwards, at Langley. Edwards briefed him regarding the Taliban attack on Alpha Base and the loss of the top-secret equipment. He ordered Simon to pull out all the stops and apply maximum pressure to get that equipment back. He also advised Simon to expect a visit from Jack Walker as soon as he recovered from the injuries he sustained in the attack.

"Walker's going to be our point man in this operation," Edwards advised. "Once you get a lead on the whereabouts of the equipment, which we believe is still somewhere within the Afghanistan-Pakistan tribal border area, he'll need an appropriate cover story."

"Don't worry about that, Director. I'll take care of all the details." After that phone call, Simon contacted his web of human assets and initiated electronic surveillance of the usual suspects. The U.S. government had offered a ten-million-dollar reward for information leading to the equipment's recovery. This morning, Simon received encouraging information. Those thoughts had no sooner passed through his mind when he heard a knock on his door. His secretary opened the door and introduced Jack Walker.

"Jack, it's nice to meet you. Please, have a seat." The two men spent a few minutes exchanging pleasantries, then got down to business. Simon began by orienting Walker on recent events. "There's been an uptick in cell phone chatter recently that lead us to believe the Taliban cut a deal with the Chinese, meaning the Chinese have probably made the Taliban a monetary offer for the stolen equipment. I just got off a phone call this morning with a trusted source, and he corroborated that information. We have a mole inside the Chinese Ministry of State Security. He's informed us that a Taliban warlord named Amir Sharif Kahn contacted the Hang Shen Import-Export Company in Karachi about shipping some mining tools to Penang, Malaysia. He thinks those 'mining tools' are our missing drone hardware. Your job, Walker, is to find that package and bring it home." Simon waited a moment and expected a response from Walker, but all he got was a blank stare.

"Walker, what's going on inside that brain of yours?"

"Huh—oh, sorry—I was thinking. Why Penang, and why Malaysia? And then on to China?"

"I don't know. That will be up to you and your partner to figure out." Simon's comment about a partner caught Walker off guard. He had never partnered with anyone before on a field assignment.

"Partner? What partner? I work solo on things like this—what are you talking about?"

"Well, Walker, remember we are not alone in this world. Some of our allies are also interested in this AI drone deal, Australia for one. And they are also in line to purchase this equipment. Consequently, they have offered to assist us in any way possible to help in the return of said equipment.

"Additionally," Simon continued, "the director wanted me to come up with a cover story for you. After giving it a lot of thought,

I decided a male-female team would be the most effective. First of all, four eyes are better than two, and a male-female couple will draw less attention than a lone, seedy-looking male. You and your new girlfriend will pose as tourists on vacation. As far as aliases go, you're an accountant, John Wilson, working for Lockheed Martin, and she's a United Airlines pilot, Susan Vella, and you both live in Denver, Colorado. You're traveling through Southeast Asia without an itinerary using her airline travel benefits, which entitles you to discounted travel."

"I see my reputation precedes me. I suppose the director still doesn't completely trust me after that thing in Venezuela, but I don't need a babysitter—"

"She's not a babysitter," Simon interrupted. "Her name is Stark, and she's an accomplished field agent in our sister agency, the Australian Secret Intelligence Service (ASIS)."

Walker rolled his eyes and muttered, "Oh, brother."

"Don't be so quick to dismiss her. Ms. Stark has spent the last six years in the field, has an impressive record, and comes highly recommended. She participated in covert operations against the Jemaah Islamiyah Islamist terror group in Indonesia and the Abu Sayyaf terror group in the Philippines. She's also an expert scuba diver, mountaineer, skydiver, and an Australian Air Force Reserve major. In addition, she's got about five thousand hours flying their E7A Twin Engine Jet Reconnaissance plane. For her day job, she is an international first officer for Qantas Airways on the Boeing 747-400."

This time, Walker, irritated by the discussion of a partner, interrupted. "OK, OK, she can fly a plane—a big plane—and do those other things, but I still don't think I need a partner."

"That matter is out of your hands. I don't know how to put this gently, so I will be brutally blunt. Our missing equipment is so technologically advanced that if it falls into the wrong hands, every member of the American Armed Forces, as well as the Foreign Service people staffing our embassies, are at increased risk. An adversary could exploit that technology to create a swarm of stealthy assassins. Therefore, you and your partner have been green-lighted to take whatever steps necessary to retrieve or destroy the missing equipment. That directive comes from the top," Simon leaned in and emphasized, "AND, I mean the *very top*. Got it?" Without saying a word, Walker rubbed his chin and nodded.

"Now, this is how it's gonna go down . . ."

Simon talked for the next twenty minutes, and Jack listened, noting the details and asking about his resources. The embassy made a room reservation for Walker at the Islamabad Marriott Hotel, where he would meet his new partner. The next day, the two would fly to Karachi, where the couple would try to determine if the mining tools shipment also contained the stolen drone hardware.

Walker arrived at the Marriott and decided to wait for his partner before checking in. He might as well play this right, he thought. *It might look suspicious if we're supposed to be a couple, and we check in separately.* After his tense meeting with the station chief, Walker had only one thing on his mind. *Man, I need a drink. I'm glad Simon, at least, told my new partner to meet me in the hotel bar.*

CHAPTER SEVEN

The Marriott enjoyed a cozy bar in the basement that served alcohol to foreigners, and Walker had the place to himself. The drinks were pricey, and the selection limited, but Walker found a scotch acceptable to his taste. The solitude and a glass of scotch on the rocks helped him relax. He lifted the glass to his lips, took a sip, swirled the elixir in his mouth, and swallowed. *Ahh, just what the doctor ordered.* Before taking another drink, he heard a female voice from behind ask, "Excuse me, are you Jack Walker?" He turned in his seat and saw a tall, statuesque brunette standing behind him.

Jack stood up to face her. He couldn't believe his eyes. It was Addison from Sydney. Not remembering her last name, he didn't realize that agent A. Stark was HER! His surprise showed on his face.

Addison enjoyed the *gotcha* moment as she recognized his genuine surprise. She stepped forward, lightly grabbed his shoulders, and pulled him toward her, kissing him on his cheek. "So nice to see you again, Jack! Your girlfriend has arrived, and she is ready to travel SE Asia with you. You better behave."

Jack was frozen, staring at her, as Addison moved around the table and sat down. Disarmed by his surprise and her striking good looks, he squirmed a little in his seat and groped for words. "Addison, it's been a long time. Wow! OK! You're here! This may sound corny after six years since we were together, but I have thought about you many times, wondering where you are and how you've been."

Addison, busy taking in his actual presence, was mentally comparing it to the pictures in her head. She also remembered that she too had thought about him many times over the years. "It was quite a surprise for me to be offered this assignment. Yes, I accepted but did not mention to my boss that I had made your acquaintance some years ago when I was in agent training. And seeing you now, you are still looking pretty good for an old man!"

They sat quietly for a moment while a waiter came over, taking their order.

"So, now you are my girlfriend and traveling companion for this mission through Southeast Asia," remarked Jack. "This time, we will have plenty of time to get to know each other."

The couple spent the next half hour getting reacquainted, after which Jack said, "Well, I guess we better go check-in."

Addison smiled, and the two walked arm in arm up the staircase to the hotel lobby. After all, she thought, they were traveling together as a couple.

They approached the lobby desk, and the clerk greeted them, asked their names, then asked for passports while looking up the reservation.

Jack considered himself a good judge of people, and something about the desk clerk seemed odd. He spoke English well, but something about his behavior was out of place. He kept glancing from side to side as if looking for someone, and Jack thought he detected a nervous tone in the man's voice when he spoke. Jack knew from experience to trust his instincts, and his inner self screamed, "danger!" The clerk finished the check-in process and extended his hand, returning the passports and then offering two keys.

"Mr. Wilson, Ms. Villa—your keys."

Addison noticed a concerned look on Jack's face and a faraway look in his eyes. She approached the counter, stood alongside him, and took the keys from the clerk's hand.

"Thank you. Come on, John. Let's get to our room and relax," she said. The words rolled off her lips in a soft, beckoning tone while she cast a sideward glance at Jack.

To complete the charade, Jack put his arm around her waist as they strolled toward the elevator and said, "At your service, m'lady."

Halfway to the elevator, she whispered, "Don't get any ideas—this is all for show. When we get to the room, *I* get the bed, and *you* sleep on the sofa—got it?"

Jack smiled and nodded, "Yeah, I got it."

Their third-floor room was halfway down the hall from the elevator. Jack inserted the key in the door lock, paused for a moment, turned his head toward Addison, and put his left index finger up to his lips, signaling silence. He removed a cell phone-size device from his jacket pocket with his other hand. Jack believed there was no such thing as being too careful. That belief protected him from bodily harm on more than one occasion, and the desk clerk's peculiar behavior increased his presumption in taking all necessary precautions. Addison's eyes widened in acknowledgment when she recognized the RF (radio frequency) detector.

Jack opened the door, stepping into the room. He moved the sensing device from side to side, checking for electronic emissions as he walked through the room and into the bathroom. After leaving the bathroom, he approached the clothes closet, and the LED lights on the detector began flashing. The same thing happened when he held the sensor over the end tables beside the bed. Jack touched Addison's arm and waved his left hand in a "follow me" motion as he headed toward the door, never once speaking a word. Once outside the room, Jack's pace picked up as they moved toward the elevator.

"That room's got more bugs than a termite mound—probably a combination of cameras and microphones. Someone knew we were coming. The embassy made our reservations, so we can't trust going back there."

"So, what do you suggest we do now?"

Jack, his mind whirling, pushed the elevator button for the second floor. "We'll get off on the second floor and walk down one flight of stairs. I don't want the lobby clerk to see us get off the elevator and leave. We'll use the side entrance coming in from the parking lot, walk a block or so away from here, and grab a cab."

"And then what?" Addison asked, letting Jack take charge. *Jack was on a roll!*

"And then we go to a different hotel. We're also not going to fly to Karachi tomorrow. The embassy made those reservations too. Tonight, we'll stay in a hotel near the train station, and tomorrow, we'll take the train to Karachi."

Addison nodded. "That's exactly what I would do."

The Iranian military attaché posted to the Iranian Embassy in Islamabad began his morning activities and read Tehran's latest communique. Javid Kazemi's post as military attaché also included supporting the activities of Iran's Ministry of Intelligence (MOI), which, in the recent past, occupied most of his time. He finished reading the MOI's latest operational status report when he heard a knock on his door.

"Enter."

The door opened, and the MOI's senior operative in Pakistan, Rehyan Abed, entered Kazemi's office. "Greetings, sir. May Allah be with you."

"And with you, my brother. Please, have a seat. I just finished reading the MOI's latest operational status report. It said you would fill me in on the most recent information regarding the missing secret American equipment and the American spies trying to retrieve it."

"Yes, sir. We've had a small setback regarding that. Allow me to explain. As you know, one of our friends in the Pakistani Inter-Services Intelligence Agency alerted us of the Taliban's intent to sell the secret American equipment to the Chinese. We also have a keen interest in American drone technology and have been ordered by Tehran to prevent that transaction. The Americans have dispatched their agents to track down the whereabouts of the equipment and recover it."

"And how do you know that?"

"We have a source within the American Embassy who informed us about a meeting between their CIA station chief and one of their operatives. Their operative was to stay at the Marriott Hotel overnight and fly to Karachi this morning. Our technical people placed hidden cameras and microphones in the hotel room. One of my men also posed as the desk clerk and verified the same American male who visited the embassy and an Australian female checked in together. We believe their respective intelligence agencies have provided them with identities that allowed them to pose as tourists. We know they went to their room, but, unfortunately, they disappeared."

"Hmm, that's not good news. Your superiors, I'm sure, are not happy about that."

"No, sir, they're not, but we haven't given up. We know the American and his companion didn't get on their flight to Karachi this morning, but one of our agents did. The only other good way to get there is by train. My man will be in Karachi before the morning train arrives and try to pick up their trail.

"If the Americans manage to get their equipment back, we will steal it from them. Otherwise, if the Chinese manage to thwart the American attempts, we'll simply wait for a suitable time and steal it from them."

"Thank you for updating me on your plans. May Allah protect you."

Walker awoke and knew it was early by the absence of sunshine when he gazed in the direction of the window. He sat upright and winced when he felt the pain in his lower back. "Damn hard couch," Jack groaned as he rubbed the pain out of his back. He glanced at Addison, who had a contented smile on her face as she lay sprawled across the king-size bed. *This sleeping situation sucks*, he thought. *If we can't share the bed, we're going to at least take turns on the couch.*

Walker raised his stiff frame from the couch, got dressed, and walked to the small coffeepot on the counter next to the dresser. He made two cups of coffee, walked to the side of the bed, and nudged Addison's shoulder with his hand. "Wake up, Sleeping Beauty. It's 0600. We gotta be at the train station in an hour."

They rode in silence as the cab bumped its way along one of Islamabad's better roads on its way to the train station. Walker had a plan in mind but was not planning to share it with Addison until they reached a safe place. Their experience at the Marriott convinced him someone else knew who they were and their mission.

The cab came to a halt in front of the station, Walker paid the fare, and they stepped into the morning's coolness. Addison pulled her unbuttoned jacket tighter together against the morning chill and hurried toward the entrance doors.

"Wait," Walker said. "Come this way." He pointed in the opposite direction and started walking.

"What? I thought—"

"Change of plans. I didn't want to say anything until we were out of earshot of any eavesdroppers. There's a car rental office three blocks in this direction. If someone knew we were staying at the Marriott, they probably knew we had reservations to fly to Karachi this morning. I suspect there's a welcoming committee waiting for us at the Karachi airport, so when we don't get off the plane, it won't take a genius to figure out that we probably took the train. That's why we're going to drive."

"What? Are you nuts? That's an eighteen-hour drive!" Addison glanced at Walker, rolled her eyes, and thought, *Oh brother*.

Walker smiled a silly smile and kept walking. Addison caught up to him and knew protesting his decision would be futile. Walker let her calm down a bit and then shared his plan. "We rent a Toyota Camry, drive all night, and take the most direct route: National Route 5. In Karachi, the Agency has a safe house a short distance from the port. We'll use that house as our base of operations. Then we'll stake out the Hang Shen Import-Expert Company until we ID Peter Chen or David Lee. We'll tail them, and hopefully, they'll lead us to the missing equipment."

Addison followed a half step behind as Jack pushed forward to the car rental counter. Before starting this assignment, the Australian military attaché in Islamabad briefed Stark on the highlights of Walker's personnel file sent to him by the CIA's director of Operations. According to his file, she knew Walker was strong-willed, decisive, self-confident, and a highly competent field agent. They said self-confident. *Boy, did they get* that *right*, she thought. But his diversion plan was brilliant!

Car ride to Karachi

Their trip through Pakistan to Karachi took them through breath-taking and contrasting scenery, which helped relieve the long drive's boredom. National Highway 5 paralleled the Indus River. They viewed snowcapped mountain peaks, and their journey through the fertile Indus River valley showcased its surrounding forests and desert.

They were silent for more than an hour, and Stark wearied of looking at the scenery. She decided this would be an excellent opportunity to learn more about her new partner. *There has got to be more to you, Mr. Walker*, she thought.

"So, Walker, six years later, you are still an agent for the CIA, and a good one, I've been told. How does *that* work for you?"

Walker, keeping his eyes on the road, slowly formulated an answer. "It does work for me. I've always liked it. It's been exciting, sometimes *too* exciting, sometimes dull, but it's always been interesting. Generally, I work alone and have to live with my decisions, good and bad. I have access to a great support team when in the field, and they have always been there for me."

Addison listened carefully, thinking of her professional career.

Walker continued to talk. "By the way, after our short time together in Sydney, I didn't want to leave you. I was attracted to you. Saying goodbye as we did made me feel ah—incomplete—I wanted more. Then back in the USA, I got busy again and being on the wrong side of the earth, my job just took over my existence."

Addison nodded her head, knowing how the job can sometimes take over your everyday presence. "Yes, the job can take over sometimes. It happened to me also—a relationship going dry from just being out of sight, unavailable for a couple of months.

"Hey, Walker, since we'll be living together in the safe house, can you cook?"

Walker raised his eyebrows but rose to the occasion. "I do OK."

Stark quickly responded, "OK, then—let's alternate every other night if that's all right with you. We'll have to find a market for shopping." Now, they were both thinking ahead to Karachi.

After pausing in their own thoughts, Jack was the first to speak. "My boss said you distinguished yourself in the Philippines chasing information on the Abu Sayyaf guerrillas. Sounds like the edge of danger for an attractive, blue-eyed female, standing out in a foreign environment."

"Yes, there was some truth to that in the Philippines. The Abu Sayyaf group was a descendent through marriage to the Osama Bin Laden terrorists of the Middle East. They functioned in southern Mindanao, near Zamboanga City. The group supported itself by kidnapping travelers, nurses, missionary couples, even targeting Red Cross personnel for ransom and extortion. In December 2011, they seized a former Australian army soldier-turned-university teacher, Warren Rodwell, from his home in Zamboanga. My job was to get on-site, collect, and report back any information that would help with his release. I did exactly that, and although it got a little dicey a couple of times, I got back to Australia in one piece. With the help of certain Philippine officials, Australia negotiated a $AUD 94,000 payment for 'board and lodging' expenses, paid by his family, securing his release in March 2013.

"Wow," Walker said. "Glad you made it out of there in one piece! And now, you are a proven agent of the ASIS."

Again, there was silence for another mile or so, both driven to his/her own thoughts.

Next, Stark popped the question. "Hey, Walker, ever been married?"

He took his eyes off the road for a second and glanced at her. "Huh? What'd you say?"

"I asked if you've ever been married."

"Me? No, and I never had the time to commit to a permanent relationship. I guess you can say I'm married to my job. How about you?"

"No, me neither. I've been too busy enjoying life and my work. I guess we have a lot in common like that."

Minutes later, Walker glanced at Stark a second time and saw she had her head turned toward the window. Stark's questions served one good purpose; they broke the ice. Then the couple slowly meandered into conversations about their lives from childhood to the present. Their conversation helped the time pass as quickly as the scenery. After a long, uneventful journey, the duo arrived at the CIA safe house on Karachi's outskirts. Walker's legs were stiff, and his back ached, evident by his halting motions as he exited the vehicle. His actions did not go unnoticed by the ever-observant Addison Stark, and she could not resist the opportunity to poke fun in his direction.

"Whatsa matter, old man? A little drive too much for ya?" Before Walker could reply in kind, Addison threw her head back, laughed, and through a smile, she said, "Just busting your chops—every muscle in my body aches too. Do you think our house has any white wine in the refrigerator?"

Addison and Jack stood on a crushed stone path outside the small cottage. For almost the first time, their eyes met, and neither was in a hurry to leave the other's sight. Walker smiled and offered his arm to escort her up the walk. She took it, and they walked side by side to the front door.

After assessing the condition and resources inside the property, Walker discovered a bottle of Sauvignon Blanc in the refrigerator. Finding a wineglass on an overhead shelf, he poured it half full and handed it to Addison. She quickly noticed that he had poured only one drink.

Walker knew he had to cover their tracks.

"Stay here," he said to his partner. "I'm gonna ditch the rental car. There's another car in the garage that we'll use from now on."

In addition to a Toyota Corolla, two bicycles were in the garage. Walker tossed one in the Camry's trunk and drove ten miles to the opposite side of town. He ditched the car in a secluded alley, hopped on the bike, and peddled his way back to the safe house.

On return, Jack found Addison lounging on a floor cushion in the small main room, sipping on her wine. She had taken a bath, put on a T-shirt and athletic shorts, and with legs curled up underneath her, was quietly awaiting his return. As he entered the room, she suggested, "Jack, clean up a little and join me. I'll pour you a drink." And with a little smile, she added, "Don't take too long."

After freshening up, Jack reentered the room. She beckoned to him in a friendly voice, "Come sit next to me." Somehow, the same attraction that had gripped them in Sydney was beginning to take over again. He sat down, put his arm around her, and their eyes met yet again. He kissed her unhurriedly on the lips. She kissed him back, hard. There was no talking now from either of them, just hot, delicious breath. After a few minutes, he maneuvered to pick her up and carried her to the bed in the next room. There was nowhere else to be tonight but in each other's arms—and in a safe house.

CHAPTER EIGHT

The dawn of a new day greeted Walker and Stark with a few fair-weather clouds playing peek-a-boo with a rising sun still low on the eastern horizon. They sat facing each other at the kitchen table with their hands curled around a cup of hot coffee. She held her cup of coffee a few inches from her lips. Stark confessed, "I've spent too much time around you 'Yanks,' and you've corrupted me. I now prefer coffee over tea."

Both realized this chatter was small talk compared to the elephant in the room—their emotional entanglement could be a problem on the mission. Someday, they could be compromised, putting themselves in danger by being too slow to react or making an emotional decision at the wrong time. Being professionals, they knew better.

Jack said, "Last night was beautiful. I don't regret a thing!"

"For me too!" she murmured. "But, Jack . . . the mission—"

"Yes, I know. Of course, you're right. We will have to agree to 'cool it' till the mission gets resolved; that is the only way. We will have to be on our best behavior, hands-off, super agents for the next days and weeks. Seriously, we can do it. We have to."

After a few full minutes of silence, Addison spoke up. "So, what's our plan for today? I know you want to locate your missing equipment. Just how do you propose we do that?"

"I've been giving that a lot of thought. Unfortunately, we can't just storm into Chen's warehouse and demand he gives it back to us, so we'll have to be a little more creative and covert."

Stark put down her cup, and with her elbows on the table and her chin resting on her hands, she said, "This ought to be interesting. Go ahead—I'm listening."

Walker raised an eyebrow in response to his partner's loaded comment, but he let it go. During their day-and-a-half road trip, he learned that she was a strong woman, confident in her skin, and would challenge him when appropriate.

"OK—here's what I'm thinking. We'll split up. One of us will stake out Chen's office building while the other one stakes out his warehouse in the shipyard. After finishing their shifts, many of the workers would socialize at a nearby tea house—to unwind with some tea and parathas—you know—that flat, unleavened bread they fry on the walls of a clay oven—"

Stark reached across the table and firmly clutched the back of Walker's hand. "Walker, listen. Before you continue, let me explain something. I've spent some time traveling and working in this part of the world, so I'm very familiar with the local customs and foods. Please don't feel as if you have to explain everything to me. If I don't know something, I'll let you know."

There was her independence and self-confidence percolating to the surface again. *I kind of like that*, Jack thought, *and she has soft hands too.* "As I was saying, I think if I disguise myself and hang around that tea house closest to the port entrance at the end of the workday, I may pick up some careless conversation about activity in the warehouse or even the whereabouts of our equipment."

Stark nodded affirmatively and offered that she would set up a post near the front gate with a view of the offices and try to pick up any patterns of any officials and their comings and goings. Walker nodded. Now, Stark nodded and said in her all-business tone of voice, "OK, let's get going."

Ditching the Camry on arrival at the safe house proved a smart move. After Walker and Stark failed to show up at the airport or the train station, the Iranians decided their quarry must have driven to Karachi. It took a couple of days and numerous bribes to verify their suspicion. After leaving the rental car office in Islamabad, Iranian MOI agent Rehyan Abed hurried to the airport to catch Karachi's next flight with new information. *Allah willing, I'll find the infidels in Karachi before they locate and retrieve the package.*

Hang Shen Import-Export Company, Karachi

David Lee knocked on his boss's door. He opened the door in response to a muffled "Come" from the inside and entered the spacious office. Peter Chen stood at the large window overlooking the vast Karachi shipyard and turned as Lee entered the room. "Ah, good morning, David. What news do you have for me regarding that special package headquarters instructed us to deliver to Penang?"

"Good news, sir. The package is in our possession in Warehouse Five. It is being prepared for shipment to Penang. First, it's being repackaged in wooden boxes and then included on the manifest as part of a shipment of iron ore mining tools for delivery to Britannia Mining in Bukit Besi. Once the shipment arrives at Penang's Butterworth Terminal and clears customs, we'll separate the package from the mining tools. The tools will continue their journey to Britannia Mining, and we'll transport the package to the freight forwarder's warehouse near the Penang Airport. There's one other thing, however—"

"I don't like the sound of that," Chen interrupted.

"It's not a big deal, sir. Our contact in Islamabad informed me that an Iranian MOI operative is tracking the package. My contact suspects, he intends to—how shall I say—'liberate' it from our possession. The Iranians are desperate for Western technology, especially anything pertaining to drones and artificial intelligence. We've taken precautions to protect the package, and as far as I know, the Iranians don't know that it's in our possession. As you know, we're one of five Chinese-owned shipping companies in Karachi." With a smug tone in his voice, Lee continued. "By the time they figure it out, the package will be on a Malaysia Airlines flight to Beijing."

"Good. Please keep me posted on the progress. That's all for now."

Lee bowed his head in acknowledgment, turned, and left Chen's office.

He walked the twenty feet separating his office from Chen's. Less spacious and less neat than Chen's, Lee entered his office, sat back in his desk chair, and rubbed his forehead. His role as the company's director of operations challenged his maturing physical and mental abilities, but he also juggled a hidden agenda known only to him. He worked for the CIA as a double agent. He knew American agents had placed a high priority on recovering their stolen secret equipment. That information had been passed to him by the CIA station chief Simon at the American Embassy in Islamabad after Lee informed the station chief that the equipment was in his company's possession. Simon instructed Lee to contact his agents and tell them how Lee intended to ship the 'package' and its final destination. Those thoughts occupied his mind as he reflected on his decision to betray his country. His mind drifted back to an earlier time, marred by one tragic event.

China's "one-child" policy resulted in only one son to Lee and his wife. The boy grew into a strong and handsome young man. Working for the Chinese government, Lee and his family enjoyed a lifestyle full of advantages not enjoyed by most of his countrymen. Life was good . . . until a fateful day twenty-five years ago.

Lee paused in his thoughts, lowered his head, took a deep breath, and forcibly held back a tear from the corner of his eye. *My son, beautiful Su Lee*, he called out. *They murdered my beautiful son.* Lee's mind flashed back to June 1989, at the height of the Chinese pro-democracy movement. Being a student activist, the twenty-year-old Su Lee was the target of government retaliation. During a demonstration in Tiananmen Square, government soldiers brutally murdered him and hundreds of other demonstrators. Lee and his wife never recovered emotionally from that traumatic event, and Lee vowed revenge. He bided his time, and ten years ago, a chance meeting in Islamabad culminated with his recruitment by the CIA. This meeting was when Lee chose to use his remaining time on earth to work against a country that placed so little value on its citizens' lives. Now, in his twilight years, he began to recognize that revenge would not bring his son back after all. *I need to extricate myself from the "spy" business—somehow—and soon! My exit will be well planned.*

CIA Safe House

The encrypted satellite phone was ringing on the table. They were expecting a call from Walker's boss, Josh Edwards, who wanted to brief them with some new information. It had been three days since their arrival in Karachi, and Walker and Stark still did not know the whereabouts of the missing AI equipment.

Walker picked up the phone, and Josh began speaking.

"You just missed it. Two days ago, the package left Karachi by ship, bound for Penang, Malaysia. It will arrive in two days. You can pick up the trail there.

"Soon, we expect to have the essential flight information, date, and time, for the package to leave Kuala Lumpur—"

"Excuse me, Josh," Walker interrupted. "Addison and I were wondering why Penang. How did that ever happen?"

"Yes, Jack, that's a good question. It seems the Chinese have used the Penang-Kuala Lumpur-Beijing route before and feel comfortable using it again. In recent years, SE Asia, in general, and

Malaysia, in particular, has modernized their industry, building modern plants and producing products to Western standards, utilizing their cheaper labor. They make all kinds of products for the West, like electronic parts for computer use, hard drives, telephone accessories, household items, etc. IBM, Motorola, and others are now big players in these countries. In Northeast Penang, Motorola owns a manufacturing facility that builds lithium-ion batteries and cell phone charging systems. After careful packaging, it goes to Penang, through customs, and is delivered to Malaysia Airlines Kargo for routing to Beijing. The shipping of cell phone parts occurs two to three times a week on this route. Usually, after delivery to Malaysian Airlines, the airline trucks them to Kuala Lumpur, and they catch the next flight to China.

"On arrival in Beijing, it is trucked to Tianjin, where they are assembled with other components into your common cell phones for sale in the West. The Chinese are comfortable with their 'assets' moving on this generally secure commercial transit system and can easily manage the customs requirements of Malaysia with a few 'extra' dollars."

"Wow, quite a new world system of production," Jack acknowledged. "For the mission, however, thinking ahead, it seems we may have a chance to retrieve it on the ground between Penang and Kuala Lumpur, or in flight, with our plane making an unsuspecting detour." Jack started to smile as he glanced over to Addison.

Josh was quick to respond. "Jack, two things. First, position yourself late this afternoon at the ChaiWala Bukhari Tea House located three blocks from the Hang Shen Import-Export Company office building. A friend of ours will approach you, and he will have some important information for you and Addison. Details on what to expect in Penang.

"Second. We'll talk again after you arrive in Penang. I hope you can put together a working plan for intercepting and retrieving the package. Also, have a good backup plan in case there are any unexpected events. You have the full support of the 'company' to do what is necessary to get the equipment back in safe hands! Advise us of any resources you may need. We'll talk soon."

Josh Edwards intentionally failed to mention to Jack that David Lee of the Hang Shen Import-Export Company was the friendly contact with the information; Lee was also a double agent. Walker knew the CIA had an asset in Karachi but did not know Lee was their man. On the other hand, Lee knew Walker was CIA and surmised he was nosing around and trying to get a lead on the missing equipment's whereabouts. Both men also knew how to conduct a clandestine meeting using code words.

Walker followed a group of workers into the tea house and sat one table away from them on the outside patio. The four men talked among themselves, and Walker smiled to himself as he eavesdropped on their conversation.

Whew, they're speaking Punjabi, he thought. *I'm sure glad I paid attention in language school. Since about half the people in Pakistan speak Punjabi, I guess I lucked out.*

When Walker sat down, the table behind him was unoccupied. A voice from behind startled him when he heard, in perfect English, just loud enough for him to hear, "How do you like this weather?" He resisted the temptation to turn around because he recognized the coded question. If he answered the question with a negative response, that meant a dangerous situation existed and to discontinue the conversation. An affirmative response meant, "Let's talk."

Still looking straight ahead with his back to the voice, Walker replied, "The weather's beautiful; couldn't be nicer."

"I have some information for you," the voice continued. "The package left Pakistan on a container ship some days ago bound for Penang, Malaysia. The ship should dock the day after tomorrow at the container ship terminal on the mainland opposite the George Town cruise ship terminal. From there, it will be trucked to a freight forwarder's warehouse on Penang Island, repackaged, and combined with a commercial shipment of lithium-ion batteries and then forwarded to Kuala Lumpur for air shipment on one of Malaysia

Airlines' numerous daily flights to Beijing."

"Do you know which flight? What day—"

"I don't know those details yet. When I do, I'll reestablish contact. I should go now. I've been here too long already. Wait five minutes before you leave, and don't turn around."

Walker waited seven minutes, rose from his seat, and as he headed for the exit, glanced behind him and saw only an empty table. *Well, that was helpful. I better collect my partner and get our asses to Penang ASAP*, he thought.

———◉———

That evening, back at the safe house, Walker and Stark collected their thoughts, and Jack made airline arrangements to get to Penang. Walker punched the end-call button on his cell phone and exclaimed, "It never fails. When you've absolutely, positively got to get somewhere fast, it takes forever."

"Why? What's the problem?"

"There are no direct flights to Penang, and they all make at least one stop. I booked us on a Malaysia Airlines flight to Penang via Bangkok. It's a little over eleven hours, gate-to-gate. Son of a bitch!"

"That's better than one week on a boat, don't you think? When do we leave?"

Walker frowned at Stark for a couple of seconds before he replied. Jack was tired and frustrated. He found her sour reply with that Australian accent irritated him. He quickly decided to keep his mouth shut and abruptly departed from the living room toward the bedroom and said in a louder-than-normal voice, "Plane leaves at 0800!"

Addison sat on her floor mat, smiled, and said in a low tone, "Grumpy!" She rose from the rug, stood upright, and retired to the other bedroom.

She was tired from the day's stressful activity—playing cat and mouse with suspected terrorists—but she had one last thing to do before calling it a night. Sitting in a comfortable chair next to the bed, she lifted a notebook from the night table next to the bed and documented her day's activity in a coded text. After finishing her two-sentence entry, she closed the book, sat back in the chair, and let her mind wander. She thought about her life's journey so far and considered herself a lucky woman in some ways, but not so lucky in others. She briefly reflected on her childhood, growing up in Brisbane's middle-class suburb. *I'm incredibly thankful for both my mum and dad*, she thought.

Addison's mother noticed an interesting development in her young daughter—she was always looking up in the air—first, it was birds and then airplanes. Whenever a plane flew overhead, she would look up, point to it, and say, "Look, Mummy, a big bird." As Addison matured, her interest in aviation grew. She read books and magazines with aviation themes, and after saving money from baby-sitting, she began taking flying lessons when she turned fifteen. The mother watched the daughter blossom and often told her, "Don't listen to anyone who says you can't do something because you're a girl. You can do anything you put your mind to."

Addison placed her journal on the nightstand, stood, and turned down the blankets on the bed. As she lay in bed in the darkened room, she thought one final thought before drifting off to sleep. *I've pursued my dreams and am happy with my career choices, but it has come at a price—like being alone tonight in Pakistan. I've always put my career before relationships, and as a result, I've not been very successful in that area. Maybe someday, I can open up to a special someone who will accept me with no conditions.*

CHAPTER NINE

The following morning, Walker and Stark boarded a Malaysia Airlines Airbus A-330 and departed Karachi on time for the first leg of their eleven-hour journey to Penang. The large jet, capable of carrying up to two hundred eighty-nine passengers in two classes of service, was nearly full. Walker could not believe his luck. Checking again last minute with the gate agent, he and Addison scored two last-minute seats together in the economy cabin's forward section. Their good fortune had two benefits. First, an aisle separated their two seats—A and B in row nineteen—from the nearby section of four seats in the cabin's center. Walker wanted to use this opportunity to discuss their growing plan to intercept the package on the ground while it was en route to Kuala Lumpur Airport. The seating arrangement afforded the couple privacy to engage in that conversation. Second, the forward section of economy seats had extra legroom, which caused Walker to smile.

Stark glanced at Walker, saw the smile, and asked, "Why are you happy so early this morning?"

"If you were six foot two, you wouldn't have to ask."

At that moment, a flight attendant delivered a cup of hot coffee on the tray table in front of Walker. He smiled again, grabbed the cup, and reclined his seat another notch.

"OK, Walker, now that you're comfortable and wide awake, what is your latest plan? We have to intercept the package before it gets on that plane to Beijing, right?"

"Right. We have an informant at the cargo warehouse facility near the Penang Airport. The informant is the owner. He provides services as a freight forwarder—a business that collates smaller shipments together as one for the airlines. The KL station chief told me he is in contact with the informant regularly. The package arrived at the container port today, so we're about twelve hours behind it.

"Our freight forwarder will take possession after the cargo clears customs. The 'package' will be separated from the mining equipment and repackaged at the freight forwarder's warehouse for delivery later to Malaysia Airlines MASkargo unit at Penang Airport. MAS then trucks it overland to KL. That window of travel will be our opportunity to retrieve it.

"Our freight forwarder friend, named Ahmad Osman, also provided the station chief with interesting additional information."

"How so?"

"The freight forwarder informed the station chief that he was instructed to bundle the package with a shipment of Motorola lithium-ion phone batteries and then process the whole shipment through Malaysian customs—the batteries and the 'package'—as a single shipment of batteries."

"Wait a minute—you said he was instructed. Instructed by whom?"

"I was saving that for later, but since you asked . . . The freight guy is a freelancer who works for anyone willing to pay for his services. Right now, he works for both the Chinese Ministry of State Security and us—"

Stark interrupted, "Wow, that guy has a big set. Talk about a toxic work environment." Her comment caused Walker to smile.

"Like I was saying, the station chief didn't go into detail, but he said the freight forwarder had been very helpful to us in the past. This time, he's letting us know the Chinese instructed him to consolidate the 'package' with the lithium-ion battery shipments. They have numerous shipments every week earmarked for Beijing from the nearby factory. He cautioned me that it was important we don't do anything that would jeopardize the identity or safety of the asset."

"Of course, I agree. So what's the plan?"

"I have a basic plan A and then backup plan B. First, plan A. We'll try to intercept the shipment on the ground while traveling from the MASkargo facility on Penang Island to Kuala Lumpur Airport. The station chief will arrange for three additional field operatives to meet us at our hotel. After picking us up at the hotel, the five of us will travel together to the intercept point, a desolate stretch of highway in central Malaysia. We'll set up a roadblock, pose as local police, stop the truck, tase the driver, and drive the truck off the road into the jungle. You and I will be waiting there, off-road. I know what we're looking for, so we'll load it into our van when I find it, and we all ride off into the sunset. The station chief is trying to arrange either a small, fast boat at a sleepy coastal marina or a friendly helicopter to take the equipment out of Malaysia to safety in nearby Singapore."

Addison glanced at Walker, and by the look on his face, she knew he was pleased with his plan. *It sounds like a good plan*, she thought. "If plan A doesn't work out, and somehow the package gets to Kuala Lumpur and on the plane, then what? What's your plan B?"

Walker turned his head, glanced over his shoulder, made sure no one was near, and then looked at Addison before answering. "Well, we don't have a lot of good choices. We get on the flight and hijack the plane."

⋰⋱

Kuala Lumpur

The sun had broken above the eastern horizon half an hour earlier and had begun its climb into a cloudless blue sky when Zara turned his flight simulator off. His steps faltered as he departed the room, now exhausted both physically and mentally. It was his day off, and he looked forward to spending most of it sleeping. By two o'clock in the afternoon, his bladder and rumblings in his stomach awoke him. His all-night flight simulator session exhausted him, but it remained the most satisfying hours of his otherwise miserable existence. He sat up in bed, rubbed the sleep from his eyes, and decided, first things first. *I better relieve myself before I explode*, he thought. With that priority taken care of, he then shuffled to the kitchen. Since he slept through breakfast, he began preparing a lunch to quench his growling stomach. His depression over his marriage had also depressed his appetite. He was not eating much these days and usually waited for his stomach to announce his hunger. Still in his bathrobe and slippers, he filled a small pot with water, put it on the stove, and adjusted the flame to a medium height. He decided three hard-boiled eggs and fruit would suffice. Zara sat down on one of the four chairs circling the kitchen table, picking his usual chair. He leaned back in the chair and let his mind wander as he waited for the water to boil.

He faintly smiled as his memories transported him to a time when he was nineteen and his future wife, Nurul, had just turned seventeen. Before their arranged marriage, the two teenagers knew each other from their limited participation in school functions, the mosque, and social sightings around town. As is customary in many Southeast Asian Muslim countries, teenagers can become willing participants in the marriage arrangement. They can have yes and no input into the discussion and negotiations by their families. Sometimes, families stipulate that there shall be no children for the first two years—should the husband and wife truly not get along. In this case, however, they both were excited to proceed.

Romantic attraction, youthful hormones, and cultural anticipation blinded the young couple to the actual realities of what it meant to have a life together. A serious individual by nature and from a family with deep religious convictions, Nurul would do what was good for the family and be an obedient wife as dictated by her religion. Zara, by contrast, was more secular in his beliefs, had a practical personality, and yearned to be successful. But the sudden death of their daughter had turned their respective worlds upside down.

As his marriage fell apart and feeling more isolated every day, he could not resist the easy flirting with female crew members assigned to his flights. Not known to him, he needed this companionship to fill the deep hole in his heart. Zara thought, *My dear Nurul, what happened to us? Why did we drift apart?* Zara knew the answer to his rhetorical questions, which only deepened his depression and guilt. *I only have myself to blame.*

The sound of boiling water brought Zara's mind back to reality. He stood, walked to the stove, and dropped the eggs into the boiling water, and six minutes later, they were ready. He shelled them, sliced them, and ate them with freshly sliced mango. After finishing his meager meal, he left the kitchen and prepared for another day alone. He satisfied his physical hunger, but he longed for relief from the emotional pain of his deepened sadness. As he returned to the bedroom to get dressed, he stopped at the bathroom and grabbed a bottle of pills from the cabinet. He stared at the bottle before opening it and removing two of them. Then he half-filled a glass with water, threw his head back, and swallowed his drugs. The meds took the edge off his pain an hour later, even as he longed for a more permanent solution.

Later that day, Zara felt more like his old self just reading and going for a long walk along the tree-lined streets of his neighborhood. For now, his mood had stabilized. *I wish things could stay this way*, he thought, *but I know they won't. The Xanax helps, but I wish it didn't make me so sick. Maybe I should see my doctor.* He shook his head and dismissed that thought. He feared Malaysia Airlines would find out and ground him if he saw a doctor.

After a light dinner, he sat in front of his home computer. He logged onto Malaysia Airlines' scheduling application to confirm for a second time the actual check-in and departure times for tomorrow night's five-and-a-half-hour flight to Beijing. With that task accomplished, he focused on the crew assignments and saw one name that brought a smile to his face—*my beautiful Aishah will be there. It must be two months since we were last together. She wanted us to meet in KL, but I put her off and said I'd call her later.*

Zara's eyes continued to scan the crew manifest, and he saw Hashim Merican identified as his first officer. Zara knew of Hashim but had never flown with him.

Born in Malaysia twenty-seven years ago, Hashim was an intelligent, disciplined, and personable individual whose bright, huge smile filled his face and made others smile in return. A week after his twentieth birthday, the Langkawi Malaysia Flight Training Academy accepted him as a cadet into their professional pilot flight training program. Two years later, Malaysia Airlines hired him for flying duties in Kuala Lumpur. His enthusiasm, academic, and technical excellence impressed both his superiors and his peers. He completed his Boeing 777 ground school procedures and simulator training two months ago and has flown with other training captains since then. It's called Initial Operating Experience (IOE) in the industry—a structured on-the-job training experience. Friday's flight with Zara would be his last training flight. If his performance met strict airline standards, as decided by his last check airman, Zara, Hashim would assume line-flying duties without further supervision.

Zara reviewed Hashim's electronic training folder and saw the notation that Hamid had completed his previous IOE flight from Kuala Lumpur to Frankfort, Germany, one week ago. The favorable comments by the other training captains impressed him. Zara read their remarks out loud. "First Officer Hashim always seems well prepared. His system and procedural knowledge are excellent. His application of that knowledge is impressive. Hashim displays good situational awareness."

This type of favorable review, showing excellent progress with his first officer duties from another check pilot, essentially said Hashim was ready to be an everyday line pilot. Zara's job should be easy on Friday's flight with not much instruction needed: just verify he is ready to be released from training and given normal line flying status.

Zara pushed back his desk chair, closed his eyes, and rubbed his forehead. The pounding in his head had returned, and he wondered if the pills he had taken before he sat down in front of his computer this evening were to blame. His pain had caused his thoughts to turn dark, and feelings of despair welled up inside of him. Those very thoughts took over and replaced the positive thoughts he had earlier when he focused on his upcoming trip. Zara projected ahead to his "final solution" plan on Friday's flight and considered the possible hurdles with dealing with Hashim in the cockpit.

I should give him a call, he thought, *and build up his trust in me.* Zara repositioned himself in front of the computer, pulled up the MAS pilots' call list, and punched Hashim's phone number into his cell phone. Hashim Merican picked up after three rings.

"Hashim, this is Captain Zara here in Kuala Lumpur. I see we are flying together on the March 8 flight to Beijing and back. I just wanted to call and introduce myself and welcome you to the triple-seven fleet."

"Good evening, Captain. Thanks for the call."

"From the records, I see you have been flying the Airbus 330 for the last two years. How has the change to the Boeing 777 been treating you?"

Hashim replied, "The instructors at the triple-seven school have been both friendly and very helpful. I have been 'thinking in French' with my Airbus flying for the last couple of years, but now I'm back to Boeing engineering concepts and procedures, which I first saw on the B737 years ago. And the triple-seven is so big—three hundred tons!—yet so maneuverable when hand flying it. I think I like the control yoke design better than the side-stick controller design of the Airbus."

Zara, not thinking, emitted a half smile. "Yes, I can relate to that. I too prefer the central control wheel design, and in my opinion— it just feels more natural. In the pilot world, passengers and pilots alike are judgmental regarding landings; you know, the smoothness of the touchdown and rollout. How have your landings been during your IOE trips?"

"Yes, sir, I consider landings to be my greatest challenge. That's why it feels so good to hear passengers applaud after you 'stick' a landing."

Zara chuckled. "Yes, I agree. That's a good feeling. I see that your course objectives and phase checks have all been certified, pretty much on schedule. Have your trainers answered all your questions along the way?"

"Yes, sir. My instructors and training captains have been great, and I feel ready to move on."

"Excellent. If any questions come to mind, give me a call, or I can address them in person when we fly together. I want you to feel comfortable and confident in your new position as the first officer on this jumbo jet." By Hashim's tone of voice, Zara felt that their conversation achieved his goal of gaining Hashim's trust. As Zara prepared to end their discussion, Hashim interjected a piece of personal information, feeling comfortable.

"Sir, I appreciate the call and your interest in my professional development, but the last few weeks have been a busy time for me. Two weeks ago, the director of flight operations called me to ask if I would cooperate with a news article about younger pilots in S. E. Asia coming of age in the piloting profession. It was a travel industry piece highlighting Malaysia Airlines using the industry's best practices. CNN travel industry expert, Richard Quincy, showed up in Hong Kong a few days later, with a camera crew in trail, filming me flying the return trip to Kuala Lumpur. It was an exciting day! A few days later, I became engaged. A week ago, we celebrated the event with an engagement party. My fiancée is also an airline pilot on a competing airline based here in Kuala Lumpur."

"Wow, you have been a busy fellow. Getting married! Congratulations to you and your fiancée. Please tell me more about your television video experience when we meet. I'd love to hear about it. Concluding the call, Zara ended with, "See you Friday night."

Hmm, Hashim will probably do very well on his final check ride.

Hand-picked by upper management for his publicity role as a new first officer. Aiming to please, he should also be very compliant if I ask him to do something, like leaving the cockpit to attend to a matter in the passenger cabin. Yes, I can see this working to my advantage.

PART 3

Preparing the Package

CHAPTER TEN

Penang Island, Malaysia

I've never been more grateful for a trip to end, Walker thought. *What an ordeal.* Twelve and a half hours after he and Stark stepped on their flight in Karachi, they stepped off in Penang. The pair traveled light with only one carry-on bag apiece. Stark had never been to Penang Island before: she got excited about their arrival after reading about its reputation as an international crossroads and transportation hub in SE Asia for raw materials, rubber, tea, and spices, all going to England in the olden days. George Town, established as a British Crown Colony in 1867, is the island's capital and just five degrees north of the equator.

They followed the terminal exit signs and emerged right behind the taxi stand into the midday brightness. Jack opened the taxi door for Addison, and they both collapsed into the backseat.

"Where to?"

"Hotel Equatorial," they both said at the same time. Walker gave Stark a good-natured jab in the ribs and commented, "Just like an old married couple, hey?"

Stark smirked and thought, *Married? Or, on second thought, never say never.*

The seven-kilometer ride took ten minutes. The consulate had reserved a deluxe twin room for them, and check-in was quick and efficient.

"Your keys, sir. Happy hour begins at five-thirty tonight in the hotel bar, and complimentary breakfast in the lobby starts at six thirty tomorrow morning. Have a good evening."

Stepping away from the reception desk, Walker checked his watch. "Hah, only one hour until happy hour begins. Boy, can I use a drink."

Stark shot him a sideward glance and just shook her head. "I plan to soak in a hot bath for an hour, and then we have business to take care of, right?"

"You're such a killjoy."

"Make you a deal, Walker," Stark jabbed back quickly. "I'll join you at 5:00 p.m. in the lobby bar for drinks if you promise to accompany me to one of those food streets in 'Old Town.' I want to try nasi lemak— pieces of fried chicken with egg, tiny, salted fish, and spicy sambal sauce alongside fragrant coconut rice. Now, am I a killjoy?"

Penang International Airport

After completing a one-hour flight from Singapore, a Chinese-registered Gulfstream 5 business jet slowed to a stop on the Executive Services ramp at Penang International Airport. The jet's door opened five minutes later, and four Asian men descended the stairs and stood on the concrete ramp as a black limousine approached. As they waited for the limo, the Gulfstream's copilot removed three medium-size, hard-sided suitcases from the cargo compartment and placed them next to the four men. The limo driver stopped abreast of the four men, and a fifth Asian man emerged from the limo's rear and greeted the Gulfstream's passengers. The driver placed the suitcases in the trunk while the five men entered the limo and occupied the rear passenger seats. After completing the task, the driver sped toward the airport exit. The four visitors comprised a scientific team of two scientists, an engineer, and a team leader. In true Communist fashion, the team leader had no scientific credentials but was a Ministry of State security official. The four men sat in silence until addressed.

"I trust you had a good flight," David Lee asked.

The team leader, Shen Chow, acknowledged Lee's question with a nod.

"Good, we have a five-minute drive to the warehouse facility, which is just on the other side of the airport. The equipment you are interested in seeing has been separated and placed in a secure room for your inspection. If everything meets your approval, we will release the balance of funds to our Afghan friends." Shen, still with a stoic expression on his face, nodded again. "I notice you brought luggage," Lee continued. "I was told you would be here for only a couple of hours. Have your plans changed?"

"No," Shen replied. "Those suitcases contain test equipment and computers my team needs to perform their inspections. We will return to Beijing immediately after we finish."

Lee felt a nervous shudder track through his body. He participated in other clandestine activities, such as drug smuggling and money laundering, but this operation was high stakes and very personal. He took a deep breath. *Wow! I need to get out of this business . . . and soon!* The drone hardware with its artificial intelligence software captured from Alpha Base by the Taliban could be a game-changer on future battlefields. The Chinese wanted it and were willing to risk everything to get it, and the Americans would do whatever was necessary to get it back. *And here I am, right in the middle,* Lee thought, *but I'll do what is needed to avenge my son.*

The freight forwarder's warehouse, a modern, white, two-story building with blue trim, loomed in front of them. Office space occupied the second floor, while the entire first floor consisted of four loading docks on the outside, which serviced one-quarter million square feet of warehouse space on the inside.

Lee tapped the driver on the shoulder to get his attention. "The entrance is ahead one hundred yards, on the right." The limo driver navigated the maze of access roads and stopped in front of the lobby's twin glass doors.

"We'll get out here," Lee instructed. "Our host will be waiting for us inside." Lee held the glass door open for his guests and joined them in the spacious lobby. A frail-looking Malaysian man in his mid-fifties stood as Lee and his four guests approached. "Mr. Shen, this is Ahmad Osman. He is the freight forwarder responsible for getting your equipment ready for shipment to Beijing." Ahmad acknowledged Lee's introduction with a smile and a slight bow. "Ahmad, please show our guests the way to the room where you have the equipment ready for their inspection." Ahmad again acknowledged Lee's request with a slight bow, and with his left hand, motioned in the direction of a sliding glass door. "Please, gentlemen, follow me this way."

The inspection room lay at the warehouse's rear and was a quick two-minute walk from the lobby. Upon their arrival, Ahmad punched the five-digit code into the keypad to the door's right, followed by an audible click. Upon entering, the men saw three six-foot-long tables covered with an assortment of mechanical and electronic equipment. Shen barked an order, and his three-person team sprang into action. They opened their wheeled, hard-sided plastic suitcases and removed an assortment of equipment and laptop computers. Their first task was to photograph the equipment laid out before them as their computers and test equipment powered up.

Shen turned to Ahmad and said, "From this point, it will take them about two hours to complete their inspections and evaluations. Is there a quiet place I can make a private phone call?"

Ahmad nodded and gestured toward a small conference room at the rear of the larger room. "Sir, you may use that room for your call." Without acknowledging Ahmad, Shen did a military-style pivot on his right foot and walked toward the small room.

Lee's eyes followed Shen for a moment. *Arrogant bastard*, he thought, and then he turned in Ahmad's direction. "Thank you. You may leave and get back to your work. When these men finish, I'll let you know what has to be done next." Ahmad nodded, smiled, and turned to leave. Lee's eyes followed Ahmad as he walked ten feet to the door. *His limp seems more pronounced,* he thought. *Probably aggravated by the long walk here.*

Lee admired Ahmad's courage and resilience. Ahmad's private opposition to China's crackdown on the Uyghurs, a Muslim ethnic minority group in Xinjiang, China, caused him to suffer a near-death accident at a Malay street protest gone violent. Surgeons had to reconstruct his right femur with rods and screws and repair his right knee's tendons and ligaments, leaving Ahmed with a painful limp. However, instead of discouraging Ahmad, his suffering had the opposite effect. It steeled his resolve: He engaged in a personal war of harassment that focused on misdirecting China's shipments and working with other countries' intelligence agencies to disrupt China's attempt to steal Western technology. Lee did not have to ask Ahmad twice for his help. *And an envelope with five hundred U.S. dollars didn't hurt either,* Lee thought. Fifteen minutes after Ahmad's departure, Shen finished his phone call and returned to the group.

"Mr. Lee, there is going to be a change of plans. If my team finds the equipment acceptable, my superiors instructed me to inform you that my team and I will accompany the equipment on its trip to Beijing. They ordered me not to let it out of our sight." Shen's words caught Lee by surprise and caused his mind to race. He knew the American and Australian agents planned to make a ground intercept to retrieve the "package" before going to Kuala Lumpur. Still, he also knew they were not expecting extra company. One truck driver would not pose a problem, but a car full of Chinese citizens would.

"Mr. Lee? Is everything okay?"

"Yes, I'm sorry. Everything's fine. I was just thinking about the final shipping arrangements to Kuala Lumpur Airport. Ahmad will get me that information, but I'm sure it will be a day or two before this equipment gets merged with the cell phone battery shipment and passes customs' inspection."

Lee noticed a slight furrow on Shen's brow and decided to answer Shen's unasked question. "Don't worry. The inspectors here are quite accommodating," adding with a slight smile, "This local customs' office has been useful to us before."

The Chinese team finished their work two and a half hours later. Lee, Shen, and his team relocated to the small conference room where each man approached Shen and took turns giving him their assessment of the equipment's capabilities and technology level. Stoic Shen sat in silence and occasionally nodded his head while listening to his team explain their findings. They were impressed and excited. Chow Sum Li, the engineer, summed up their assessment. "Sir, this equipment represents a significant leap in developing and using artificial intelligence on the battlefield and is at least ten years ahead of our state of the art."

After Chow summarized the team's assessments, Shen asked, "Will reverse-engineering the technology you saw today level the playing field between our American enemies and us?"

"Yes, sir, without a doubt. If we build on this technology, we can surpass the Americans in probably two years instead of being ten years, or more, behind."

"All right then. My superiors said they would authorize the release of the balance of funds if our evaluation were successful. Mr. Lee, you may tell your Taliban friends that we will release the remainder of the money to them within the next three days. Our consulate has arranged lodging for us at a nearby hotel. Lee, you will advise me when the shipment is ready to leave, and we will ride in an automobile behind the delivery truck to its destination at Kuala Lumpur Airport. Our work here is done. Pack up your equipment, and we'll proceed to our hotel."

Lee listened in silence as the Chinese team packed their equipment. He knew further work was needed to be done. He knew the CIA agents tasked with retrieving the equipment expected only to intercept a delivery truck. A car full of Chinese nationals accompanying the truck changed that scenario. A gunfight on a Malaysian highway was not in anyone's best interest. His mind searched for a solution but found none.

I'll pass this information on to the Americans, he thought. *It is out of my hands, and they'll have to decide how they want to proceed.*

CHAPTER ELEVEN

Kuala Lumpur

As Zara busied himself cleaning up the kitchen, he heard the Westminster door chimes signaling someone was at the front door. He paused, turned off the water, and moved in the direction of the front door. The chimes rang a second time, annoying him.

"All right, all right, I'm coming." He looked through the peephole and grimaced when he saw his best friend, Haziq. He was not in the mood to see anyone. Upon opening the door, he greeted his friend with a shrug. "So, what brings you here?" Not waiting for an answer, Zara continued, "All right, come in."

Zara and Haziq became best friends during their eighteen months in the Philippines, attending Malaysia Airlines' cadet flying school. They had much in common as their close working and living conditions created a brotherlike bond. Upon their return to KL, their professional careers advanced initially first officer and to captain flying duties, and their friendship deepened. Their wives also became friends, and the couples enjoyed each other's company at airline employee parties and family birthdays and anniversaries. Over the years, the families had shared the joy of each other's successes. They also grieved together after Zara's youngest child died. Haziq's wife was a great comfort to Nurul in those trying times. Now, workplace gossip caused Haziq to worry about his friend, and he came to offer his help.

Haziq stepped into the house and followed Zara to the living room. Zara waved his arm toward the couch and offered, "Have a seat, my brother, and tell me what you want."

"First, here's a six-pack of your favorite beer. I know Nurul disapproves, but she left your house months ago, and that's why I'm here." Zara broke eye contact with Haziq, took the brown paper bag from his outstretched hand, and placed it on the coffee table. Zara frowned as both men sat and faced each other.

Zara said, "So, you know. I guess even bad news travels fast. What have you heard?"

"Well, you know Nurul and my wife are friends, just like you and me, and Nurul confided in her that you two are having problems—that she just couldn't put up with your infidelity any longer. Also, several pilots at work have asked me about you. They wondered if you felt okay because they said you seemed distracted lately. They said—and these are their words—'you seem to have lost that spark and zest for life.' They know you placed great importance on crew resource management, and they respected you for that, but now they're talking about your lack of communication and leadership in the cockpit. They said you used to relish personal engagement in the past, but now, you have become withdrawn and joyless."

Zara looked sheepishly to the side as Haziq continued to speak. Zara thought about what he said, especially his comments about Crew Resource Management (CRM). During the classroom part of his flight training, Zara's and Haziq's instructor drove home the value of communications and proactive workload management to eliminate cockpit hazards and mitigate human error. The instructor concluded his lecture with examples of how a breakdown in CRM led to tragic outcomes. Most notable among those examples were: United Airlines Flight 173, which ran out of fuel while holding near Portland, Oregon, and crashed; Flying Tiger Line Flight 66 collided with terrain on approach near Kuala Lumpur because of the crew's confusion over altitude requirements; Eastern Airlines Flight 401 descended into the Florida Everglades while the crew focused their attention on a simple landing gear warning lightbulb that was out. Those lessons made a strong impression on Zara, and he swore he would never allow himself to be careless in the cockpit. Now, he seemed not to care about such things, and other people noticed the change.

"Maybe you should talk to someone, my friend; you know, a—"

"NO! I know what you're going to say, and I don't need to see a shrink—and I won't! You know what that'll do to my career. They'll ground me. I can't live with that. I'd rather be dead!" Zara sat up straight, his back stiff, and with a quickened pulse, looked at his friend and pleaded, "I'm fine. I am just going through a rough patch at the moment. You know—losing Misha, Nurul rejecting me, and my foolish behavior with our flight attendants—I know it looks bad, but I'm getting it under control. I just need a little more time to get it all sorted out. Trust me, brother, if I thought I was putting my safety and my passengers' safety at risk, I'd ground myself," he lied. "No, I got this. You'll see."

"I trust you'll do the right thing. You've got a good reputation, and you're a good man. Zara, I understand your concerns, but safety must come first. But only you know your state of mind, so please give this situation some hard thinking."

After a few moments of silence, Haziq continued, "Hey, my wife is out of town next week. How about lunch one day, after you return from your next trip? You pick the spot."

"Sure, okay, Haziq. I'll call you when I return," Zara answered, forcing a smile.

———◦※◦———

Kuala Lumpur

Iranian agent Rehyan Abed could not believe his luck. After he lost Walker and Stark's trail in Karachi, he did not think he had any chance to intercept them again or the package. *It's a big world*, he thought, *and I'm trying to find the proverbial needle in a haystack.* That picture changed when he received a call from the military attaché in the Iranian Embassy in Kuala Lumpur, who requested the two meet to discuss an important matter. As Abed relaxed in the Malaysia Airlines flight bound for Kuala Lumpur from Karachi, he reflected on his good fortune. *It's fortunate for us that bribery works well in this part of the world. Our previous successful dealings with the MASkargo freight forwarder, Osman, in Penang are still paying dividends. He reports a Chinese front company in Karachi instructed him to conceal some "sensitive" equipment in a shipment of batteries to avoid detection by Malaysian custom authorities—with the destination of that shipment being Beijing, China.* After arriving in Kuala Lumpur, Abed made his way to the row of cabs waiting outside the terminal. He opened the first cab's rear door and made himself as comfortable as possible in the cramped backseat.

"The Iranian Embassy, and please hurry."

The cab stopped in front of a closed gate representing the only opening through an eight-foot-high stone wall topped by a four-foot-high fence of curved steel bars surrounding the Iranian Embassy compound. Seconds after the cab stopped, the gate opened inward, allowing the cab to proceed along the circular driveway before it stopped in front of the main building's ballistic-proof glass doors. Abed exited the cab, entered the building, and was met in the lobby by the military attaché, Rashid Muhad.

"Come, my brother. Let's go to my office and talk for a while. Did you have a good flight from Karachi? Would you like something to drink, perhaps a cup of tea?"

"Thank you, sir. Yes, tea sounds good."

Both men walked down a door-lined hallway before standing in front of a wooden door that Muhad pushed open. "Please, come in and make yourself comfortable." The two men entered just as a staff member approached them with a tray containing two cups of tea and some light pastry. The staff member placed the tray on Muhad's desk and left the room.

Abed made himself comfortable in a padded red leather chair in front of Muhad's desk and asked his host, "Sir, I understand you have some information for me . . . about some 'sensitive' equipment. What is your—"

"Just one minute," Muhad interrupted as he held up his right index finger, picked up his phone, and punched the zero button with his left index finger. "Yes, please send in Farzad. Thank you. Sorry for the interruption, but there's another person who should hear this information. He's going to be your partner in this operation."

Partner? Operation? Abed thought.

Five seconds later, the office door opened, and a twenty-something young man with a baby face entered.

"Rehyan, this is Farzad Bahadori. The Ministry of Intelligence director sent him here to assist you in an important operation. Please sit, Farzad," Muhad said, while pointing to a second red leather chair. "Our country's leader has decided it is in our best national interest to intercept and take possession of the equipment stolen from the Americans that is now on its way to Beijing."

"Excuse me, sir," Rehyan said, "but won't that anger our Chinese brothers?"

"Yes, it probably will, but that matter is for others to deal with. Your orders are to hijack the flight, uh, Malaysia Flight 370, leaving Kuala Lumpur at 12:30 a.m. this Saturday, and force the pilot to fly to Zahedan—"

Rehyan nodded. "I am familiar with that city near our eastern border with Afghanistan."

"Yes, that's correct, and that is why you were selected for this honorable task. Zahedan is within the plane's range, and its airport's runway is long enough to land a large airplane."

Muhad continued with the specifications of the mission. "I've arranged a conference room downstairs for you and Farzad and two additional agents to meet and discuss the details of your assignment. Farzad and his associates were schooled in Iran in preparation for this hijack task. Now, given we know the type of plane involved, a Boeing 777, the four of you can familiarize yourselves with the aircraft, seating arrangements, and decide on your options to control the two cabins while you get the pilots to fly to Iran. Two of you will be sitting in the forward business section. When one of the pilots opens the cockpit door to leave, you will enter the cockpit and force the other pilot to change course or be shot. The other two agents will be managing the economy section passengers in the rear, not allowing anyone to come forward.

"You'll need weapons. Our engineers have perfected a 3D printing process to produce a handgun molded from a strong plastic like polymer; the same as the ammunition. The gun can be disassembled and is undetectable by X-ray in a carry-on bag. You are authorized to use whatever force is necessary to accomplish your mission.

"If the pilots refuse to cooperate, you are to kill both of them and crash the airplane. If we can't get the secret American equipment, then neither will the Chinese."

Muhad's last statement caused Rehyan's back to stiffen, and he sat straight up in his chair. He glanced at Farzad sitting next to him and saw no reaction at all—not a flinch or a twitch—just a stoic calmness. *Now, I understand,* he thought. *My so-called partner is here to make sure we are both martyred if we can't accomplish our mission.*

"Good, then our meeting here is over. You will pick up your weapons downstairs before you leave. Praise Allah."

CHAPTER TWELVE

Penang Island, Malaysia

Zara's wife, Nurul, sat at the small table tucked into a breakfast nook next to the kitchen. Three large windows opened the room to sunlight and made it bright and cheery. She would sit and stare outside for hours. It was her favorite seat in the house. Her home's location on Penang Island offered stunning views of the coastline just south of George Town, the capital. The cheeriness of her environment and the beautiful memories of happier times buoyed her mood most of the time, but this morning, nothing seemed to help as she stirred her now-tepid cup of tea. She left her husband and their home in Kuala Lumpur eight months ago and hoped she could cope while adjusting to her new reality by spending time in her "happy place." She knew couples broke up for many different reasons, but her mind kept going back to that tragic event many years ago when their daughter drowned on a family vacation. That was the turning point, she admitted.

Maybe I wasn't fair to Zara. That seems to be the time our life together began falling apart. We didn't talk, and when we did, we argued. I wish we would have gotten some counseling, but Zara was adamant we could work this out ourselves. And then his womanizing. I just couldn't take it any longer. Nurul lowered her eyes, her fingers still curled around the now cold cup of tea, while tears formed in her eyes and began to roll down her cheeks.

The loud, cold, and compassionless ring of her cell phone, lying on the table, startled her. Its announcement of an incoming call snapped her attention back to reality. She picked up the phone and smiled when she saw the call was from her son, Jamal.

"Hello, Jamal, how are you?"

"I'm fine, Mother, and you?" The two exchanged the usual mother-son pleasantries for a couple of minutes before Jamal stated the reason for his call.

"I got a call from Haziq, you know, Father's pilot friend, the one Father trained with in the Philippines. He didn't want to bother you, but he wanted us to know his concerns about Father's behavior—"

"What's wrong?" Nurul interrupted. She continued with an edge of sarcasm, "Your Father's having lady trouble?"

"Mother, please, I'm serious, and, no, that's not the problem. Well, yes, that's a problem, but not the one Haziq called me about. He's concerned about Father's health. He, other pilot friends, and other airline employees who interact with Father daily have noticed a big change in his personality. Haziq said Father appears anxious, distracted, and moody. He's also been complaining about headaches and nausea. Haziq visited Father today to check up on his friend and to try to talk to him. Haziq said Father almost threw him out of the house when he suggested Father seek professional help. Father said he wouldn't do anything to jeopardize his flying career and that he had everything under control."

"That doesn't surprise me," Nurul said. "I haven't talked to your father, as you know, in a couple of months. Your father never shared his inner feelings with me or anyone else. He always thought he could overcome anything by the sheer force of his will. Thanks for letting me know, but I can't think of any way to help. He has a serious job flying those big airplanes. I hope whatever is going on with him doesn't cloud his judgment. Even though we aren't together anymore, I wouldn't want anything to happen to him or anyone else." After Nurul ended the call with her son, she sat alone and stared into space. She faced an uncertain future but thanked Allah for the love and support of her only child.

Penang, Malaysia

Addison had finished her one-hour soak in a tub of hot water and felt rejuvenated. After long hours of sitting in cramped airline seats, her muscles ached, and the hot water did wonders to ease her pain. She entered the bedroom with a large towel wrapped around her otherwise naked body and used a second towel to dry her hair as she walked. "You know, Jack, the benefits of a hot bath are so under-rated. You should try—"

"I think we may have a problem," Jack interrupted. "I just received a text message to expect a call in the next hour from my boss, Josh Edwards. He has new information and new instructions to relay. Our plans may go down the drain, and we should be prepared."

Addison's pulse quickened. "When you suggested plan A, the ground intercept, it sounded very doable to me. When you mentioned the hijack option for plan B, I first thought you were just trying to be funny. Then I got that you meant it. I think plan B could be the problem. I fly Boeing commercial airliners for Qantas, and taking over an airliner in flight is no easy task, especially since 9/11."

Sitting on the edge of the bed, Walker's hands clasped together, forearms resting on his knees as he stared at the floor. Stark gave him reason after reason why a plan B wouldn't work. "—there's the possibility of Air Marshals on board, the cockpit door is fortified, tight security screening—"

Walker raised his head, looked at Stark, and interrupted. "Yeah, you're right, and probably a dozen more reasons why this would be nearly impossible to pull off for two ordinary people—but that's where you come in."

"Excuse me?"

"Do you think we were teamed together just because we've got pretty faces? No, it was because the operation planners at Langley wanted to cover all the bases. They knew we'd probably have opportunities to intercept and retrieve our equipment—on the ground and, failing that, in the air.

"So, the CIA thinks hijacking an airliner full of passengers on its way to Beijing is a good option?"

"There are no good options. We can't let this equipment fall into Chinese hands. We need to have a better idea of what we can do—in the worst situation possible." Walker continued, "So, between now and the flight, we need to figure out how to force the pilot and copilot to fly us to Diego Garcia."

"Diego Garcia? You mean the American military base on that small island in the middle of the Indian Ocean?"

"Exactly. The press will go bonkers, but our fake identities will provide us cover. The story will go something like this—we demand a hundred-million-dollar ransom and a yacht waiting for us at Diego Garcia, or we start killing passengers. The U.S. agrees to pay the ransom. We land, they arrest us, and the passengers are released. While that drama plays out, our military personnel retrieve the package, and everyone lives happily ever after."

"Easier said than done, Walker . . . Okay! Let me get dressed first, and we can continue this conversation. Now, I need a drink. Would you mind turning around?"

"I'll do better than that." Walker stood and walked toward the room's door. "Happy hour starts in ten minutes in our sitting room—when you're presentable. Maybe a couple of drinks will stimulate our imaginations." He closed the door behind him and left Stark still sitting on the bed as she pondered possible new instructions and a fast-changing mission.

Ten minutes after Walker left, Addison entered the sitting room. She was dressed comfortably in loose-fitting shorts, a buttoned shirt, and sandals. The room's air-conditioning system struggled to keep the hot, humid, outside air at bay. She saw Walker sitting in a straight-backed chair at the table. He was sipping a glass of what she assumed was single malt scotch. He stood as she approached.

"You clean up well, and you smell good too," he said playfully.

Subconsciously, he was beginning to appreciate Addison's natural beauty on a whole new level.

"From you, I'll take that as a compliment," she said as she pulled her chair closer to the table.

Walker said, "Can I fix you a gin and tonic from the minibar. Sorry, no lime."

"Yes, please," she answered.

Upon receiving her drink, Addison raised her glass and proposed a toast. "Here's to us pulling off this mission."

Walker lifted his almost-empty glass and clinked it against hers. "Yes, to us! Cheers."

The satellite phone rang aloud a second later, and the phone vibrated an inch across the table. Jack looked at Addison and then picked up the phone. "Okay, here we go," and pushed the answer button.

Deputy Director Josh Edwards got right to the point. "Jack, Addison, we have new information for you to digest. Our KL station chief reports our inside guy in Penang informed him that the 'package' would be delivered to Malaysia Airlines Kargo and be trucked to Kuala Lumpur Friday afternoon. It is scheduled to be on Malaysia Airlines Flight 370, a Boeing 777 jumbo jet, due to depart for Beijing from Kuala Lumpur Friday night, just after midnight. In a moment, we will talk about the intercept plan.

"Other news from our Chinese sources says that Iranian involvement is still possible, as they seem to be in the chase for the AI package. No real, actionable information yet. Separately, the Chinese have civilian scientists in Malaysia, at this moment, first inspecting their purchase and then escorting the 'package' on the ground from Penang to KL. The ground intercept is getting very complex, and civilian deaths of Chinese officials in a foreign country are not a defensible risk that our leadership wants to take. With this in mind, the powers above me have decided to abandon the ground intercept en route to KL. It's too dangerous, and the assault team idea can easily get out of hand."

Edwards continued, "Here are your new instructions—changing the objectives of the mission. The ground intercept in Malaysia to retrieve the AI package is now OFF. Similarly, any hostile takeover of the commercial airliner, i.e., MH370, should not occur. What if a stupid passenger wants to be a hero and gets hurt or dies? Also, we are expecting Chinese agents onboard. What if someone gets excited or makes a deadly mistake? A single stray bullet could cause a decompression and loss of jet control. It's too risky, with too many innocent lives at stake. The Washington powers at the CIA and elsewhere in the government have raised the argument that no Western, civilized country has ever hijacked a commercial airliner to date. Therefore, the inherent risk is unacceptable."

Jack and Addison looked at each other as this drama was playing out and could see plan A was out, and there was no support for plan B. When Edwards paused after recounting the above instructions, Jack responded, "Okay, boss, we got it. No retrieval attempt on the ground and no takeover attempts in flight for MH370. So, where does that leave us?"

"Jack, we do have a plan in mind. Let's call it plan C. You and Addison will continue to travel with the package to Beijing to assist the plan C special ops team of mercenaries waiting there to attack and destroy the 'package' while in transit to the Motorola factory. The risk of this operation is much less, while the reward is acceptable. We will simply build another drone to replace the one we destroy."

Later that evening, Walker had finalized their KL-Beijing flight reservations. He wanted seats in business class upfront, close to the cockpit and front galley. With the help of the American Embassy staff in Kuala Lumpur, they managed to get him and Stark seats 2A and 2C, a window and an aisle seat. The entire exhausting process took two hours.

"Whew, that was a pain in the ass," Walker sighed as he sat on the couch in front of his laptop computer. He closed the laptop and turned to Addison. "We're all set. Finally!"

"Isn't it ironic," Addison smirked, "that with our new mission directive to escort the package and assist in keeping it on time for a scheduled meeting later on the ground in China, we may be required to protect the cockpit from third-party intruders. Wow!"

"Right. I guess we should be ready for anything," responded Jack. "That's why the station chief told me to check the life vest compartment between our seats for a weapon. He didn't elaborate, but I'm assuming it's some kind of firearm—"

"For God's sake, Walker, do you realize how dangerous it is to discharge a firearm on board an aircraft in flight? The cabin is pressurized, and if that bullet goes through a window, the rapid decompression could suck one of us through the window, and I don't have to tell you what *that* would mean. Also, if it severs a wire bundle of the fly-by-wire flight control system, it'll be impossible to control the aircraft, and we'll crash. I swear, you Americans and your guns."

"Yeah, I know all that, and I don't plan on shooting the place up or shooting anybody if at all possible. But it will give us leverage with the crew and hopefully deter any passengers from getting involved."

Stark gave him a sideward glance and, in a softer voice, said, "You're right, of course. I just hope we can pull this off."

<hr>

They awoke early Friday morning, gathered their things, ate a quick breakfast in the hotel restaurant, and prepared to leave for their trip to Kuala Lumpur. The couple had decided to drive, and while they ate breakfast, the concierge made arrangements for a rental car. The driver parked the car next to the curb, and the concierge handed Walker the keys. "Have a good day, sir, and a safe trip."

The couple climbed into the front seats of a brand-new Ford Fusion. "Okay, kiddo, buckle up. We've got a five-hour ride ahead of us, four if we don't stop."

Still looking straight ahead, Stark replied, "Roger that, and don't call me kid."

"You're right," Walker said, "You are no kid! I'm sorry. You are a great agent and an essential asset to this team." Walker continued thinking to himself, *You are no kid; instead, you are a beautiful woman to be much appreciated.*

PART 4

Kuala Lumpur International Airport

CHAPTER THIRTEEN

Malaysia Airlines Maintenance Ramp, KLIA
Friday Afternoon, March 7, 2014

Boeing 777, registration number 9M-MRO, sat on the ramp in front of Malaysia Airlines' maintenance hangar at Kuala Lumpur Airport. The B777 is the largest twin-engine aircraft globally, famous for replacing the now expensive 747 four-engine behemoths on international routes. Nearly two hundred feet from wingtip to wingtip and two hundred nine feet long, capable of seating configurations carrying three hundred sixty-eight passengers, the triple seven is loved by the airlines, passengers, and crew alike. The Malaysia Airlines marketing department had it scheduled to depart just after midnight on a nonstop flight to Beijing. MAS maintenance technicians had completed their preflight inspections, but one final task required completion before the maintenance dispatcher signed off the aircraft for flight.

A maintenance technician approached the aircraft in a truck equipped to service the aircraft's crew oxygen system. On the aircraft's previous flight, the captain noted that the crew oxygen system pressure was low and required servicing in the aircraft's technical log. The technician opened the access panel on the fuselage and connected the charging lines. The whole process took only minutes to complete, but he had one more task to accomplish. He looked around his immediate vicinity and saw no other personnel. The technician climbed the boarding ladder and entered the cabin at the front of the business class section. He glanced into the cockpit and saw no one. He stretched his neck to look past the forward bulkhead and saw no one in the main cabin. Then he reached into the pocket of his coveralls and withdrew a quart-size Ziplock bag which contained a small black object and a piece of paper with three numbers scrawled on one side. He opened the life vest compartment between seats 2A and 2C and pushed the plastic bag to the rear. He closed the compartment, took one last glance around, and left the aircraft.

Zara's Residence, Kuala Lumpur
Friday Evening, March 7, 2014

This evening, Zara's preparation for an all-night flight had begun just as many others before it. Zara awoke from a late-afternoon nap, took a shower, ate a light supper at home, and then changed into his uniform. He backed his car from the driveway at nine p.m. and followed his usual route to the airport, three-and-a-half hours before he would captain Flight MH370. He drove the route hundreds of times before and always looked forward to arriving at his destination and the challenge and excitement of flying a large commercial airliner. In his country, commercial airline pilots enjoyed a rock-star status. Under normal circumstances, he enjoyed the attention and adoration, but a different mood engulfed him tonight. The two Xanax pills he took an hour earlier nauseated him and gave him a headache. He thought food would help, but it did nothing. Worse than his physical discomfort was his deepening paranoia. He began to debate with himself, questioning his judgment but getting defensive. *My wife and son hate me. My so-called friends talk behind my back. Tonight, I can make all that go away*, he thought. *I can stop the pain.* He backed into a crew reserved parking space in the airport parking lot and placed his keys under his seat. *I won't need these anymore*, he thought. He exited his car without locking it, walked the one hundred yards to a guard shack, presented his ID, and proceeded to the terminal.

After a short walk, he entered the Malaysia Airlines dispatch office. A few other pilots were in the room to one side, sitting at tables, with an extended countertop dividing dispatcher personnel and desks on the other side.

Zara put on a forced smile. "Good evening, Kim. I see your flight plans here on the counter. Have you anything special for Flight Three-Seventy to Beijing that I should be aware of this evening?"

"No, sir, nothing special. It looks like a textbook flight tonight. You've got the flight plans. Here are your en route weather, cargo manifest, crew assignments—all the usual stuff."

Zara took the paperwork from Kim's outstretched hand, walked to a nearby table and chair, and sat down. He spent the next ten minutes reviewing the various documents. The computerized flight plan calculated their en route time to Beijing and also their fuel burn, including reserves. Zara decided to wait for his first officer to arrive and review the flight planning information with him before signing off on it.

He turned his attention to the crew manifest after his review of the flight papers and saw Aishah's name as the chief purser. He lowered the paper and stared ahead. *Aishah will be flying with me tonight*, he thought. *Ah, we've had some wonderful trips together.* His temperament went from blissful reminiscing to a bottomless pit of despair—as if someone flipped a light switch—when he recalled the events of his troubled life and projecting tonight's events

On one such eventful day, Nurul answered his cell phone while he showered, noticing the call was from their son. When she finished talking to her son, she saw a notification for a new text message. She respected her husband's privacy and would not snoop through his phone, but curiosity got the best of her. The text contained a picture of Aishah with the Tower of London in the background. She did not know Aishah, but she knew her husband worked with female flight attendants, and he had recently been to London. It seemed harmless enough, and she thought little of it until two months later when she found a note in his uniform pocket: *"Thank you for our wonderful trip together. Love and Kisses, Aishah."* That note started a series of discussions that soon spiraled out of control. Conversations became arguments, which devolved into shouting matches and, in time, resulted in the destruction of trust and their marriage.

Zara lowered his head, raised his right hand, and rubbed his forehead. After several minutes, he stood and approached the dispatch counter.

"Kim, do me a favor. Can you pull the weather for the central and eastern Indian Ocean?" Kim responded with a silent, confused look. After all, Zara's flight was in the opposite direction. "Please indulge my curiosity; it has nothing to do with tonight's flight," Zara lied. Kim complied. Fifteen minutes later, Zara read the new weather data and began to visualize the elements of his plan.

———◄◉►———

Zara had signed in for duty at 10:50 p.m., followed by First Officer Hashim twenty-five minutes later. The two men sat together and looked over the flight plan and other documents. Zara quizzed Hashim on details of the fuel load calculation, and after a couple of minutes, both men agreed with the final fuel load. Zara then noted, "The weather looks good en route, maybe a little turbulence halfway due to a cold front, but clear at our destination. Everything looks in order. Hashim, do you also agree or want to make any changes to our flight plan?"

Hashim knew the captain purposely included him in the flight's planning aspects and the final fuel load required, testing his planning processes. So he responded, "Yes, Captain, looks good to me, as we have no obvious contingencies to concern us."

Zara continued the conversation. "We have another shipment of lithium-ion batteries tonight, very common on this Beijing trip. MAS HazMat folks signed off the paperwork, so we can assume they're packed properly and in the appropriate-type containers. These are your common cell phone batteries that could self-detonate if they overheat or were overcharged or not packed properly." Zara, always the professional instructor, then briefed Hashim on the significant elements of the hazardous cargo paperwork.

He continued, "Hashim, in 2010, these same batteries exploded in flight and took down a United Parcel Service Boeing 747 cargo plane in Dubai, killing both pilots. Many batteries went 'thermal' and burned in a chain reaction that could not be stopped. Today, we know better—they are packaged with specific separation requirements and must be less than 30 percent charged for transport. Be watchful for the appropriate signatures on the HazMat forms that verify that the proper packing and procedures have been followed."

With all briefing items complete, Zara and Hashim stood, walked toward the dispatcher's counter, and Zara called to Kim. "No changes on three-seventy's planned fuel load—forty-nine point one kilos looks good."

Kim nodded and placed a call to the fueling service to fill the giant Boeing with forty-nine thousand one hundred kilograms—approximately one hundred eight thousand pounds—of Jet A-1 fuel. That fuel load gave the flight an airborne endurance of seven hours and thirty-one minutes, including reserves. The planned flight duration to Beijing was five hours and thirty-one minutes.

———◍———

Jack Walker and Addison Stark arrived at Kuala Lumpur Airport two hours before their scheduled 12:30 a.m. departure. They each had a small carry-on bag. They proceeded to the gate with no bags to check and were pleased to find only three people ahead of them at the security checkpoint. Jack went through the metal detectors first, and stopped ten feet beyond and turn to watch Addison come through. Addison put her bag on the conveyor belt and began walking through the metal detector.

"Excuse me, ma'am, is this your bag?" Addison looked in the direction of the voice and saw a security guard holding up her carry-on bag.

"Yes, it is. Is there a problem?"

"Please step over here to the table. I have to inspect the contents." Addison expected this scrutiny and was ready.

Jack watched closely as Addison began to maneuver. He keep seeing her with new eyes, and beyond the fact that see looked gorgeous to him, she was so dammed strong and independent. His feelings for her keep growing.

The guard pulled two twelve-inch-long devices from her bag that contained a rubber mouthpiece and what looked like a small, pressurized cylinder. "Uh, what are these?" he asked, holding up one of the devices.

"It's an underwater breathing device," she said innocently. "We've been on vacation and have been doing a lot of skin diving. I carry one of these on me when I free dive, you know, without scuba gear, as a safety precaution." Jack thought, *She's charming him!"*

"Yes, ma'am, but you can't take a pressurized cylinder onboard the aircraft, even if it's a small one—"

"Oh, these cylinders are empty," Addison interrupted. "See, if you push this purge button, here, nothing comes out." The guard nodded, pushed the button a couple of times, and returned the items to Addison's bag.

"Have a good trip, ma'am."

Addison smiled, took her bag, and continued walking to the gate. Walker watched all of this without saying a word until they were out of earshot of the security guards. He glanced over his shoulder and then leaned closer to Addison's ear as they continued walking to the gate.

"What the heck was that all about?" he asked. "Do you expect us to go swimming before we complete this mission? Besides, how are a couple of empty emergency breathing devices gonna help us anyway?"

Addison turned her head slightly toward Walker and smiled. "We're going to be flying over a lot of water, and I believe in being prepared. Our naval aviators, and yours too, have these devices in their survival vests. These devices are not empty. They're charged to their full capacity, which is about thirty breaths."

"But I saw you push the purge—"

"Yes, I pushed the purge button to convince the guard they're empty, but the button is fake. You don't think you Americans have a monopoly on spy gadgets, do you? Our tech geniuses modified these devices so they can appear to be empty when, in fact, they're fully charged."

Walker shook his head and muttered, "Well, I'll be damned."

———※———

The four Iranian Ministry of Information agents passed through security with no trouble. They split up into two teams of two, with Rehyan and Farzad together and their two other associates nearby. Their disassembled plastic handguns passed X-ray inspection without detection.

The boarding area for MH370 began to fill with the over two hundred passengers expected to be on this evening's flight. When the Iranians arrived in the boarding area, Rehyan glanced around and spotted two empty seats for Farzad and himself. They also spotted Walker and Stark. Abed leaned closer to Bahadori's ear and said, "Our American friends are here." Then nodding in their general direction, he continued. "Over there, to the left of the gate agent's counter."

"I see them. The American and Aussie agents will receive the first two bullets from our weapon." Abed acknowledged Bahadori's comment with a smile. He sat back in his seat, and the Iranian agents blended in with the other passengers waiting to board Flight 370.

———※———

Elder Ruth Mah is a passenger tonight on MH370 to Beijing. She and her daughter arrived early at the gate area to make sure her wheelchair boarding of the flight went off without a hitch. Ruth will be meeting her husband in the morning in Beijing: He works as a consultant for a Malay mining company with Chinese ties.

Hope Lee is her loving daughter, a barrister educated in England, and a consultant advocate in government affairs. She lobbies the Malaysian government concerning new medical legislation. Hope is a good-looking, single, thirty-something professional woman with a big heart. She devotes much of her time to her mother, who suffers from type 2 diabetes with severe neuropathy in both her legs

———◈———

Captain Zara and F/O Hashim walked toward the door leaving the dispatch area to proceed to the gate. Zara and Hashim were joined by the ten flight attendants assigned to tonight's flight in a hallway leading to the terminal. They walked as a group to the departure gate. Everything looked normal to the casual observer.

Zara considered, *If I can make it to the aircraft without anyone suspecting me, I'm home free.* Until isolated in his cockpit cocoon, Zara would appear professional and businesslike, especially when dealing with his coworkers. He did not want anything to appear out of the ordinary. That meant forcing his depression and gloomy feelings into the recesses of his mind. He hoped he could hold it together long enough for him to accomplish his goals.

Passersby glanced at the group in the terminal and smiled, impressed by their sharp-looking uniforms and professional swagger. Malaysia Airlines flight crews enjoyed a high social status, based on their airline's reputation for professionalism and customer service. Aishah walked at the front of the flight attendants and quickened her pace to catch up with Zara. When Zara felt a light touch on the back of his arm, he swiveled his head to the left and saw Aishah walking behind him.

She was always the consummate professional in front of her peers. She addressed her captain, "Sir, may I have a word with you?" Zara slowed his pace and then stopped walking as he turned to face her.

"Hashim, you and the crew, please, go on ahead. We'll join you at the gate."

Hashim nodded and started walking again, followed by the flight attendants. As the group weaved around Zara and Aishah, no one made eye contact, but many conceded their understanding of the couple's relationship with faint smiles.

With the group now out of earshot, Aishah said, "I just want you to know that I'm looking forward to our trip together and our layover in Beijing. It's been a while since we last flew together, and I've missed you. I wish we could see more of each other in Kuala Lumpur, but I understand the need to maintain distance because of our careers. That's all. I just wanted to tell you—while we had some privacy before boarding—how I felt and how much I'm looking forward to being with you."

"And I with you, Aishah. Beijing awaits us." In the moment, Zara began to recognize the old feelings of attraction and desire for Aishah, so beautiful and vibrant. But his traditional thinking warned him, *there is a price to pay for these indiscretions and feelings of guilt*. Thus, he concluded the relationship was poisonous and destructive. This was his karma.

"Come, let us catch up with the crew. We've got a flight to catch," he finished with a forced smile. His depressive mood had deepened, and he felt sick to his stomach, but he forced himself to sound and appear normal. *Yes, especially as we go through security*, he thought. *Many cameras are scattered around the airport, but most are before and after the security checkpoint. When the investigators look back on this evening, I want everything to look normal and aboveboard.* As Zara and his chief flight attendant continued walking down the hallway, a final thought came to mind. *Yes, dear Aishah, we will be together tonight, but not how you imagine.*

As the ten cabin crew members entered the gate area, Aishah broke from the flight attendant group to approach the gate agent's podium. The agent briefed her, "You have no special needs passengers tonight, except for Mrs. Ruth Mah, who will need help boarding and wheelchair assistance in Beijing. We will bring her down to the airplane as an early boarder when you're ready to accept passengers."

Aishah walked over to Ruth, nodded to Hope Lee, and said, "Nice to have you with us tonight, Mrs. Mah. My name is Aishah, and I will be taking care of you tonight onboard our flight to Beijing. You will be boarding early in a few minutes, and I will see you on board. I'll save a pillow and blanket for you if you like." Then again, smiling toward Hope, Aishah turned and headed toward the jetway door where the other flight attendants had gathered to board the aircraft.

The pilots and cabin attendants boarded the aircraft thirty minutes before passenger boarding began. As part of their flight preparation, airline policy required the captain to conduct a crew briefing. Because different departments at the airline schedule crews, airline pilots would often joke that if it were not for this required briefing, the first time a flight attendant might see and meet the captain would be in an emergency. Zara and his eleven crew members squeezed into the limited space around Door One-Left and the first couple of rows in the business class. Zara stood in the aisle at the head of the group with Hashim at his side.

"Good evening, everyone," he began. "I'm Captain Zara. Your first officer tonight is Mr. Hashim Merican. By the way, Hashim is a six-year veteran of the 737 aircraft and is now joining us in the 777 fleet. We should have an almost full flight tonight, and we are planning a flight time of five hours and thirty-one minutes en route. The en route weather looks good, so your service to passengers is expected to be normal this evening. So far, we estimate arriving in

Beijing on time. Beijing weather is good for our arrival and layover. Fueling is complete, and catering has us loaded up with a lot of goodies." A few smiles and giggles followed Zara's last comment, but he continued. "Tonight, I would like to share some happy news; We should congratulate Hashim. He just told me that he recently became engaged to be married." Hashim had only told Zara about his engagement during their conversation the night before.

After a chorus of oohs and aahs, numerous congratulations and pats on the back followed. The unexpected announcement caught the shy Hashim off guard and caused his face to turn a deep crimson. Zara finished. "Okay, that's all I have right now—thank you, everyone. Miss Aishah, do you have anything to add?"

"No, sir, we are fully briefed."

"In that case, everyone, go to your stations, resume your duties, and prepare for boarding."

————— ◉ —————

Zara and Hashim entered the cockpit and stowed their luggage. Zara reminded Hashim that he would be the pilot flying the aircraft this evening from takeoff through to landing.

"Hashim, as part of the preflight tonight, please load the flight plan into the flight management computer. I'll do the exterior walkaround inspection."

Zara put his hat on and strutted out of the cockpit. Going down the jetway stairs to the ground, he would take the next five minutes to visually check the aircraft itself, proving it was ready for flight. Then with his eyes and head swiveling left and right in a panoramic sighting, he caught the whole of the B777 in his view. *Wow! No matter how many times I've walked around this aircraft, it still astounds me how big it is!*

He stopped at the left engine and looked inside the cowling. Zara saw the slow-turning outer fan blades, rotating freely because of the light breeze passing through the engine. *All is good here.* Turning to his left, Zara inspected the nosewheel tires, struts, and nosewheel doors that were now open. The pushback tractor and tow bar were attached to the nose gear, ready to push the aircraft off the gate into the larger ramp area behind.

Walking around the nose to the other side of the plane, Zara saw the right engine and a cargo loading ramp pushed up against the forward cargo pit. The last cargo containers were rolling into the cargo compartment, containers filled with commerce to Beijing. Just then, a ramp supervisor, with papers in his hand, came walking up to the captain.

"Good evening, Captain. I have a Hazardous Materials manifest for MH370—lithium-ion batteries—in the forward cargo pit. Packaging all looks good." Zara looked at the manifest and nodded, acknowledging the supervisor's comments. "Have a good trip tonight, sir," the supervisor concluded and walked away.

"Thank you," Zara returned.

Zara continued around the plane, all two hundred feet from wingtip to wingtip and two hundred ten feet nose to tail. The tires looked good. There were no leaks from the engines or fuel tanks and no dents or holes in the fuselage caused by collisions with ground equipment. All doors and hatch covers were closed and latched. Walkaround completed, Zara headed back to the cockpit.

"External walkaround looks good," Zara reported. He saw Hashim just about to finish the flight plan entry into the computer.

He proceeded with his captain's setup of the left side of the cockpit: All switches and displays with the correct settings for departure, including a test of the oxygen mask, mask microphone, and overhead speakers. Next, Zara independently checked the flight plan in the computer—it matched precisely the dispatcher's filed flight plan with their navigation routing to Beijing. In minutes, both had completed their respective duties on setup, and Captain Zara called for the preflight checklist. Hashim changed the flight management computer display menu to "checklists" and began reading from the appropriate one. Working together, reading from their LED display screen, where one pilot asks the other questions and the other pilot answers with the verifying response. Checklist completed, they now simply waited for the passengers to complete the boarding process and for the cabin doors to close.

As part of Hashim's last "on-the-job" training flight tonight, Zara told him to expect questions about various technical and procedural requirements pertaining to tonight's flight. Hashim expected quizzing during the entire flight. This technique was not so much a test, as a chance to share information and give some perspective from the senior pilot to the more junior pilot coming to this new aircraft, the 777 model. Indeed, this teaching method also allows the newer pilot to ask questions about his new job, responsibilities, and real-world techniques—info not found in the books. As this is the last scheduled training event, the check pilot will determine that the student pilot is safe to assume regular duties as a first officer without any additional pilot training or instructors assigned. In these sessions, however, the pilot being trained is always aware of his performance and accepts the pressure to perform and "pass the check" in the allotted time. Hashim's knowledge and enthusiasm impressed Zara. *Yes*, he thought, *Hashim will be a perfect crew member tonight: he is eager to please.*

———◉———

The gate area was becoming crowded. Almost all the seats were occupied; one hundred fifty-three Chinese, thirty-eight Malaysians, six Australian citizens, and others, including children, ready to go to sleep, all planning to come on board MH370 for a total of two hundred twenty-seven passengers.

The flight began to board thirty minutes before its scheduled departure time. As the passengers started to queue up in front of the jetway entry door, a harried Chinese agent Shen Chow arrived at the gate with his technical team in tow. A late departure from their hotel, a longer-than-expected cab ride, and a long line at the security checkpoint conspired to delay the four Chinese passengers. When they arrived at the gate, Shen breathed a sigh of relief. *Whew*, he thought, *we're not too late. My superiors would have been very unhappy if we missed this flight and the "package" in the cargo bin below arrived without us.*

Everything about the passenger boarding process proceeded in a routine and orderly manner. First, those with disabilities or families with small children boarded, followed by frequent flyer elite status, then business class. Then after a brief pause, general boarding for the economy began.

The normalcy of routine of the boarding process stood in stark contrast to the dark thoughts going through Zara's mind. He rationalized his intention to take over control of the plane and make it disappear as the only way to relieve his pain and not disgrace his name, his family, and the profession he loved. Of course, no one in their right mind would agree with his logic, but Zara was not in his right mind.

The cockpit intercom chime sounded and ended Zara and Hashim's question-and-answer session. When Zara lifted the handset to his ear, he heard a familiar female voice.

"Captain, we're finished boarding, and the cabin is secure. Request permission to close the cabin door," Aishah reported. The sound of her sweet voice made Zara smile.

"Thank you, Aishah. Go ahead and close all cabin doors. We'll be pushing back off the gate in five minutes."

PART 5

Flight MH370—Vanished!

CHAPTER FOURTEEN

After the final cabin door closed, the ground crew outside and below on the push tractor reported ready to push back. Zara instructed Hashim to contact Lumpur ground control and request clearance to push back from the gate and start engines. Ground control granted Hashim's request at 00:27 past midnight local time, three minutes early. Below, the ground crew pushed back the aircraft to a designated spot on the ramp, requested brakes set, and told the cockpit to start the engines. Hashim started the two Rolls-Royce Trent 892 engines. With the engines starting and operating normally, Hashim requested clearance to taxi. Ground control cleared the flight to taxi to runway 32 left and hold short of the runway. When at the hold point, call Lumpur tower on frequency.

"MH370, 32 Left, you are cleared for takeoff with no delay." Lumpur tower cleared the flight for takeoff at 12:40 a.m.

Zara taxied the plane onto runway 32 left and lined up the plane's nose on the runway centerline. He turned his head to the right and spoke to Hashim. "You have control—I have the radios." Hashim responded by taking the controls, declaring, "I have control." Pilots use this specific language to avoid ambiguities regarding who is working the flight controls. Hashim released the parking brake, stood up the thrust levers, and called for "takeoff thrust." The aircraft lurched forward, energized by two engines of ninety thousand pounds of thrust each. The big jet picked up speed as it accelerated down the runway. Hashim lifted the plane off the ground approximately halfway down the runway, executing a flawless takeoff, pointing MH370 skyward.

Two minutes later, Lumpur Departure Control cleared the flight to climb to Flight Level 180—the aviation term for eighteen thousand feet. Additionally, "MH370, you are cleared direct to IGARI intersection. Proceed on course."

As the flight continued, seasoned and novice travelers alike filled the cabin with a low hum of excitement as they marveled at the night-time beauty of Kuala Lumpur's city lights scattered on the ground in random patterns. The passengers in window seats on the plane's left side had a breathtaking view of the twin Petronas Towers rising one thousand four hundred eighty-three feet above the city's sparkling lights. The air was smooth above ten thousand feet, so Zara turned off the seat belt sign, and a chime sounded in the cabin. That signal alerted the flight attendants to begin their service, and tonight, that service would be quick. Many passengers were already hunkered down in their seats, window shades down, and pillows and blankets in place.

At 12:46 a.m., air traffic control cleared MH370 to climb and maintain FL250. Four minutes later, air traffic control cleared MH370 to climb and maintain FL350. Eleven minutes later, Zara made a radio call. "MH370 maintaining FL350."

Now level, the plane sped toward the IGARI intersection, the end of Malaysian-controlled airspace, and the beginning of Vietnamese responsibility for traffic separation. The Xanax dosage Zara had taken earlier in the evening tied his stomach in knots and had made him physically sick to the point of his vomiting in the terminal restroom on his way to the gate. His mental state suffered, and his need to be free of this pain caused his thoughts of suicide to flood his consciousness. Zara decided, *Enough! The time has come to set my plan in motion.*

Captain Zara turned to his copilot and said, "You know, Aishah, our chief flight attendant, is a special friend of mine. Earlier, when I mentioned to her that you are engaged to be married, she was very happy for you." Hashim nodded and wondered where this conversation was going. "Yes," continued Zara, "she wanted to talk with you some more about your fiancée and your wedding plans." Zara's eyes moved down and slightly left, stopping on the cockpit door camera display. These displays came into service after the 9/11 tragedy. A single button push brought up the cabin video system on the multi-function display, three camera angles of the front cabin—the view of the cockpit door entry area, the area around the left-side passenger entry door, and a picture of the forward galley workspace, near the right-side service door.

"I can see her—she's in the forward galley. In a few minutes, I'll make the position report to Ho Chi Minh at IGARI. So why don't you go visit with Aishah if you wouldn't mind, and while you're out, can you please bring me back some black tea?"

At first, Hashim thought Zara's request was strange but harmless, but Zara was the flight commander, and he was also evaluating Hashim's performance on tonight's final check ride. Hashim nodded, removed his headset, released his seat belt, and slid his seat to its full aft position. "Sure thing, Captain. Be right back." Hashim walked behind Zara's seat and out the cockpit door. Zara glanced over his shoulder to confirm Hashim's departure. He looked down at the center console and pressed the cabin door lock switch. Now, he was alone in the cockpit.

———

In Kuala Lumpur Area Control Center (KLACC), controller Abdul Hoqq sat in front of his two radar scopes. He was one of two controllers on duty tonight and a junior controller trainee and data planning controller. At 1:19 a.m., Hoqq contacted MH370. "Malaysian three seven zero, this is Lumpur Control. You are approaching IGARI. Radar service terminated. Contact Ho Chi Minh frequency one two zero decimal nine."

Zara acknowledged those instructions four seconds later with, "Good night. Malaysian Three Seven Zero."

Hearing that radio transmission from MH370, the KLACC controller Hoqq assumed his duties and responsibility for MH370 were complete. That was the last recorded transmission anyone would receive from MH370 that evening.

Completing his radio call, Zara closed his eyes and took a deep breath. Then, opening his eyes, he stared at the flight management computer for a moment. *It's time to begin; no turning back now.*

Tonight, Zara planned to duplicate a flight he had created on his home flight simulator and one that he practiced just this last month. He removed a small notebook from his flight bag and opened it to a marked page. Using the flight management computer's keypad, he entered Penang's latitude and longitude coordinates. He thought, *One last look at my beautiful hometown—so many wonderful memories.* His next input was the coordinates for a navigation waypoint over the Andaman Sea near the MEKAR intersection northwest of Penang. The third and final waypoint he entered was a location in the southern Indian Ocean.

He looked up and glanced at the navigation display, essentially a moving map, and saw he was currently arriving at point IGARI, the edge of Vietnam airspace. *Now, it's time to become a ghost*, he thought. *I don't want to disgrace my family or my ancestors, so when I end my life tonight, I will do it in such a way as to leave no trace or clues to betray my actual intent.*

He reached down, located the transponder switch on the aisle control stand, and set it to the "standby" position. His deliberate action turned off the aircraft's radar transmitting function that caused the aircraft's "blip" to disappear from the air traffic radar screens of Kuala Lumpur, Ho Chi Minh City, and Bangkok. Next, he selected the "Communications Page" on his flight computer display and turned off the aircraft's automatic ACARS satellite reporting system. Zara's actions severed his communications' connection to the aviation world and caused his plane to disappear at 01:20 local time.

The Ho Chi Minh (HCM) air traffic controller watched MH370 approach Vietnamese airspace at the IGARI intersection and expected the pilots to check in with a radio call at any minute. Distracted by another controller's question, he later returned his attention to watch his two assigned radar screens. Suddenly, the HCM controller remembered, "Did MH370 call in? Oh! Where did MH370 go?" There was no radar blip on his screen for MH370 like before, nor any ident tag showing a call sign "MH370" or displayed text reporting his assigned altitude of thirty-five thousand feet. It had already been minutes since MH370 should have reported on the assigned frequency to HCM.

The controller waited no longer. He called MH370 directly on the assigned frequency. "Malaysia three seven zero, this is Ho Chi Minh Control. Do you read?" The aircraft did not return his call. "Malaysia three seven zero, Ho Chi Minh Control. Do you read me?" Still, there was no radio contact nor any radar contact. The controller became very concerned.

At 01:38 a.m., the HCM controller called his counterpart controller, Hoqq, at KLACC, on a direct phone line, asking, "Where is MH370?—He never reported my frequency. I have called him many times. I no longer show him in radar contact."

Abdul was startled. His stomach dropped. "What the—? What's happening?" *Why is HCM calling me?* He had not been watching continuously in the last minutes after instructing three-seventy to contact HCM, and the Malaysian Airlines flight to Beijing had since disappeared off his radar screen. At first, he thought, *Maybe something is wrong with my radar display.* So, he called out to his fellow controller sitting nearby. "Singh, do you have MH370 on your display?"

"No, I have negative contact with three-seventy. I haven't seen him for a while."

A feeling of dread welled up inside Hoqq. *What happened to MH370? Did I do something wrong? It has been over eighteen minutes since my handoff of MH370 to HCM.* Beads of sweat wet his brow, and he felt his pulse quicken. "Hey, Singh, have you seen the watch supervisor tonight? Do you know where he is?"

"I saw him about an hour ago. He said that it looked like a quiet night, so he would take a nap. He's probably sleeping in the rest area."

Hoqq was exasperated. MH370 was gone! He instinctively called MH370 on the frequency two more times, and each time, his radio call went unanswered. The silence almost made his heart stop. He kept looking at the radar screen, unconsciously hoping MH370 would appear again. *Why didn't the pilots call if they had trouble?*

Abdul yelled for the junior controller sitting nearby and instructed him to wake the watch supervisor and immediately bring him to the radar room. When the watch supervisor walked in, Abdul gave him a quick brief on MH370 disappearing off the radar screen, not answering any radio calls from either KLACC or HCM, nor had three-seventy made any distress calls. Abdul could barely contain himself thinking, *Did MH370 crash into the sea?*

At 01:57 a.m., HCM called again to repeat that MH370 had never reported in by radio to HCM at IGARA. His supervisor had instructed the Vietnamese controller to make this call, squarely putting it on the record that HCM had no radar contact, no radio report, and therefore, no responsibility for MH370. KLACC's Hoqq assumed, on that quiet night, just like every other night, that MH370 was flying normally, continuing flight into Vietnam airspace. Now, KLACC could no longer validate the handoff to HCM. KLACC was now on the spot and responsible for explaining MH370's whereabouts as they were the last air traffic control station to have managed the aircraft.

The KLACC watch supervisor, nervously standing between Abdul and Singh, quickly picked up a landline telephone and punched in the requisite numbers on the console for Malaysia Airlines' Operation Dispatch Center (ODC). Airlines have a dispatching department that is independently required to "flight follow" their aircraft. *"Maybe they will know what's happened to*

MH370." But to his dismay, ODC told him, "Standby; we'll get right back to you."

The KLACC and Malaysia Airlines ODC talked numerous times over the next twenty-five minutes. In those minutes, the Malaysia Airlines duty manager mistakenly analyzed its computerized flight following system, sharing three separate, erroneous messages to KLACC authorities. Malaysia Airlines said, "MH370 is still flying," "MH370 is in Cambodia," "MH370 position report is N14.90 E109.155," and the "aircraft is still downloading signals." MAS operations control simply had no concerns—everything seemed okay—the computer program said so. The KL ATC watch supervisor, trusting the airline's operations department reporting, was content that MH370 was still flying, well north of Malaysian airspace and beyond any KLACC responsibility. Around 02:30 a.m., he returned to the rest area to finish his nap.

But those erroneous messages from the airline only served to confuse the HCM and KL controllers as their radars showed nothing flying! Cambodia had called back and told an inquiring HCM that Cambodia had no flight plan or radar sightings for MH370. They all wondered why their radar scope couldn't see MH370. "Is the airplane still flying, or has it crashed? Why hasn't the flight radioed in or transmitted a Mayday distress call?" Questioning phone calls between the region's air traffic controllers continued for the next two hours.

KL controller Hoqq, who was very concerned, got halfway out of his chair and stopped. At first, he thought he would leave his duty station, go to the bunk rest area, find his supervisor, and report that he suspected three-seventy had crashed. His second thought caused him to sit down again. If he awoke his supervisor and his suspicions were wrong, he would be in big trouble. Asian cultures did not reward initiative. Authority rule—right or wrong—was paramount, so Hoqq decided to err on the side of cautious self-preservation. He sat silently for a moment and, in his mind, rationalized his decision. There was no distress call, and no other aircraft were in three-seventy's vicinity requiring traffic separation. Maybe MH370 had a communication system failure. *I'll give it some more time and wait until my supervisor wakes up before I report it.*

At 0430 a.m., MAS ODC called to reveal that the flight following system had been misinterpreted. The information previously passed to KLACC was only a computer program's *projection* on the plane's position, solely based on its takeoff time and not a real-time report of its location. Also, all internal airline attempts to contact MH370 had gone unanswered. Essentially, they had overstated their confidence that MH370 was okay and still flying. In fact, MH370 was incommunicado at best . . . and not even flying at worst.

Controller Hoqq became physically upset and again instructed the junior controller to wake the watch supervisor and bring him to the radar room. At 0530 a.m., as Hoqq watched the supervisor enter and walk across the room, the phone from MAS ODC rang. A senior MAS duty manager was calling. Hoqq reached up and handed the phone to the supervisor, watching his facial expressions change from annoyed to wide-eyed upset! He had just been told that MH370 most likely had "never left Malaysian airspace."

The watch supervisor put the phone down and tried to collect his thoughts. *This can't be happening to me! Where did MH370 go?* He turned to the data planning controller and said, "Issue an **Alert Phase** message on MH370. Establish a Rescue Coordination Center (RCC) for the KL region. MH370 is position unknown and without communications."

One hour later, at 0632, more than five hours after the MAS flight had disappeared off the radar scope, KLACC issued the highest alert message possible, a Distress message, **DETRESFA**. Hoqq wondered to himself, *Has the aircraft been down for five hours now? Did all those passengers and crew die in a crash, or are they waiting in their life rafts in the sea below to be rescued?*

RMAF Butterworth, a Royal Malaysian Air Force Base, was situated five miles from the town of Butterworth in Penang province. This base was the headquarters of the Integrated Area Defense System. Its mission was to respond to aerial and surface threats to Malaysian national security. The station used powerful military radar units and a squadron of US-supplied F-18 fighter aircraft to accomplish its mission. Tonight, an RMAF air traffic controller sat at his console and monitored air traffic in the country's northern sector, including neighboring borders of Vietnam, Cambodia, Thailand, Indonesia, and the Indian Ocean to the west.

The north sector controller spoke, "Sir? I think we have a problem."

His superior, who stood a few feet behind him, turned and replied, "What's wrong, Sergeant?"

"Sir, a few seconds ago, I had a commercial aircraft—MH370— displaying tracking information as it approached the IGARI intersection, and now, it's gone. I mean—I still see a primary 'blip,' but its ID, altitude, and heading information are gone—like someone turned off the transponder. So I assume it's a civilian transport aircraft—it's big enough—but it is flying suspiciously parallel to the Vietnam, Thai, and Malaysian border."

"Or maybe he had a communication systems failure? For example, did he squawk 7500 or 7600 or transmit a distress call on the Guard frequency?"

"No, sir, no distress calls and no distress transponder codes. It looks like he made a left turn, coming in from the South China Sea, and is heading right at us. Should we scramble the F-18s and check him out?" Scrambling fighters for an unusual, noncommunicating aircraft had almost become an international protocol since the 9/11 attack in New York City years earlier.

"Hmm, I'd have to run that up the chain of command, and it's the middle of the night. If I wake the general, and this turns out to be nothing important, I may as well kiss my career goodbye."

"Yes, sir, but what if the plane is not friendly or it's been hi-jacked? What if it turns toward Kuala Lumpur? You know, those Petronas Towers—"

"Not likely, Sergeant. If it were a hijacking, he would have squawked the emergency code 7500. If he lost all communication capability, he would have squawked 7600. So, no, just stand by and keep him in sight. You just keep doing your job, Sergeant, and I'll do mine."

The sergeant returned his attention to the radar screen. He thought about calling his counterpart in Lumpur Air Traffic Control via their direct telephone line to ask questions about MH370 but decided to "follow orders" after his supervisor's rebuke. The sergeant had a bad taste in his mouth, though—*something was very wrong with his unannounced radar intruder.*

CHAPTER FIFTEEN

Zara had set his plan in motion, but, unbeknownst to him, three groups of people in the cabin had their individual agendas, and it did *not* include his suicide. Walker and Stark were escorting the "package" and quietly talked about the cancelled ground intercept plan, evolving into a destroy mission after they landed in Beijing.

Stark sat in the window seat, and although it was night, she could tell by the absence of city lights that they had crossed the coastline outbound into the South China Sea, and were heading toward Vietnam. She nudged Walker's arm, and he turned his head toward her.

"We just crossed the coast," she advised. "Beijing, here we come."

Meanwhile, Walker could not wait any longer. He bent over and opened the life preserver compartment between their seats. He reached to the back and pulled out a Ziploc bag containing a small 9-millimeter Beretta pocket pistol and a piece of paper with three numbers, five-seven-six scrawled on it. Stark smiled when she saw the confused look on Walker's face.

"The pistol I get, but what's with the three numbers? Do you have any idea what the numbers mean?"

"As a matter of fact, I do. So, you mean, there's something *I* know that *you* don't?"

"Don't bust my chops. Now is no time for joking around."

Turning serious, Stark replied. "That's the unlock code for the cockpit door. Maintenance and operations personnel have that code to gain access to the cockpit for maintenance or emergency purposes. Whoever left you that bag of goodies knew we might have to get into the cockpit. Airline and most government policies these days, since 2001, forbid the pilots from opening the cockpit door for any reason, and I mean ANY reason, even the threat of death to hostages, passengers, or crew."

Stark touched Walker's arm. "Look," she said, throwing her eyes forward. She had a clear view of the cockpit door from her seat and saw it open. Hashim emerged and walked to the forward galley and began a conversation with one of the flight attendants.

Walker remained in his seat. He put the small pistol in his pocket. At that moment, and unbeknownst to Walker, Stark, the Chinese, and Captain Zara, the Iranians decided to make their move.

With one pilot leaving the cockpit, the four Iranian agents began their prearranged hijacking plan. They removed the plastic gun parts from their carry-on bags and assembled the weapon quietly and carefully. Rehyan and Farzad were in business class and would work together to manage an assault on the cockpit. They planned to take a hostage—they did not care if it were a flight attendant or one of the pilots—and force one of the pilots to fly them to their destination in Iran. With guns in hand, they both unbuckled their seat belts and started walking to the forward galley from their fourth-row seats on the aircraft's right side. In the economy section of the plane, the two other Iranian agents were positioning themselves to the forward section of that cabin to best control any form of passenger interference.

Meanwhile, in the cockpit, after having successfully disappeared from radar, Zara's next move was to change course to the west. His left thumb pressed the autopilot disengage button on his control wheel, turning the autopilot control off. Then he began "hand flying" the big jet. He made an unusually steep left turn that exceeded the standard limit of thirty degrees of bank. This caused the "g-forces" on the aircraft and occupants to double. Seated passengers were pressed hard into their seats, but the two Iranians walking in the aisle toward the galley stumbled and almost fell. They grabbed some seatbacks to prevent hitting the floor. The two agents in the back also went down to their knees, where they simply held on until the g-force abated.

First Officer Hashim and the rest of the flight crew seized anything stationary to prevent their falling. *That's very strange that the captain would make such an aggressive maneuver without warning. I better get back to the cockpit*, he thought.

The steep turn caused Stark to glance out the window. It was night, and moonlight reflected off the water below. Zara's change in course caused the reflections to change their position relative to the aircraft's wing. Due to Stark's many hours of flying experience, she had developed a keen "seat of the pants" flying sense, and she knew what they just experienced was a steep left turn.

Walker turned his head and looked at her. "What the hell was that all about?"

"The pilot just made a steep turn to the left—he changed course almost one hundred eighty degrees. So we're heading back to Malaysia, but westbound, not toward Kuala Lumpur. I don't know why, but let's wait a minute and see how this plays out."

Before Zara's steep left turn, Hashim and Aishah had engaged in a friendly conversation, discussing Hashim's upcoming wedding plans. He leaned on the galley counter with his left forearm, and Aishah had her back to the business class cabin. Neither one saw the approaching Iranian danger. After Zara completed the turn and rolled the big jet straight and level, the two Iranians recovered their footing and balance. Farzad Bahadori reached the galley first, put his left arm around Aishah's neck, and pulled her to one side. Rehyan Abed followed and pointed his gun at Hashim.

"Open the cockpit door!" he demanded, "or I will begin shooting people, starting with you two."

Everyone within earshot froze in place, and time seemed to stop. Walker and Stark stared in disbelief as other passengers gasped and mumbled indiscernible comments. "QUIET! You will all be quiet. We don't want to hurt anyone, but we will if the pilot doesn't meet our demands. You," nodding toward Hashim, "open the door—now."

Hashim raised his hands and pleaded with Abed. "Please, don't hurt anyone. What do you want? I can call my captain and tell him your demands."

Abed's eyes darted from side to side as he composed an answer in his mind. "We want you to divert this flight to the airport in Zahedan, Iran. Our interest lies in your cargo, not in hurting any people. If you cooperate, the Islamic Republic of Iran will see to your safe return. If not, we have orders to destroy this aircraft and everyone aboard."

"Did you hear that?" Walker whispered in Stark's ear. "They want the cargo—the package—holy shit! That looks like some kind of firearm he's pointing at them. I was hoping to avoid using a gun on board this plane, but this certainly complicates things. He said they want to go to Iran, and we're no longer heading to China."

"I will ca-call my captain," Hashim stammered as he pointed to the intercom phone next to the left-side boarding door. Zara happened to glance at the cabin video camera display and saw what was happening on the other side of the cockpit door—a man was holding a gun on his copilot and Aishah and was walking toward the intercom phone. This unexpected development startled him, and a new surge of anxiety flowed through his body. *Those men are taking hostages. They probably want to get into the cockpit. Things are getting out of control. My plan!*

In an instant, Zara decided on his next move. Maybe he could salvage most of his plan and get to a remote area in the Indian Ocean before crashing the plane, but he had to act fast. He opened a panel next to his left hip and grabbed his oxygen mask. Unlike the masks in the passenger cabin, the pilot's mask was donned over the head and covered his face from forehead to chin. After he donned his mask, he felt a slight, cool wisp of air across his nose that confirmed the oxygen flow. He leaned to the right and looked up at the overhead control panel. He paused for a minute, took a deep breath, and realized there would be no turning back from the consequences of what he was about to do. He located the LEFT and RIGHT air-conditioning "Pack Switch," pressed them both, turning them off. Those switches controlled the pressurized air into the cabin, keeping the cabin's altitude at a breathable eight thousand feet while the outside altitude was thirty-five thousand feet. Zara's eyes searched across the overhead control panel until they came to rest upon another set of switches. His fingers rested upon the switches that would manually open two external doors—outflow valves built into the forward and aft body fuselage. For Zara, nothing else mattered except stopping his pain: the fates of others did not matter. He pressed the switches and opened both doors. A rapid decompression swept the aircraft's interior, pushing the pressurized air of the cabin out of the plane now. In the cockpit, the Red Master Warning System alert confirmed that the cabin air was now too thin for survival.

Zara's actions caused all hell to break loose in the passenger cabin. The noise level, caused by the fast-moving air, increased to where normal conversation was impossible. Violent surges of air whipped the passengers. Their minds, senses, and physical well-being were under attack. Fear and anxiety gripped their minds like a vise, leaving each passenger to wonder, *Is this the beginning of the end? Am I going to die?* The smell of the air changed—a metallic solvent smell replaced the odor of brewing coffee. Loose paper, drink cups and their contents, and personal items swirled around the cabin, animated by surging currents and struck everyone's bodies. As the cold outside air displaced the warm, conditioned, interior air, condensation formed, and an undulating fog hung halfway between the ceiling and floor. The raging air even lifted the dirt out of the carpets and peppered passengers' bare skin with a painful abrasive spray.

"Damn," Walker shouted over the cabin noise. "This is like being on the beach in a hurricane."

"Grab your mask," Stark yelled, "and sit back to stretch the tube to get the oxygen flowing." Walker followed her instructions, and oxygen began to flow freely to his relief. Unfortunately, the Iranians did not fare so well. When the cabin depressurized, First Officer Hashim, who was moving toward the interphone and left-side entry door station, grabbed one of the two masks hanging there. Abed, who was escorting Hashim, panicked. Lacking formal training with the depressurization drill, he did not see the second mask hanging and twisting with the air currents near the forward entry door. His panicked mind told him to get back to his seat where there was a mask for him. His partner, Bahadori, let go of Aishah. Now free, Aishah stepped sideways, grabbing one mask above a flight attendant's seat at the service entry door.

With his back against the right-side service door, Bahadori froze like a deer in the headlights of an oncoming car. At their current altitude of thirty-five thousand feet, the "time of useful consciousness" was twenty to thirty seconds, depending on a person's physical health and condition. Bahadori, a heavy smoker, felt the effects of hypoxia even sooner. The first stage imitated mild intoxication, followed by a sense of dizzy foreboding, then the loss of consciousness, followed quickly by death. Twelve seconds after the cabin depressurized, Bahadori lay unconscious on the galley floor.

In Abed's panicked attempt to return to his seat and the safety of its life-sustaining oxygen, he caught his toe on a seat post, stumbled, lost his balance, and ended up spread eagle on the floor. His plastic gun slipped from his hand and slid on the floor, coming to rest at the feet of the Chinese agent Shen Chow. Abed raised himself on his elbows and tried to stand. "Tired, must rest . . ." he mumbled and lay back down on the floor, now unconscious. Shen and his colleagues wore their oxygen masks while observing the commotion from their aisle seats as the Iranians tried to hijack the plane.

Shen Chow's mind raced as he looked down at the gun, which came to rest inches from his right foot. *This is not good. Those Iranians want our package. I think they're dead now from a lack of oxygen, but something has happened to this airplane to cause this depressurization. I just may need that weapon before this is over.* He leaned forward, bent down, and retrieved the plastic gun. As he returned to the upright position, he placed the weapon in the seatback pocket in front of him.

After the cabin depressurized, Walker and Stark remained seated with their masks on. Now, Stark nudged Walker's arm. He glanced at her, and she yelled, "Something's wrong!"

"Yeah, no shit! What tipped you off?"

"No, that's not what I mean. Standard operating procedure after losing cabin pressure is to descend as quickly as safety permits. We haven't started to descend yet."

"Maybe the pilot's dealing with some emergency. Besides, we're on oxygen, so what's the big deal?"

"The big deal is that the oxygen generators for each of these masks produce a finite amount of oxygen—only about twelve minutes' worth. *That's* why we should be descending." Immediately after she spoke, she felt an increase in g-force pressing her into her seat again. "Damn, he's climbing! This guy in the cockpit is trying to do us in. He is *not* our friend!"

Zara had decided that all his passengers would die with him tonight. He decided to hasten the process by climbing the airplane higher to thinner air. It would also eliminate any further interference while implementing his "final solution." The passengers' oxygen generators would cease making oxygen in a few minutes. At thirty-five thousand feet, they would succumb to hypoxia in twenty to thirty seconds, and at forty thousand feet, that time would cut in half.

The cockpit door was ten feet from the forward entry door station where First Officer Hashim had taken refuge when the masks deployed. *If there's an emergency, why isn't he descending?* Hashim removed his oxygen mask, ran to the door, and turned the handle. It was locked. He banged hard on the door and yelled, "Captain . . . Captain, unlock the door!" Repeatedly, he slammed his fist on the door while trying to turn the handle with his other hand. He entered the three-digit unlock code on the emergency access keypad, then turned the door handle again, but the door remained locked. Finally, Hashim realized *Zara has overridden the code. He wants to keep me out!*

Hashim hurried back to the entry door station, put the mask on again, and sat down on the empty flight attendant's seat. He removed his cell phone from his pocket and made one last desperate attempt to get help. He thought if he could make a call to his fiancée in K.L., he could ask her to contact the aviation authorities and try to establish radio contact with the cockpit. He selected her phone number and pressed the send button— nothing. Before he could try a second time, his oxygen supply ran out. He knew he had waited too long. He was only a few feet away from an oxygen bottle in a nearby overhead compartment that the flight crew called a walkaround bottle. It contained an hour's worth of oxygen and was used to assist a passenger having a breathing emergency during the flight. He whipped the mask off his face and hurried toward the overhead compartment containing the life-sustaining oxygen bottle. He unlatched the compartment handle, stood still for a moment as his body slowly wavered back and forth, then his knees buckled, and he collapsed to the floor—unconscious.

Hashim's futile effort to reach the walkaround bottle occurred right in front of Walker and Stark. An airline pilot herself, Stark knew what happened to Hashim. She also knew it would happen to Walker and herself unless she took action. So she bent forward and reached for her carry-on bag under the seat in front of her. She pulled the bag onto her lap and grabbed the two emergency breathing devices. She activated one and handed it to Walker.

Slumped in their seats or collapsed on the floor, the entire crew and passengers were nearing unconsciousness or already gone.

"Here, put the mouthpiece in your mouth and breath slowly. Our seat masks probably only have a few seconds of oxygen left."

Walker was bleary-eyed, but he was still able to follow her directions. Before she put the mouthpiece of the second device in her mouth, she warned, "We've only got about thirty breaths of oxygen. We won't be able to communicate with these things in our mouth, so listen up. Grab that walkaround bottle," she said, pointing at the overhead compartment in front of them, "just in case your breathing device runs out of air before you get back. Walk to the back of the plane and grab the second bottle from the rear galley's compartment. Bring it back here for me. In the meantime, I'll try using the unlock code to get in the cockpit. GO!"

Walker sprang into action and did as Stark instructed. He stood up and grabbed the walkaround bottle from the overhead compartment in front of his seat and slung its carrying strap around his neck. The violent air currents caused by the rapid depressurization had subsided, but the cabin air had turned bitterly cold. With a free hand, he grabbed ahold of the seatbacks to steady himself as he made halting progress toward the plane's rear. He came up to the beginning of the economy section and stopped momentarily. Looking left to the cross-aisle, he saw two bodies lying on the floor: the two Iranians had gone to sleep. Moving through the economy section now, the harsh reality of death permeated his thoughts as he passed row after row of limp bodies. All these people look peaceful as if they were asleep, but no—they were all dying or already dead. He shook his head to clear those thoughts from his mind and focused on the task at hand. *I got to push those thoughts out of my head. Got to get that second walkaround bottle, or Stark and I will join these folks in their eternal sleep.*

Still wearing her portable breathing device, Stark followed Walker out of the row. She made a left turn, stepped over Hashim's body, and walked ten feet to the cockpit door. Due to the bone-chilling cold, she punched the three-digit code into the keypad on the aisle wall just outside the cockpit door with an unsteady hand. She entered five-six. "No, wait. Dammit, that's wrong," she mumbled. "It's five-seven-six. Got to clear that entry and try again—"

When Stark initiated her first entry attempt, the "door access" warning system alerted Zara that someone was trying to gain access to the cockpit. "How can this be? Everyone should be passed out by now." He looked down at the video monitor and saw a woman on the other side of the cockpit door with a strange-looking apparatus on her face. He found the switch labeled "door access denied" and pressed it.

Watching the on-camera action just outside the cockpit door, Zara became frantic and desperate to bring his plan to fruition. His panic caused several final thoughts to flood his mind. *I've been found out. My plan is failing—They are coming for me—I will have disgraced my family.*

The minus thirty-degree Fahrenheit cold numbed her fingers and mind, but Stark entered the correct code on her second attempt. *I hope this works*, she thought. Unfortunately, when she tried the handle, it would not budge. "Rats—it's still locked," she mumbled indiscernibly. "He must have denied access from inside. Damn!"

Walker had retrieved the second walkaround bottle and struggled forward toward the cockpit to join his partner. Upon entering the business class cabin, he noticed an unusual object protruding from the seatback pocket that an Asian man occupied. He recognized the object as the gun brandished by one of the Iranian hijackers. The Asian turned his head and stared at Walker with saucer-wide eyes. In his weakened condition, the man sucked a final breath; then his head slumped against his chest.

Jack saw Addison ahead. *She hasn't got the door open yet. What the hell is wrong?* This was not the time to panic, and Walker knew it. He forced himself to relax and recalled his SEAL training, which taught him to perform under extreme physical and mental stress. *If I could survive that, I can surely survive this*, he thought.

Stark's attention remained entirely focused on opening the cockpit door. Walker approached her from behind. When he put his hand on her shoulder, her startled reaction caused her to jump and recoil from him. He was wearing the walkaround bottle face mask, and although his voice was muffled, she could hear his apology.

"Sorry 'bout that. Here, put this on." He handed her the second walkaround bottle he had retrieved from the rear of the plane and added, "Your little scuba device is probably running out of air. Mine ran out halfway returning from the rear." She took the bottle from Walker, put on the O2 mask, and slung the strap around her neck.

"Thanks, I owe you one, even though you scared the bejeebers out of me. We've got another problem, though. The door is locked from the inside. That's the bad news. The good news is that the lock-out function is on a timer. If the pilot forgets to reset it in sixty seconds, the keypad becomes active again."

Panicking after seeing two people on the other side of the cockpit door, Zara had decided on his final move. He did not want to risk failure with additional cabin interference. He reached over, placed his right hand on the engine throttles, hesitated for a few seconds, and then pulled them aft to the idle power setting. With the autopilot on, he programed a three-thousand-feet-per-minute descent. His actions caused the big plane to aggressively descend toward terra firma.

This is not my plan to disappear, but it will have to suffice. Zara performed one final act in his tragic play. He reached up, grabbed the regulator hose and oxygen mask, and ripped it off his face. Ten seconds later, with his last breath, he sighed, *"My darling Misha!"*

Walker and Stark were still standing in the aisle in front of the cockpit door, trying to warm their bodies by stomping their feet and rubbing their hands together when Stark noticed the change in noise level. "What the hell, now? He's pulled the engines back to idle."

Walker cast her a worried look as if to ask, "And?"

Without waiting for him to verbalize his unspoken question, she replied, "And that means we're going down, and the last time I looked, we were over nothing but water."

Two minutes had passed since Stark's last unsuccessful attempt to unlock the cockpit door. "All we can do is keep inputting the code and hope the lock timer resets. We don't have much time—maybe a couple of minutes before impact. This better work." She input the code again, and taking a deep breath, she turned the cockpit door handle. Not knowing what to expect, Walker stood next to her with the small Beretta in his right hand. She heard a click, and the handle rotated its full travel. She thrust her weight on the door, and it swung open.

"Thank God," Walker exclaimed. "Good job!"

They barged into the cockpit and saw Captain Zara slumped in his seat as his oxygen mask lay askew on his lap. Walker approached him from behind and placed two fingers on his carotid artery. "He's gone—no pulse."

Stark jumped into the copilot's right seat without waiting and assessed their situation without wasting a second. *Thank God the control panels are set up like the 747 -400 I fly at home!* Then Addison spoke aloud very methodically, "Autopilot is ON, throttles at idle. We're descending and picking up speed. The altimeter's reading five thousand feet and dropping. Thank God this ship is still flying. Another few minutes, and we'd be swimming with the fishes." She advanced the throttles, programed the autopilot for a higher altitude, and began climbing the big jet. *Pressurization*, she thought as her eyes surveyed the overhead control panel. Her disciplined search stopped when she saw the air-conditioning Pack Switches were OFF. She pushed both ON. Her scan also discovered the two outflow valve doors were open, and she pressed the switches to close them, sealing off the cabin. Her actions caused the airflow entering the plane to increase and pressurize the interior cabin. In thirty seconds, the cabin altitude stabilized at its normal level of eight thousand feet.

While Stark took control of flying the aircraft, Walker accomplished the grim task of removing Zara from his seat. He unlatched the pilot's seat belt, and from behind, straddled both his arms under Zara's armpits, clasped his hands across Zara's chest, and dragged him from his seat, through the cockpit. Then he laid him in the aisle outside the cockpit door. When Jack returned to the cockpit, he looked at Addison, who had removed her mask and had full control of the flying situation. She pulled back on the throttles a little and leveled the aircraft at thirty-one thousand feet.

"The aircraft's fully pressurized now, so you can take your mask off," she advised. Jack lifted the mask off his face, took a deep breath, and ran his fingers through his tousled hair.

"Jeez, man, I knew there was a good reason why I brought you along." With a slight turn of the head, she gave him a long, dirty look from the corner of her eye. *A weak joke! After all this hard work . . .* Stark retorted quickly, "And I'm glad I brought you along!"

------◈------

Five minutes of silence followed Walker and Stark's takeover of MH370. Stark busied herself checking and rechecking the aircraft systems. Walker stared through the side window at the black nothing of the night sky. Finally, Stark broke the long silence. "Amazingly, after all that, we're headed southwest in the general direction of Penang. The flight plan that the captain had programmed into the flight computer takes us over Penang and then northwest toward the Andaman Sea and into the Indian Ocean. But that can be changed. So, where do you want to go?" Walker turned his head, looked at Stark, and nodded. "Yeah, that's great to hear, except none of this turned out as we planned. We have a plane full of dead people. That wasn't supposed to happen." With an exasperated tone in his voice, Walker continued. "Who the hell could have known we'd have to deal with a suicidal pilot, not to mention those other characters who tried to hijack the plane before us? Jeez, what a mixed-up mess of bullshit this night has turned out to be."

"Yes, for sure, crap everywhere. But look at it this way. We're still flying, and we have options. I've found the air traffic transponder turned off, so we're currently off civilian radar scopes. Once over the Indian Ocean, we will be out of range of any ground-based radar. We could go direct to Diego Garcia as we once planned. At least, it will be a friendly place. I figure we'll land there in five hours with about one hour of fuel left in the tanks."

Stark continued. "Back in Penang, before Josh Edwards changed our mission from 'intercept and takeover' to 'escort only,' you mentioned that you had discussed the details of 'takeover' operation with your station chief in Kuala Lumpur, and he instructed you to fly to Diego Garcia and maintain radio silence as long as possible, right?"

Walker nodded and wondered where this line of conversation was going but decided to hold any questions. "Yeah, that's what he said. Since it's the weekend, there'll be a minimum of personnel at the airfield. Their flight operations branch had also canceled all arriving and departing flights for the entire weekend to have the entire airfield to ourselves. The tower will keep the runway and surrounding airspace clear until eight o'clock Saturday morning. If we haven't shown up by then, they'll consider our mission a bust."

"So, what do you want to do?" Addison asked. "All the passengers are dead. The Chinese are dead; the Iranian hijackers are dead. We only have so much fuel left. We can land back in Malaysia, Thailand, or Singapore, or we can go to a friendlier place like Diego Garcia."

Walker looked at Stark and saw a small smile on her face. Her smirk aggravated him because it indicated she knew something that he didn't. "Okay, what's so funny?" he said, annoyed.

"Not funny, but it's good to hear they're expecting us . . . sort of . . . because we won't have to talk to anybody." Her remark confused Walker and caused him to wrinkle his brow and narrow his eyes. "You'll be happy to know," she continued, "that this aircraft comes equipped with an automatic landing system. So I can program the flight computer to utilize their instrument landing approach, and the autopilot will fly this beast to the ground—hands-off."

Walker, tired from all the night's exhausting activities, finally got a clear picture in his head of what to do. *Unfortunately, I cannot change the tragic outcome of what has occurred. But like Addison said, we have options.*

"Yes! Diego Garcia, here we come," he said. Addison nodded her agreement.

Stark became busy reprogramming the flight computer. "First thing to do is delete the pilot's southern Indian Ocean destination coordinates." She accomplished that task with five keystrokes. "Second, I add the latitude and longitude coordinates for Diego Garcia Island. There—done. Now we sit back and let the plane do the rest—as we wait."

Walker began thinking and turned to Stark. "It would be great to call ahead and let them know we are proceeding to D.G.—so they can prepare. Addison, is there any way to send a discrete message to our facility in Diego Garcia from this commercial airliner?"

For a minute, Addison was deep in thought. "With our onboard systems, there is no way to send a secure or coded message through government channels. It would all go through civilian channels. However, we could make a very short radio call to Diego Garcia, say, at two hundred miles out, with a disguised message. I'll bet facility personnel are still on alert and know this mission was active at one time, and the flight has gone missing. So if we descend low, approaching D.G., and then making a radio call, there is a good chance that no one else would hear us or see us."

CHAPTER SIXTEEN

Four hours later, Stark had navigated the big jet within two hundred miles of Diego Garcia. *Time to start our descent*, she thought, *and put this bird on the ground*. Down lower now, she knew that the VHF radio range of a transmission would be less and limit any unfriendly monitoring of the frequency.

Walker had worked on a short message, disguised to be meaningless except to the intended recipient. On the Diego Garcia tower frequency, Walker transmitted for twenty seconds:

"Delta Golf Tower, this is Jack Airlines. Highest priority for Josh Echo HDQ Langley. Retrieval complete in 1 hour. Prepare!"

Stark's attention shifted to the flight management computer, and she typed the name of the initial approach fix for ILS runway 31. After inputting the initial approach fix, she listened to Diego Garcia's automated weather broadcast. From that broadcast, she received the wind velocity, direction, altimeter setting, and suggested runway. Her navigation database suggested maintaining a two-thousand-foot altitude, and a thirteen-hundred-foot altitude was safe within one hundred miles of the island. She initiated the descent and thought, *Not a lot of tall buildings out here.*

She decelerated the 777 to maneuvering speed below five thousand feet while lowering the flaps—"Flaps 5." Intercepting the final approach course, she commanded herself to execute "Flaps 20," gear down, and then final landing flaps, "Flaps 30." As the jet descended further on glideslope, through fifteen hundred feet, the autopilot message announced "LAND 3," which indicated "all systems go," for the automatic landing she promised Walker a few hours earlier. Stark had flown automatic approaches like these dozens of times during her flying career—this was old hat for her but not so for Walker.

As he sat in the left seat, his gaze would shift from Stark to his left-side window. Not usually unnerved, the calm, cool, and collected Walker witnessed firsthand this big jet flying itself to a landing without a human at the controls. Feeling his heart pounding in his chest, he questioned his trust in Boeing engineers and prayed for a successful landing. Walker was not a fan of automation, especially on this scale.

At first, a speck of an island appeared out the front window on the horizon. The ocean's surface continued to rise underneath them. Walker wondered—and hoped—that they would reach the edge of the growing island before they plunged into the water. He took a deep breath, held it, and just when he thought they would hit the water, a runway's hard surface appeared under them, and the main landing gear contacted the ground with a characteristic tire screech.

Stark smiled. "You can start breathing again, Walker. We have arrived." Walker frowned at her, irritated again by her smile . . . and then exhaled a long swoosh of air.

When the plane's wheels touched down, the computers commanded the throttles to move to the idle position and applied automatic braking. The plane traversed two-thirds of the runway's twelve thousand feet of concrete as it coasted to taxi speed. Stark disengaged the autoland system, took manual control, and taxied the jet to the first taxiway turnoff. A pickup truck greeted them at that intersection with a large "Follow Me" sign mounted on its rear cargo bed. That's when Walker and Stark knew their message made it through—they were waiting for them.

Stark turned the big jet onto the taxiway and followed the pickup to a giant hanger. She nudged the throttles until the jet's nose was only a few feet from its front door. Then she set the brakes and shut down the left and right engines. Without any additional communication, the hangar doors began to open on cue. Within minutes of the giant hangar doors fully opening, a tow tractor and three military personnel appeared and positioned themselves in front of the nosewheel. Two of them hopped from the tractor and attached a tow bar to the big jet's nosewheel. With that task accomplished, one of the men positioned himself to the left of the cockpit side window and flashed a thumbs-up to the cockpit. Walker saw the signal and relayed it to Stark. She released the parking brake, and Walker showed a thumbs-up to the ground personnel. The tractor driver began towing the Boeing jet inside the hangar. After the plane's tail cleared the door, a fourth man pushed a button on the wall-mounted control panel, and the giant door rumbled at first, then closed with a loud thud.

Walker glanced out his left-side window. "They're wheeling out a boarding ladder, and it looks like we've also got a reception committee waiting for us."

He and Stark removed their headsets, raised themselves out of their seats, and stretched their muscles as they exited the cockpit. Walking toward the left-front entry door, Stark could not resist the temptation of letting her eyes wander into the passenger cabin. Her gaze revealed a cabin full of lifeless victims, and the scene caused her body to shudder. *How could anyone commit mass murder on this scale?* She shook the thought from her mind and focused on disarming the door. Looking out the small window in the middle of the entry door, she could see the metal stairs being pushed against the fuselage. She turned the handle when she heard a "thump" and opened the door.

Three marines stood at the foot of the rolling staircase with their raised M-16 rifles pointed at her. Standing behind her, Walker saw the marines, raised his hands, and yelled, "It's okay; we're unarmed." Then without saying a word, one of the marines motioned with the muzzle of his weapon that they were to deplane. Walker stepped in front of Stark and, with hands raised, started down the stairs. Two officers appeared from a hallway, crossed the hangar floor, and stood behind the marines when they were halfway down.

"I guess this is the rest of the welcoming committee," Stark commented.

"Marines! Stand down," one of the officers ordered. Then on his command, the marines lowered their weapons and stood to one side of the boarding ladder. "Mr. Walker and Ms. Stark, welcome to Diego Garcia. Please, follow me. We have a conference room for our use, and I'm sure we have a lot to talk about." Walker turned his head toward Stark and, in a whispered tone, said, "That's an understatement if I ever heard one."

Upon seeing the two officers, Walker noted they were of equal rank, but one was an air force colonel, and the other was a navy captain. *That makes sense. The U.S. Air Force and Navy share this base, and we'll probably need the help of both services to get out from under this mess. I'm sure these guys were briefed on our original mission*, he continued to think, *but, boy, has that changed.* The group of four walked in silence and entered the conference room. Colonel Metzger broke the silence.

"Please, have a seat, folks, and make yourself comfortable." As he continued to speak, he pointed to a small table against the far wall. "There're sandwiches on that table and some cold drinks. Sorry I can't offer you something a little—"

"Colonel, sorry for the interruption, but our original plan has gone to hell in a handbasket. There's a plane full of dead people in your hangar, and we've got one hell of a long story to tell you." Walker started talking as fast as he could because he had a plan C in mind but had to explain to the two officers what had happened. For the next fifteen minutes, Walker detailed the gruesome events that played out aboard MH370 after their takeoff from Kuala Lumpur until their successful appropriation of the flight. As Walker's story progressed, the two officers exchanged glances and an occasional raised eyebrow.

After Walker finished, there was a moment of silence until Colonel Metzger asked a question. "So, you think the pilot intended to commit suicide from the beginning, and it was just coincidental that he was scheduled for this flight with the package onboard?"

With a firm tone and a nod toward Stark, Walker replied, "Yes, sir, we do. Ms. Stark and I also believe, based on the flight path he programmed into the flight computer, that he had intended to crash the plane into a remote spot in the south Indian Ocean. He probably hoped that no one would ever discover the plane again."

"Damn," was the only word Metzger could stammer.

A moment of thoughtful silence followed his comment until Captain Allison suggested, "George, let's go back to your office since it's closer and call Sec Def. It's early evening in DC. We may ruin a few dinner plans, but we've got to immediately report this up the chain of command. In the meantime, we'll remove the package from the cargo compartment and secure it for shipment back to the States while we try to figure out what to do with the fatalities. You two stay here. Have something to eat and drink. You must be starving."

The two officers stood and turned toward the door when Walker spoke. "Aah, sirs, I have a suggestion." His voice caused the two men to stop and turn to face him. "I was going to say, when you discuss this situation with Sec Def, let him know that Stark and I discussed a plan C while we were flying here. If you want to keep the lid on this, we can continue flying the pilot's course to the south Indian Ocean and ditch the plane in the sea as he planned. While we're here, you can remove the bodies and give those folks a decent burial, but make it look like the pilot succeeded in his suicide mission. Stark and I discussed this at length on our way here—"

"Let me continue from here," Stark interrupted. "In addition to removing the bodies, we should remove all other light items like seat cushions, luggage, personal items—in other words—anything that would float. That way, after I ditch the plane, and it breaks up into large pieces, it'll sink without leaving a trace. We should also remove the emergency location transmitters (ELT) and the voice and data recorders. The ELTs are water and g-force activated and radio out the current position coordinates. The voice and data recorders have special batteries lasting 30 days and send out pings detectable by sonar, bringing listening ears to their vicinity. Furthermore, if we top off the plane's fuel tanks, I can fly it farther than the pilot originally intended, and when they start searching, they'll be searching in the wrong part of the ocean." The two officers looked at each other, nodded, and continued walking out of the room. Walker looked at Stark and said, "I don't know about you, but I'm starved."

CHAPTER SEVENTEEN

Colonel Metzger and Captain Allison returned one hour later. They had just finished a marathon series of phone calls. Lights were burning bright in every building in Washington, D.C., pertaining to national defense, homeland security, and intelligence. That flurry of activity produced an agreed-upon and coordinated response in record time. Waiting, Walker and Stark had succumbed to exhaustion and had their heads resting in their arms on the table when the officers burst into the conference room. The noise of heavy footsteps and a slamming metal door roused them from their light, twilight-like sleep.

Metzger dropped a folder thick with papers on the conference room table in a not-so-gentle manner. The loud thud caused Walker and Stark to raise their heads and rub their eyes.

"Wake up, you two; we've got work to do."

Still rubbing his eyes, Walker stood, and with halting steps, walked toward the coffee urn on the side table. "If we're going to have a serious conversation, I need some coffee to clear my cobwebs."

"While you two were enjoying your beauty sleep, the captain and I talked to half the people in D.C., including the House and Senate leadership and the president's national security advisor. Suffice it to say that our course of action going forward has the full support of the United States government."

Walker returned to his seat at the table with two cups of coffee, one in each hand. He placed one in front of Stark and sat down. "You've got our attention, Colonel. What's our next move?"

"The consensus is that we don't want this thing to go public. It would have been easy to explain a hijacking supposedly motivated by money. Still, a plane full of dead passengers with the only survivors being an American and an Australian would create many questions that would be difficult to answer. Our original priority was to retrieve or destroy the stolen equipment while on the ground in transit. Now we have a plane full of dead people. There's no way to explain that away easily. The international community would not believe us."

Colonel Metzger looked at Walker then Stark. "You said the pilot was actually on a suicide mission, right?"

Walker and Stark nodded. "Yes, we believe so," said Walker. "After the first officer came out of the cockpit, the captain took the airplane off course with a steep turn, even before the Iranians announced the hijack attempt. Later, we found the flight computer with other waypoints to fly into the south Indian Ocean, and we found the ATC transponder turned off. None of these actions seemed coordinated with the Iranians in the cabin."

"When Addison and I finally made it into the cockpit, and Captain Zara was dead in his seat, the aircraft was in a steep dive to crash into the sea. So, yes, the captain had his own plan to take down the airplane."

"Well, we'll just keep the story line that way . . . a pilot suicide mission. We'll remove the bodies and respectfully inter them at a location yet to be determined, but in the meantime, we'll keep them in a refrigerated warehouse here on base. I've already instructed our personnel team to begin removing the bodies and anything in the cabin that would float. The leadership concurred with your suggestion, Ms. Stark, to fly the pilot's original suicide course and ditch the plane in the south Indian Ocean. They left it up to us to work out the specific details to make that happen."

"The air force secretary brought a Boeing engineer into the conversation when we discussed the feasibility of ditching in the sea. He concurred it would be possible and offered two suggestions. First, he suggested you bail out of the aircraft just before it runs out of fuel. Then the plane would be in a controlled descent on autopilot before impacting the sea. The impact would be at a shallow angle, hopefully causing it to skip once or twice; you know, like throwing a flat stone across the water, but still hard enough to break it up into larger pieces. He estimated the pieces would sink in no less than fifteen minutes. He thinks your chance of surviving impact forces would be low.

"If you were to ditch the aircraft manually and survived, exiting a broken aircraft underwater presents many additional problems affecting your survival. He recommended removing the external avionics bay door located on the fuselage's forward belly, which mechanics use to access the electronics bay on the ground. The access door can only be removed from the outside. So we will have to remove it on the ground before you take off. Since the opening is large enough for a man and his equipment to get into the plane, we think it's also large enough for a man or woman to bail out of the plane. With that big hole in the belly, however, you wouldn't be able to pressurize the aircraft after takeoff, but you should be okay if you fly at ten thousand feet.

"Before the engines flame out, you'll engage the autopilot, get to the avionics bay, and bail out of the open hatch. That avionics bay is accessible internally by lifting a floor panel under carpeting at the forward entry door and then descending a metal ladder. This exit will also minimize any possibility of your body hitting any portion of the plane's tail."

Walker's attention, fueled by a strong dose of caffeine and this extraordinary escape scheme, caused him to squirm involuntarily, and the more he heard, the more anxious he got. Addison listened intently and nodded. She could picture very clearly the escape the engineer was describing. For Jack, however, the plan caused him even more concern as a hundred questions popped in and out of his head.

"Wait a minute. Are you guys serious? Why can't we just demolish the plane here, on this island, and bury the pieces?"

"Don't worry, Jack. I appreciate your concern for safety, but everything the colonel said is doable and without much risk, really." Then turning her attention back to the colonel, she continued. "I'm sure your intelligence people had access to my personnel file and saw that I'm a very proficient skydiver. I've made over one hundred jumps from low to high altitudes and from a variety of aircraft, so don't worry about me."

Walker nodded. "Don't worry about me either. During my SEAL training, I made a bunch of both, high altitude low opening and high altitude high opening jumps, so—"

Metzger interrupted. "Mr. Walker, the consensus is that Ms. Stark flies this mission solo. There's no need to put two lives at risk." Walker's complexion turned beet red. His dominant nature surfaced, and he thought, *Damn it, we started this mission together, and we should finish it together.*

Walker was about to defend the idea of his going, but Stark put her hand on his arm. "It's all right, Jack. I've got this." Her superior piloting experience and skydiving abilities made her the best choice to go. "Colonel, you said the Boeing engineer had two suggestions. What was the second one?"

"Yes, thanks for reminding me. The engineer's second suggestion had to do with the plane's satellite communications system. The aircraft's SATCOM system utilizes the Inmarsat Indian Ocean Region satellite, and it enables voice and data communications between plane and ground. You told us that after you took control of the plane, you noticed that the pilot had turned off the voice and data communication feature of the system that essentially rendered the aircraft 'dark' to all but powerful military radars, right?"

Stark nodded and added, "Yes, and I left it off, and that's when we headed to Diego Garcia."

"Right, but did you know that even with the communication and data channel turned off, the aircraft still communicates with the satellite through a series of hourly 'handshakes'? Nothing of importance is transmitted or received, except acknowledging that the aircraft and satellite are connected—kind of like your cell phone linking up with the nearest cell tower. Even if you don't make a call, the linkup still occurs."

"No, sir," replied Stark, "I didn't know that. That complicates the situation if we want the plane to disappear. They're going to be many smart people looking for this airplane. Sooner or later, someone will discover those handshakes, and the trail will lead right here."

Metzger continued, "Yes, that's right, which is why one of our avionic technicians is consulting with a Boeing avionics engineer as we speak. A SATCOM system component called the Satellite Data Unit (SDU) is responsible for transmitting that handshake signal. With Boeing's help, our tech is programming a transmission delay bias and position offset into the SDU. Due to our electronic modification to the SDU, the satellite will receive a handshake time stamp and corresponding GPS coordinates consistent with the suicide pilot's original timetable and planned course into the south Indian Ocean. In reality, the SDU will be 'fooled' both in time and position--you'll be ditching the plane about one thousand miles west of their eventual search area.

Metzger said, "That's all I have. Have we forgotten anything?"

Walker and Stark looked at each other. They did not have to exchange words for conveying their concurrence—just a nod and a couple of shrugs. Neither could think of any additional points. Finally, Walker turned and shook his head, "No, sir—sounds like a plan."

Saturday morning was a quiet time on Diego Garcia with little scheduled official activity under normal circumstances. Except for the marine guards who had cordoned off access to the hangar and ramp area in front of the enormous door, there was no hint of the frantic activity taking place inside. Stark had thought of one final precaution and watched as a team of five men in white HazMat suits approached the aircraft. Each man carried a bucket filled with white paint and a long-handled brush. Their job was to blank out the Malaysia Airlines name from the side of the fuselage and cover the airline's logo seen on the tail. She would be taking off under a midmorning sun, and there was no sense in advertising the aircraft's livery.

Fifteen minutes earlier, an air force technician carrying a large duffel bag approached Stark while she was watching the painting process. "You can change in that restroom over there."

Stark glanced in the direction he was pointing, grabbed hold of the duffel bag's strap, and was surprised by its weight. She thanked him and, without wasting a moment, trudged in the direction of the restroom while she wondered, what's in this bag—bricks? Stark changed out of her civilian clothes into a military-style flight suit and returned to the hangar floor, just as the men in white finished covering the last vestiges of the big jet's markings. She laid the duffel bag containing her survival vest, flotation device, small locater beacon, and parachute on the floor at her side. She watched as other military personnel moved the ladders and work stands away from the big plane.

Walker approached from behind and stood at her side. She turned her head and acknowledged him with a nod. "Looks like everything's about done, and you'll be leaving soon. I'm concerned you're making this flight by yourself. I wish they'd let me go with you. Besides, once you take off, our work together is over. I mean, after that destroyer picks you up somewhere in the south Indian Ocean, it's going to take you to Perth, and I'll be hopping on a C-17 back to the States, so I guess this is goodbye."

She turned her head, looked at him with a pout on her face, and replied, "Why, Walker, I didn't realize you were so sentimental. You're actually a decent bloke—for a Yank."

He looked deep into her cobalt-blue eyes and quietly asked himself, *Will I ever see you again?* He nudged her arm with his, "Yeah, you're not such a bad Sheila yourself," he said, stepping forward to hug her. "Take good care of yourself."

Just as Walker and Stark finished their goodbye, Colonel Metzger approached them. "Good morning. Are you ready, Ms. Stark?" Not waiting for an answer, he continued, "Time is of the essence. We've received reports that this plane has been officially reported missing. The Malaysians reported that the aircraft would have run out of fuel by now, but there is confusion about where they think it might have gone down. Also, reports suggest search and rescue efforts are focused in the South China Sea between Malaysia and the southern coast of Vietnam. That works to our advantage, but we must hurry. I'm sure when they begin to take a closer look at the radar tracks, they'll put two and two together and refocus their search efforts in the Indian Ocean.

"Just a final word before you go. We intend to maintain radio silence, which means no ground-to-air or air-to-air communication. After we push you out of the hangar and you start the engines, you'll follow the 'follow me' truck to runway 13 - it's the closest. When you're in takeoff position at the end of the runway, look back at the control tower. If everything is still a 'go,' we'll shine a steady green light. That'll be your signal to take off. If you see a flashing red light—"

"Yeah, I know, sir. That means abort takeoff and get my butt back to the hangar ASAP, right?"

Metzger's body toughened. He was not accustomed to interruptions or harsh tones. But then again, Stark and Walker were not his usual subordinates but thinking operatives of the highest order.

"Yes, Ms. Stark, that's correct. Now, it's time to go. Good luck, Ms. Stark." Stark turned and began walking toward the boarding ladder. Glancing over her shoulder with a smile, she waved to the two men.

Walker waved back and thought, *You're pretty self-confident, Ms. Stark—gotta love that girl. Please be safe.*

Fifteen minutes later, Stark positioned the big jet for takeoff at the departure end of runway 13. She looked directly at the tower and waited. Unfortunately, she was also looking almost directly into the rising morning sun. She whispered, "Thank you, Air Force, for the sunglasses." Five seconds later, she saw a steady green light beamed in her direction from the top of the control tower. She turned her head, refocused her line of sight down the centerline of the twelve thousand feet of runway in front of her, and pushed the throttles forward. Even with a full load of fuel, the jet's acceleration surprised her until she remembered, *Oh yeah, we're way lighter than usual— no cargo, no passengers, and most of the interior is gone.* Due to the open hatch in the plane's belly, she only climbed the big jet to ten thousand feet. She ran through her after-takeoff checklist, and all systems checked green. Then she settled into her seat. *This will be a boring five hours*, she thought, *followed by fifteen minutes of sheer terror when I have to bail out.*

Four and a half hours later, a "ping" warning sound followed by a light on the master caution display caught Addison's attention. Her mind knew what it was, but she glanced at the display anyway. Yep, low fuel warning—got about twenty minutes of fuel left. That warning was her cue to get ready to bail out. She performed a few final checks out of habit.

With the autopilot ON, she set up the big jet's configuration for its final descent into oblivion. First, Stark reduced the plane's speed to a maneuvering speed of two hundred knots on a forward panel. Next, she extended the wing flaps, sets minus five hundred feet below sea level in the target altitude window, set the vertical speed to one thousand feet/min DOWN, and pulled the thrust levers back to idle. From ten thousand feet, descending at one thousand feet every minute, the big jet would hit the ocean below in ten minutes. She scanned the panel one last time to confirm the settings. A quick glance at the navigation page confirmed her position in the middle of the south Indian Ocean, one thousand five hundred miles west of Perth.

Then she pushed her seat back, stood up, and left the cockpit. The cold air in the cabin caused an unpleasant shiver throughout her body. Any warm air generated by the plane's environmental control system was being sucked through the open hole in its belly faster than it could be replenished. She removed the sport parachute from her duffle bag and strapped it to her body over her water survival suit, floatation collar, and survival vest. She felt like a bloated whale by the time she was fully dressed. She waddled toward the previously raised floor panel near the forward entry door, bent down, and, step by step, began descending the ladder. Luckily, she fit through the floor opening after bumping either side with only inches to spare. Below the main deck and looking ahead on a metal catwalk between rows of electronic equipment, she walked eight feet to the open hole on the belly where the external access door had been removed. Arriving at the edge of the opening, she sat down on the door frame, looked down at the dark blue sea passing ten thousand feet below her, took a deep breath, and pushed free, letting the rushing air suck her body through the hole.

Her body cleared the big jet's fuselage, and she established a stable free-fall position. Before pulling the parachute's ripcord, she glanced up, and for a moment, felt sad for the big jet continuing its descent to an untimely demise. She shook the thought from her head and pulled the ripcord. Her body felt the expected jerk, but the slack riser cords on her right side told her something was wrong. She looked up, and her body stiffened with fear when she saw the parachute canopy had only partially opened. She pulled the ripcord on her emergency chute, but it got tangled with her primary chute, and she was still falling too fast. She had to either clear the tangled lines or else hit the water at a high rate of speed with possibly fatal consequences. Adrenalin surged through her veins, and she fought back with every physical and mental survival trick she knew as the water below her kept getting closer. She was still struggling to clear the tangled cords when, moments later, she hit the water, felt excruciating pain, and then darkness overcame her.

PART 6

The Investigation

CHAPTER EIGHTEEN

Kuala Lumpur

On Saturday morning, the world awoke to a disturbing news event. The *Star*, the most widely read English language newspaper in Malaysia, informed the public of the grim news with the following front-page headline and article:

SPECIAL EDITION

Flight MH370 Bound for Beijing Goes Missing

Saturday, March 8, 2014, Kuala Lumpur: Malaysia Airlines confirmed that Flight MH370 went missing a short while ago. Kuala Lumpur Air Traffic Control lost contact with the aircraft at 1:40 a.m. Saturday. In a statement issued by the airlines, MH370, a Boeing 777-200ER, departed Kuala Lumpur this morning at 12:41 a.m. and was scheduled to land in Beijing later this morning at 6:30 a.m. The flight carried 227 passengers and 12 crew members. Malaysia Airlines is currently working with local and regional authorities who have activated their search and rescue teams to locate the missing aircraft.

Speaking on the condition of anonymity, an airline employee told a local TV station, "We have tried to track the flight. So far, we've had no luck. The aircraft had seven hours of fuel onboard and should have run out of fuel by 8:30 a.m. Saturday. A local TV news station reported 160 of the 227 passengers were Chinese nationals. China and

Malaysia are mobilizing their search and rescue assets and are focusing their efforts in the South China Sea vicinity. A Malaysia Airlines spokesperson said they would provide updates as new information becomes available."

After over five hours of confusion concerning the disappearance of MH370, KL ATC finally initiated search and rescue (SAR) operations for the vanished MH370. All government agencies were abruptly called into action finally coordinating their efforts to find the flight.

The Malaysian Minister of Transport also initiated action to organize an accident investigation team per the ICAO *Manual of Accident Investigation and Incident Investigation* practices. The manual requires the investigating authority to appoint an investigator-in-charge and establish three main committees: Airworthiness, Flight Operations, and Medical/Human Factors.

The MOT also established an independent, international investigation, "Team," according to ICAO guidelines that comprised nineteen Malaysian and seven Accredited Representatives (ARs) of seven safety investigation authorities from seven countries to investigate the disappearance of MH370. The Accredited Representatives were from the: Air Accidents Investigation Branch of the United Kingdom; Australian Transport Safety Bureau; Bureau d'Enquêtes et d'Analyses pour la Sécurité de l'Aviation Civile of France; Civil Aviation Administration of the People's Republic of China; the National Transportation Safety Board of the United States; the National Transportation Safety Committee of Indonesia; and the Transport Safety Investigation Bureau of Singapore. In addition, advisors to the ARs were appointed from the Malaysian states' investigation agencies and the aircraft, engine, and satellite communications systems manufacturers.

CIA Headquarters—Langley, Virginia

As the international search efforts for MH370 escalated from the South China Sea to the Indian Ocean, normal operations had returned to Diego Garcia, and Walker boarded an Air Force C-17 for his trip home. The trip, which included a stopover at Ramstein Air Base in Germany, gave him time to reflect on his mission. *I think I'm getting too old for this stuff. I feel like I've been dragged through a cactus field by a team of wild horses, but the mission was a success.* Several months of stressful, nonstop activity had exhausted him more than he realized. After arriving at Dover, the air force was kind enough to provide a vehicle and driver to deliver him to his home in Langley, Virginia.

He thought about his partner, Addison Stark, daily. He hoped she had successfully ditched the plane and had been rescued by the destroyer. But, of course, she did, he reminded himself. She was one hell of an agent. So finding out her fate was on the top of his to-do list when he returned to work.

The following day, Walker woke up feeling energized. Most days, he struggled with his inner self. One part of him wanted to get up, but the other part wanted to roll over and go back to sleep, but this was not an ordinary day. He took a quick shower, got dressed, and grabbed an energy bar and coffee as he hurried out the front door. He jumped into his car and steered it down the driveway—all before the first rays of sun broke the eastern horizon. He had a lot to catch up on and one essential thing to do.

Thoughts raced through his mind during his fifteen-minute commute to CIA headquarters. *I've been away several months, but everything still looks the same.* Upon showing his ID, the guard waved him through the gate, and he found a parking space in the front row. *One advantage of arriving early*, he thought.

His boss would not arrive for another hour, which gave Walker time to check his emails and voicemail. He stopped at his boss's office and left a sticky note on the computer monitor: *"I'm back; need to talk ASAP—Walker."*

An hour later, Walker's phone rang. His boss, Josh Edwards, was on the other end. "Jack, this is Josh; come on by, and we'll talk." Edwards knew Walker would not waste any time getting to his office. He was also sure he knew what Walker wanted. The two men knew each other for many years, and Edwards knew Walker would not handle Addison Stark's news well. He was not looking forward to their conversation.

Walker exploded when he heard the news. "WHAT? What do you mean they couldn't find her?" he screamed.

"Jack, calm down, and I'll explain. Please, sit. Mechanical trouble and bad weather delayed the destroyer's arrival at the rendezvous site. They picked up pings from her locater beacon, but they found it floating in the water attached to a piece of her survival vest, but no Stark. The beacon must have fallen off her vest or somehow been ripped off. The ship searched for four days before calling off the search. I'm sorry, Jack—they tried their best."

Jack did not hear a word Edwards said after telling him she was missing. Rage filled his mind. "I knew I should have gone with her. I knew it was too risky a thing to do by herself, damn it." He was angry with himself and everyone up the chain of command who had anything to do with the decision to let Stark fly the big jet solo. *Damn bastards, they don't care about people—just get the mission done!*

Today was not the first time Edwards had to tell one of his field agents that they had lost a colleague. It was the first time, though, that he had to tell Walker terrible news. Judging by Walker's deep red complexion, Edwards knew Jack was *not* taking the information well. He looked like a boiler ready to explode.

"Jack, I know you're upset, but we all tried to find her. We didn't just write her off as collateral damage. Please, understand. Take the day off if you need to. You've got to put this behind you and move on."

The longer Edwards spoke, the angrier Walker got, and he knew he had to get away from his boss before he did or said something he would regret later. Walker was skilled at presenting a calm, outward appearance while every muscle in his body was wound tighter than a clock spring, and his mind screamed thoughts about how much he wanted to kill someone. This feeling was one of those moments. He took a deep breath, stood, and excused himself, "See you tomorrow, boss."

"Hey, Jack, good to see ya. Welcome back," yelled a workmate from behind a cubical desk. Walker ignored the greeting from a co-worker and continued his march to the parking lot. Reflecting on the events of that morning, that coworker remarked months later that Walker, with his straight-ahead, tight-lipped stare, looked like an ax-murderer stalking his victim.

When he arrived at his car, he stopped by the driver-side door. He stood ramrod stiff, threw his head back, and filled his lungs with a long inhale of the cool morning air. He held that breath for a moment before he began a slow exhale. He hoped to expel some of his anger. It helped in the past, but not this morning.

He unlocked his car, stood still for a moment with his key in hand, and tried to shake the angry thoughts from his head. Finally, he squealed the tires leaving the parking lot as an angry expression of his frustration and made a left turn onto the George Washington Expressway—and just drove. He spent the rest of the day driving around Fairfax County with no particular destination in mind. That evening, he sat in a darkened room in front of his television, watching a show he would never remember. He held a half-empty fifth of scotch in his right hand and sipped its remaining contents from time to time. An hour later, the gold-colored elixir had begun to work its magic, and it soothed his rage. *Damn shame*, he thought. *I lost her. I should have been there to help her.*

Australian Transportation Safety Bureau
HEADQUARTERS CANBERRA, AUSTRALIA

Ana Miles lived by herself in a comfortable one-bedroom apartment in Barton, a lakeside suburb adjacent to Capitol Hill and directly south of Canberra city center. She relished her job as an aircraft accident investigator at the Australian Transportation Safety Bureau (ATSB) because every day brought new challenges. Her friends were content playing with dolls and making-believe tea parties when she was a young girl, but her interests gravitated toward model airplanes and airplane picture books. So it surprised no one when she decided to pursue an aviation career and received a master's degree in aerospace engineering from the Royal Melbourne Institute of Technology.

After graduation, the ATSB offered her a job, and she accepted their offer without a second thought. As far as she was concerned, this was her dream job. The one aspect of aviation she found most compelling was trying to determine the cause of aircraft accidents and disappearances. Two famous aircraft disappearances fueled her younger curiosity: Amelia Earhart's disappearance and the disappearance of the Pan American Airways' Hawaii Clipper flying boat. She read all the books she could find on the subject, and for her Aviation Safety course in college, she wrote a research paper on the disappearance of the Hawaii Clipper. Her research paper served two purposes: first, it was a course requirement for which she nailed an *A* for her excellent research and technical insight; second, and more importantly, she learned all things were not as they seem—that an investigator must adhere to facts and avoid the urge to rush to judgment based on innuendo and supposition.

As the Australian Airworthiness and Operations Team leader, she now had a golden opportunity to investigate a modern-day aviation mystery. As she waited for the number five bus for her morning commute to work, she reflected on her current assignment. *This is the biggest assignment of my career. A month ago, a plane full of people disappeared without a trace. The Malaysian government asked for our help and help from the Americans, Brits, French, and Chinese. My human side wants to help bring closure to the missing passengers' families, but my engineering side wants to figure out what happened and prevent this sort of thing from ever happening again. From a historical perspective, this is probably the greatest aviation mystery ever, and I'm right in the middle of it.*

Her short bus ride ended thirteen minutes later, and she walked the remaining one hundred yards to the ATSB headquarters. As she walked, she checked the time on her cell phone: 7:00 a.m. *Good*, she thought. *I have an hour to prepare for my eight o'clock team meeting.* As the team leader, she had a small private office that adjoined a large conference room.

Three lined notebooks lay open at different angles, and dozens of papers soon covered her desk as she immersed herself in preparation for her meeting. During the week, Ana would meet privately with team members and discuss their progress on individual assignments, but she held a group meeting every Friday morning. At the meeting, she and her four team members shared their previous days' activities, such as progress, problems, and issues. As she perused her notes and marked them with talking point reminders, she stopped momentarily and stared into space.

I'm fortunate to have such a great team trying to figure out this mystery. My three junior engineers have advanced degrees in three engineering disciplines: mechanical, electrical, and computer science. In addition, each has a commercial pilot's license. Then there's the American from the National Transportation Safety Board. Like me, he's got a degree in aerospace engineering but has more years' experience, especially in high-profile accident investigations where a possible rogue pilot could be considered a probable cause.

Her cell phone alarm rang as she finished her thought. "Okay, ten minutes till showtime," she mumbled to herself as she gathered the loose papers on her desk and stuffed them between the notebook pages. Then she pushed her desk chair back, stood up, and walked into the adjoining conference room. There, she greeted her team.

"Good morning, everyone," and the meeting began. One hour later, the meeting adjourned, and a low hum of conversation permeated the room as everyone prepared to return to their respective work areas.

"Brian, may I see you for a moment?"

"Sure thing, Ana. What's up?"

"As we get more and more information—or the lack thereof—I can't help but think this might be a case of pilot misconduct or third-party involvement. I know you have experience on high-profile investigations involving suspected pilot suicide; you know, EgyptAir in ninety-nine and that SilkAir mishap in ninety-seven. So I'd like to run some things by you and pick your brain a bit, okay?"

Brian Sloan, a senior accident investigator working for the NTSB in Washington, D.C., had been selected by the NTSB chairman to participate in the MH370 disappearance investigation because of his prior international accident investigation experience. It was no coincidence that the ATSB and NTSB leadership decided to pool the best and the brightest from both their organizations to aid Malaysia in determining the cause of the disappearance of MH370. The world waited—and it wanted answers.

Immediately after the disappearance of Malaysia Airlines MH370, due to incomplete reporting, incompetent interpretation, and miscommunications within the government agencies, ATC, the military, and Malaysian Airlines, days passed before a realistic picture emerged that the flight had changed course westbound and then headed into the Indian Ocean. Once convinced of that fact, Malaysian authorities suspended search efforts in the South China Sea, the Malacca Straits, and the Andaman Sea. Instead, they focused their search effort on the southern Indian Ocean.

Although the aircraft was flying "dark" at the time, one piece of electronic equipment continued to operate. The satellite data unit, or SDU, designed to transmit aircraft and telephony data, remained active. It connected seven times between the plane and a geostationary satellite over the Indian Ocean and a Perth ground station. With sophisticated analysis, the satellite manufacturer identified equal distant circles where the aircraft was located as the "handshakes" took place. Seven arcs represented a large swath of the earth's surface stretching as far north as Kazakhstan to one thousand miles off the west coast of Australia.

By March 17, 2014, the Malaysian Transport Ministry assigned the surface-search responsibility to the Australian Maritime Safety Authority (AMSA). In the meantime, the investigators, using satellite data, Boeing-supplied aircraft performance estimates, and MH370's fuel load, identified an initial search area in the southern Indian Ocean that covered almost two million square miles. The AMSA coordinated the surface search efforts of twenty-two aircraft and nineteen ships from eight countries.

Curiously, China deployed and dedicated nine ships to the search, the most of any country. At a news conference, a reporter asked a Chinese official why the Chinese government responded with so many ships. The official said he wanted the world community to know, since most of the passengers on board MH370 were Chinese nationals, that his country felt it was its duty to provide as much help as possible. But, of course, the spokesman did not discuss the downplaying of their involvement, putting those same passengers in danger by carrying top-secret military hardware in the cargo compartment below. One high-ranking Australian official wondered why China suddenly had such empathy for its people. "It just isn't consistent with their past behavior."

The search and rescue surface ships found an abundance of floating debris discarded by passing vessels, either intentionally or by accident, but nothing was traced back to the missing airliner. By late April, Australia suspended the surface rescue attempts and moved the search underwater. The results of the underwater recovery efforts provided a map of ocean depths and seabed contours.

However, oceanographers knew little about the underwater characteristics of this part of the Indian Ocean. The local geographical data lacked the detail necessary to ensure the safe operation of underwater search equipment, such as towed sonar devices and autonomous underwater vehicles (AUVs). This delayed other research vessels before they could search for an underwater aircraft debris field.

Hopes were buoyed twice during the underwater search operation: first, when the Chinese Coast Guard cutter, *Haixun 01*, and the Australian off-shore patrol vessel, *Ocean Shield*, detected pings, at first thought to be from the aircraft's voice and data recorders, and second, when an AUV spotted two anomalies on the ocean floor. The pings were heard approximately one month into the underwater search effort—but beyond the thirty days of battery life for the recorders to emit signals—and dashed searchers' hopes that they had located the flight or voice recorder. Additionally, the searchers determined one underwater anomaly was a previously unknown nineteenth-century shipwreck, and the second was a rock field. Great Britain deployed their submarine, HMS *Tireless*, to augment the surface vessel's efforts. But, again, the searchers failed to locate any wreckage or the recorders.

———————

Walker took the rest of the week off to decompress and recover physically and mentally. By the end of the week, he could no longer sit still and ached to get back in the saddle. Monday, he would return to work and try to move on in his life. Josh Edwards had left him a message that he should stop in the office after he rested up and was feeling better, and they would debrief the mission.

Monday morning in Josh's office, with coffee in hand, Jack and Josh sat at a work table exchanging pleasantries after weeks of Jack being away. Finally, Jack turned to the subject of the mission. "Josh, did we ever find out how the Taliban knew about our 'package' test program in the mountains?"

Josh thinly smiled while nodding his head. "Yes, we believe there was a leak of information as the 'package' arrived at Bagram AFB and was routed to the mountains. A local source put two and two together. Sorry you got hurt there, but nice to see you moving about so well. You and Stark did a good job of following the trail of the 'package' through the countryside—to Karachi, then Penang, and Kuala Lumpur."

"Yeah, sorry we couldn't intercept it on the ground. It always seemed just out of reach," responded Jack.

"Well, glad you and Addison were always close and could escort it, even on the flight to Beijing." Josh, then remembering a question that had been bugging him, said, "By the way, on the flight to Beijing, when did things begin to get out of control, and what triggered your actions to take it over."

Of course, Jack had written about this event in his official reports, but, naturally, Josh would want to hear this firsthand. Jack started. "Not too long after reaching cruise altitude and the cabin settling down for the long night ahead, the copilot came out of the cockpit and engaged the purser in the forward galley. Although Addison and I were fairly close to the galley, we couldn't make out any of the conversation. Then, the aircraft entered a steep turn, left, I think, throwing the copilot and purser to their knees, and some men in the aisles to the floor. The g-force threw me into my seat bottom with the most force I've ever experienced on a commercial flight. Then, two men appeared in the forward galley, one grabbing the purser and one pointing a gun at the pilot. They announced to the forward cabin to remain seated, that this was a hijacking, and that we were going to Iran. 'Cooperate, and you will not be harmed. You will be released after landing and given passage to your desired destinations.'

"About that time, the aircraft experienced a sudden depressurization. Now, there was chaos in the cabin. Anything not nailed down was flying in the cabin. I'm sure the flying pilot induced the loss of pressure to quiet the revolt on board. Most people seated put on their masks. Those with no O2 masks drifted away, falling unconscious.

Then the flying pilot climbed the plane to make matters worse. The good news was the hijackers both went to the floor quietly. The bad news was our twelve-minute supply limit was ending on the overhead masks.

"Stark was rummaging in her bags at her feet, going for the emergency scuba breathing bottles she had slipped through the security checkpoint." *Gosh. She was right again. She saved our lives!*

"By this time, only Stark and I were left conscious in the cabin, and we assumed the remaining pilot was operating in the cockpit. He had placed the aircraft into a final descent to crash. We had to get into the cockpit, but we had to breathe first. With our emergency masks on, Stark directed me to get two 'walkaround' bottles used by the flight attendants for passenger issues. She went forward to get the cockpit door open. With the new O2 bottles, we could breathe OK. And somehow, she got the door to open when the timer system reset. We got in!

"The captain was in the left seat slumped over the controls. His O2 mask was on his left knee. It looked like it had been ripped from the regulator over his left shoulder. Stark got in the righthand seat, immediately took control, and stopped our descent. She estimated later we were thirty seconds from impact.

"Josh, Stark was amazing! She got us into the cockpit and kept us flying, cool and calm. She was operating in her own element. She saved us both and the mission. Addison climbed the B777 higher and reprogramed our flight to Diego Garcia. Amazing girl!"

"Well, I guess the agencies did something right picking Stark to join the party," Josh commented. "That was a spine-chilling airplane ride you had. Glad you're back."

After a few seconds of silence, Jack asked, "How is the narrative playing out in the world, given the disappearance of MH370?"

"Well, the international press has caught hold of the story of the disappearance of a commercial airliner in this modern era as unbelievable. And it changes every day, with a new revelation and new theories proposed—search here, and now, search there—no sightings, no wreckage. The Iranians are quiet, and the Chinese are quiet and will probably remain so. The Chinese are heavily involved in the search and rescue attempts as befits their interest and respect for the 150+ Chinese on board. There is presently no hint of Iranian intelligence, Chinese MOI, or U.S. CIA involvement, and no mention of the package carried on board."

Josh's face changed as his next words were being formed in his head. "Our Chinese source in Karachi has informed us that the Chinese have a backup plan to release a story about U.S. CIA clandestine involvement, with special cargo and special agents on board the aircraft mishandling the mission and likely causing a crash in the south Indian Ocean. It's a pretty good 'cover your ass' plan for them. For us, the present confusion concerning the disappearance is sufficient to keep concerned eyes off the U.S. involvement. Maybe some disinformation can be used as needed to keep us out of the world press."

"So, the U.S. will disavow any knowledge or participation regarding the Flight MH370 to Beijing," Jack summarized. "That's beginning to sound like the story of my life."

"Anything new on Addison?" Jack asked.

"Sorry, Jack, nothing new on her," Josh responded.

CHAPTER NINETEEN

Press Conference
Kuala Lumpur, Malaysia

"Hello, my name is Hope Lee. Thank you very much for attending this conference today, where we are discussing the events surrounding the disappearance of Malaysian Airlines Flight MH370. I speak today for myself, my mother Ruth Mah, a passenger aboard MH370, and other concerned Malaysian families and friends. I want to be a voice for those missing passengers on Flight MH370."

"Today, I am asking many pointed questions. Unfortunately, I do not have many good answers. The Malaysian Ministry of Transport Preliminary Report that was made public recently delivers scant factual information about the disappearance, leaving many critical issues open. However, the following questions need to be asked of the airline and government authorities responsible to Malaysian citizens and the air traveling public worldwide. I will take no questions at the end of my remarks. Your questions need to be asked and answered elsewhere. I am no aviation expert. However, other aviation professionals and friends of the traveling public have helped me formulate these questions regarding the operational protocols, government agency responsibilities, and international expectations on handling such emergencies."

"Concerning air traffic control, we know that MH370 last communicated at 0119 local time and then disappeared off three neighboring countries' radar scopes at 0120. Did the Kuala Lumpur ACC controllers actively see MH370 disappearing off the radar screen at that moment at 0120? Was anyone watching?

"We know that Ho Chi Minh (HCM) ACC called KLACC at 0138 a.m.—eighteen minutes later—to query KL controllers on the whereabouts of MH370. Were the KL controllers surprised by the HCM call? Was KLACC aware of this disappearance before HCM called?"

"HCM initially saw MH370 approaching IGARI but still within KL airspace. Later, with no one seeing it happen, the MH370 radar symbol disappeared. In addition, MH370 never made radio contact with HCM at IGARI, and the aircraft never answered any of HCM's direct calls."

"At 0157, HCM again called KLACC and said MH370 was missing. They reminded KL that they never took control at the transfer point IGARI. Subsequently, the KL watch supervisor comes on the scene and calls MAS Operations Dispatch Center (ODC) for any information they have on MH370's position. He was told 'standby.' It had been forty minutes since the flight disappeared over the South China Sea. Was anyone ready to acknowledge the international rules that after thirty minutes of being overdue and missing, an emergency may exist with the possibility of passengers and crew having crashed or have gone down in the water below?"

"Concerning airline flight following responsibilities, MAS ODC reports back to KLACC three times in the next half hour with information, interpreted from the airlines' flight following system, that essentially said the flight was proceeding normally: (1) MH370 is in Cambodia, (2) MH370 position is N14.90 E109.155, and (3) MH370 is in 'normal condition' based on signal downloads. These assumptions, where later discovered to be totally false. The air traffic control services were confused with this information and frozen in place to rethink their own assumptions, *one hour* after its disappearance. Did not ATC trust their own systems to declare an emergency?"

"At 0430, MAS ODC called KLACC and admitted that the flight following systems information was interpreted in error! The computer program readings were only a projection of the plane's position and NOT a real-time position. At 0520, MAS ODC called again, and a MAS captain duty manager suggested that MH370 'never left Malaysian airspace'! So MH370 had been missing for over *four hours* now with *no action* taken to rescue it. Why did it take so long for the airline to admit—MAS had lost its plane?"

"Consider this: At this point, all the regional ATCs showed MH370 had disappeared, and Malaysia Airlines doesn't know where MH370 is. Did anyone think to call the Royal Malaysian Air Force controllers for further advice as the plane crossed international boundaries?"

"With respect to the Royal Malaysian Air Force, did air force air controllers actually see the 'unknown aircraft' primary radar symbol in real-time . . . or only days afterward, while looking at the previously recorded tapes? Why did the air force not scramble fighter jets, like other countries, to inspect and verify the unidentified aircraft in their airspace? How could the air force simply assume that this 'blip' was a 'friendly'? Why did the air force wait *several days* to announce they saw a 'primary target' (most likely MH370) fly across Malaysia to Penang and then to the northwest, while the ATC Rescue Coordination Center was left clueless, searching further east in the South China Sea? Are Malaysian officials scared to criticize the politically powerful Royal Malaysian Air Force?"

"Concerning pilot communications, commercial pilot friends of this investigative effort have been asked, 'What surprises you most about the disappearance of MH370?' They responded, "The silence from the cockpit. What the pilots *didn't* say!"

"The B777 has highly developed communications systems: VHF voice, HF data and voice, and Satellite Radio data and voice. Every radio has a second duplicate radio as a backup. Usually, one may go out—but not both. Despite catastrophic system failures, a functioning pilot can generally find a way to get a message out of the cockpit. Every airborne airliner maintains a listening watch, as do ground stations, on the emergency frequency 121.5 MGZ."

"Pilots are trained to talk, even in the direst situations. With air traffic control, they talk to confirm instructions and remain separated from other aircraft. Pilots share their intentions with those assisting them from the ground; i.e., their desire to proceed to an alternate destination. They can talk instantly to other airplanes, air to air, in range at any time. Even at night, pilots know there is an aircraft out there they can talk to. Even transmitting in the blind can help."

"Why didn't MH370 call Ho Chi Minh or Kuala Lumpur with their emergency? Why didn't they make a MAYDAY call on the emergency frequency? Why didn't they call MAS operations dispatch center on their satellite voice system? Why didn't they text a message? Why didn't they squawk an emergency code on their transponder? Professional pilots are very bewildered."

"Technically, MH370 disappeared from radar at 0120 local time. KLACC first issued an Alert Message at 0530, activating a Rescue Coordination Center. Then, at 0630, an official Distress message was released, and the RCC officially began the search and rescue activities. How can an airliner go missing for over *five* hours in this case without any formal action to begin a search and rescue? International protocol calls for an emergency response after *one* hour when an aircraft is missing. For ATC, it is disgraceful to lose control of an airplane. Were passengers and crew languishing below in their life rafts while the various agencies were confused by events and misinformation? Did MAS and KL ACC delay search proceedings for hours because of possible incompetence and misinterpretation of the flight following system?"

"This concludes my discussion. Thank you for your presence today."

At the end of the session, Noah Jacobs, a freelance reporter in the audience, thought to himself, *Wow, this could be a gigantic story of misconduct, even malfeasance for the countries and agencies involved, not to mention the unexplained disappearing events of the B777 itself. What was happening on board that aircraft? But, more importantly, I should introduce myself to this spokesperson, Hope Lee.*

Kuala Lumpur

Noah Jacobs sat at a small, round table outside a Starbucks in the business district of Kuala Lumpur. He cradled a still-too-hot-to-drink cup of black tea in his hands and stared into space. Jake, as his friends called him, worked as a freelance investigative journalist. He had a few desk jobs during the first few years of his career after he graduated from George Town University with a degree in journalism, but for the last few years, he worked and wrote for the highest bidder as he roamed the world. Then the ring of his cell phone jolted him back to reality. He looked at the caller ID and saw the call was from Ralph Henderson, the Associated Press's Southeast Asia news editor. In the past, Jake had worked for Henderson, most notably covering the Indonesian tsunami's aftermath in 2004, which killed a quarter-million people. Over the intervening ten years, Jacobs had built a reputation as a go-to guy for a solid story.

"Hi, Jake, this is Ralph. Got a minute?"

"You bet, buddy. What can I do for you this fine morning?" A fine morning, indeed—Kuala Lumpur, located a few degrees latitude above the equator, was already eighty-five degrees Fahrenheit at ten in the morning, under a cloudless blue sky.

"I'm sure you've been following the developments surrounding the disappearance of that jetliner. The damnedest thing—something that big and sophisticated just goes missing without a trace. Anyway, the Malaysian government gives periodic updates, but you know as well as me that those guys are as corrupt as the day is long—especially if the facts cast a bad light on them. We naturally report what they say, but if this has a bad ending, I'm sure we won't get the true story from them. That's why I'm calling. I want your help. If anyone can figure out this riddle, it's you."

"Thanks for the vote of confidence, buddy. Yeah, I agree with what you said about trying to get the truth out of the local bureaucrats. So, okay, I'll give it a shot, shake a few trees, and see what falls out."

Little did Jacobs know how difficult his job would be or how long it would take to get answers. He followed the daily news reports and had interviewed Hope Lee, and based on that preliminary information, he began to formulate a plan. Noah decided to first investigate any issues with the pilot, then the aircraft, and finally the cargo and passenger manifest. He pulled out his pocket notepad and began scribbling notes as thoughts popped into his head. By the time he finished his third cup of tea, he had six pages of notes. Happy with himself, he smiled, put the notepad back in his shirt pocket, stood up, and left the café. With a renewed purpose in life, he was anxious to tackle this newest challenge. *Yeah, solving possibly the most crucial aviation mystery since Amelia Earhart's disappearance wouldn't hurt my résumé one bit*, he thought.

Two weeks after he accepted the assignment to investigate the disappearance of flight three-seventy, Jacobs felt frustrated. He had interviewed at least a dozen Malaysian government officials, including the Transport minister and the senior members of the international accident investigation team. Using official channels did not yield much useful information. The people he interviewed only regurgitated the government's published, official position. He thought the time had come to use the back-channel approaches. Every good journalist developed contacts that would provide information off the record for a fee. Jacobs's network of anonymous sources provided invaluable help in the past, and, this time, he pulled out all the stops. The AP news editor could not officially sanction Jacobs's approach, but he was willing to look the other way if it meant getting the story.

⸺◉⸺

In Canberra, investigators Ana and Brian entered her office, and she plopped her thick notebook and portfolio filled with papers on her desk. "Pull up a chair and make yourself comfortable. Our meeting may take a while."

Brian pulled a chair closer to Ana's desk and rested his notes folder on her desk directly in front of him. "If history is any judge," he said with a weak smile, "the thickness of our folders and the number of filled notebooks will increase exponentially before we get to the bottom of this. We're only a month into this investigation, and I already feel the aches and pains from carrying around so much paper."

"Yeah, I agree, but here's what I want to go over. We know three-seventy's scheduled route was a south-to-north course from Kuala Lumpur to Beijing," Ana said as she opened an aeronautical chart depicting the Malaysian Peninsula and the surrounding countries of Vietnam, Thailand, and Indonesia. In addition to geographic features, aeronautical charts showed airways and highways in the sky that air traffic controllers use to control the separation and volume of commercial air traffic.

Miles pointed to a spot halfway between Malaysia and Vietnam using the South China Sea chart. "When MH370 reached the IGARI intersection here, he made a steep left turn, rolled out onto a south-westerly heading, doubled back toward Malaysia, and crossed the Malaysian coast near its border with Thailand." She traced a line across the map with her finger as she continued to speak. "The flight stayed close to the Malaysia-Thailand border, proceeded across Malaysia, and crossed the west coast of Malaysia just south of Penang Island, and then made a slight right turn to the northwest. He continued across the Malacca Straits and into the Andaman Sea until he was out of range of land-based radars. Why?"

Not waiting for Sloan to answer, she continued. "Here's some more confusing information. He must have made that left turn at IGARI manually because radar confirmed a very rapid turn rate which required him to bank the aircraft in excess of forty-five degrees. Autopilot use would have limited the bank angle to no more than thirty degrees, which means the autopilot was off, and somebody was hand flying the airplane. Again, why and who?"

Sloan opened his mouth and tried to answer, but Miles continued. "One last thing. When the plane flew south of Penang, the co-pilot's cell phone pinged a cell tower. The call didn't go through, but telecommunication experts say someone may have tried to make a call, but for some reason, the phone call didn't process through."

Before Miles could say "Why?" a third time, Sloan interrupted. "There's no way to answer your questions without finding the wreckage and getting the cockpit voice and data recorders. Besides, we have other position data from the Inmarsat satellite indicating that the plane turned south over the Indian Ocean before flying out of range. The consensus seems to be it probably continued that southerly course until it ran out of fuel. It's a big area to search, and the four wasted days of searching in the South China Sea didn't help."

A frustrated Ana replied, "Yeah, you're right. The inaction of the Kuala Lumpur ATC personnel, misstatements from the Malaysian Airlines Dispatch, and the lack of candid communications from the Malaysian Air Force show all groups were either incompetent or derelict in their duties. Nobody was raising the alarm when three-seventy disappeared from radar. And as you say, they wasted precious days searching in the wrong area. All parties assumed the plane went down in the South China Sea on its original flight path. So they deployed search and rescue assets to that general area. It took four days before someone took a close look at the radar tracking data and realized the plane had made that left turn at IGARI and another ten days to gain consensus to move the search from the South China Sea and Malacca Straits to the south Indian Ocean. Mind-boggling!"

Knowing that there were more questions than answers at the moment, Brian spoke up. "Let me change the subject, please. You said you wanted to discuss the possibility of rogue pilot behavior, suicide even. What's on your mind?"

Ana opened her notebook and removed six pieces of paper stapled together. "I received an email yesterday and made you a copy. Here, it's a message from the Transport minister's office with details about their police investigation of the pilot and their search of his home, including his computer. The pilot had a very sophisticated flight simulator in his home with numerous routes from Kuala Lumpur to different international destinations like London and Paris."

"Okay, sounds like the guy was really into his job, and he probably practiced flying those simulations to keep his flying skills sharp. What does that have to do with a rogue pilot behavior scenario?"

"Nothing—except for the fact that one simulation was almost the exact flight path we believe he flew into the south Indian Ocean. The police dismissed that simulation as game playing but offered no rationale for their decision. What if it wasn't a game? What if the pilot *intentionally* flew his plane to a point where it ran out of fuel and crashed?"

Sloan sat back in his seat and rubbed his forehead a couple of times. "I don't know, Ana. It seems like an awful lot of trouble to go through if you wanted to kill yourself. In the other suicide-related mishaps I investigated, the event timeline was abridged. We recovered the cockpit data and voice recorders and could piece together what happened. It went from normal to catastrophic very quickly, like in tens of minutes, not hours. I think the only way we'll ever know what happened is to find those recorders."

Ana nodded and knew Sloan was correct. "You're right, of course." She thought for a moment, then said, "I have another assignment for you. In addition to your other activity, please keep tabs on the surface search efforts. There's got to be something floating around out there that can point us in the right direction."

Sloan shrugged his shoulders and nodded. "Sure thing. You'll be the first to know."

Jacobs had several sources within the Royal Malaysian Police. Official reports said the police had searched the pilot's home, but they found nothing criminal or nefarious. However, Jacobs had a suspicious nature and rarely accepted anything at face value, so he decided to dig deeper. He made a phone call and arranged to meet one of his police sources in the Mandarin Oriental Hotel bar. Jake had a twofold reason for meeting his contact there. First, the hotel had a world-class bar, and second, if you wanted to impress someone and put them at ease, that was the place to do it. Located in the center of the city between the flowering oasis of KLCC Park and the breathtaking heights of the Petronas Twin Towers, the Mandarin Oriental had the reputation of being one of the most luxurious hotels in Kuala Lumpur. After a brief phone conversation, his source confirmed he knew more information than what was officially reported.

Jacobs arrived early on purpose. He sat at a corner table with a view of the entrance so he could easily spot his contact and, also, just as easily see if anyone followed him. As he sipped his single malt scotch, he thought, *Can't afford to be stupid or careless right now.* Finally, at ten minutes past their arranged meeting time, Jacobs saw his contact enter the lounge. The man gazed around the room, and as their eyes met, Jacobs raised his arm. The man smiled and walked toward Jacobs's table with a noticeable limp.

"So good to see you again, Minh. Please, sit. What's the deal with the gimp? Did you hurt yourself?"

Minh smiled and nodded. "Yes, about three months ago, I fell as I chased a thief. He was much younger than me. He leaped over a ditch, but, unfortunately, I didn't make it and sprained both ankles. I'm better now but still take medication for pain. Thank you for meeting me here. I've wanted to see the inside of this hotel for some time. You know, a policeman's salary doesn't leave much extra money after the bills are paid."

Jake nodded and knew where this was going, so before saying anything else, he removed a business-size envelope from his inside jacket pocket and handed it to his guest. "Here, this is something for your troubles. Take your wife out for a good dinner." Minh took the envelope, glanced at the contents, and smiled when he saw five one-hundred Malaysian ringgit inside. "Can I order you a drink?" Jake asked.

"Yes, just a cup of tea, Mr. Jake. The medication, you know."

The two men continued to make small talk for another ten minutes, and then Jacobs asked, "So, what do you know about the investigation into this missing jetliner that I can't find out reading the newspapers?"

Minh glanced over his shoulder, leaned across the table toward Jake, and spoke in a hushed tone. "The police report submitted to the accident investigators is misleading. First, the part about the pilot's normal behavior on the day of the disappearance is false, as is their report that he had no known history of anxiety or irritability. The pilot—his name is Zara—was under intense emotional stress due to his failed marriage, a bitter separation, and his son deserting him. We interviewed a pilot friend, and he confided to us that he had brought his concerns about Zara's behavior to him and advised him to seek counseling."

"And how did Zara respond to his friend's suggestion?"

"His friend said Zara got very agitated, rejected his suggestion, and told him that such a revelation would ruin his career. Zara said that he would rather die than put his flying career at risk. The friend told us that Zara's life revolved around flying and that it was all he wanted to do from an early age. Zara told his friend that he had everything under control and was taking medication to help him manage his anxiety and stress. However, we don't know what type of medication he was taking, nor did his friend. When we reviewed Zara's medical records, there were no entries of his taking any prescribed medications, not even any supplements."

Jake nodded. "That's interesting. Why wouldn't the police share that information with the accident investigators? It would lend credence to the speculation that this might be a case of pilot suicide."

"That's *exactly* why they didn't share it. You must remember, it's our national airline, and our government takes great pride in holding it up to the world as an example of the progress and accomplishments of the Malaysian people. So any evidence—or even *suggestion*—of wrongdoing that might tarnish that image is censored."

"I get it. When you called me about setting up this meeting, you mentioned two things you wanted to discuss. What's the second thing you think I ought to know?"

"It has to do with the flight simulator we found in the pilot's house. The reports about its level of sophistication are true. Our forensics people went over it with a fine-tooth comb, and what they found versus what was officially reported are two different stories."

"How so?"

"Our forensics investigation of the pilot's simulated flight, flown just weeks before the plane's disappearance which replicated three-seventies final flight, were all from one session. The official forensic report to the investigators stated that although seven flight waypoints flown by Zara were similar to three-seventy's last flight, they were isolated points—not connected—and could have come from different simulator flight sessions. The report concluded that there were no unusual activities other than game-related flight simulations. The Royal Malaysian Police are covering up the truth about the pilot's mental health and his home flight simulator. For them, it's more important to save face than tell the truth."

Jacobs sat back in his chair and stared into his half-filled glass. As he jiggled it, the small ice cubes made a tinkling sound as they bounced against its sides. He pondered for a moment before he continued. Finally, Jacobs nodded, "That's some pretty damning stuff. I think I'll sit on this for a while and try to get some corroborating information."

"This doesn't have anything to do with the pilot," Minh continued, "but we received information yesterday that the Australian government set up a Joint Agency Coordination Center at their west coast Stirling Naval Base to coordinate the international search effort. Stirling is only an hour's drive south of Perth, and many of the search personnel come ashore from time to time. I imagine opportunities exist for someone with your talents to find out information 'off the record.' But as you know, Mr. Jake, not all new information becomes public right away." When Minh finished speaking, he sat back, cracked a knowing smile, and took a sip of tea.

"Thanks for your help, Minh. Let me know if anything else comes up that I might be interested in."

Minh stood, bowed his head slightly, and left the lounge. Jacobs ordered another scotch and thought about his next move.

———◎———

Noah Jacobs had a contact who worked in the Human Resources department of Malaysia Airlines. *I wonder if Siti can shed some light on the pilot's personal life—some information they may have shared with the police or investigators but didn't get released in an official report.*

Siti Mawar worked as a personnel records specialist for Malaysia Airlines, and she managed a team of three people who were tasked to maintain all the airline's employee records. Of course, the information was confidential, but Jacobs had a persuasive way about him, and several hundred U.S. dollars did not hurt either. So over an early dinner one evening, after finishing the appetizer and engaging in a little small talk, Jacobs got down to business. He explained to Siti that he was doing an investigative piece on the disappearance of flight three-seventy and was looking for some information, 'off the record.'

Siti sighed. "And here I thought you invited me to dinner because you enjoyed my company and missed me." Before Jacobs could answer, Siti grinned and continued. "I'm only kidding. I know you pay well for information, and I do have my eye on a new designer bag, so what kind of information are you looking for?" This time, Jacobs grinned and removed an envelope from his inside jacket pocket before handing it to her. "Here, maybe this will help you get that bag.

"I've been told by another source that the pilot, Zara, had problems with his marriage and struggled with depression. Was any of this recorded in his official record? For example, was he ever given a psychological examination, and did he take any prescription drugs?"

"No, the pilot had a clean record—no record of drug or alcohol abuse. He was in good health—no complaints from other employees about his behavior. Whatever problems he may have had, he hid them very well. I'm sorry, but I haven't been much help." Finally, their meals came, and after a few moments of silence, Siti spoke again. "This has nothing to do with personnel records, but I did hear something you might be interested in."

Stuffed with a mouthful of food, Jake nodded and mumbled, "What's that?"

"I was at an employee party last weekend, and, of course, everyone was talking about the missing airplane. No one at the party had a close friendship with any crew, but two men talked about the cargo manifest. You may have heard of a shipment of lithium-ion batteries as part of the cargo, and there was some speculation that they may have caught fire and caused the plane to crash."

"Yeah, I've heard that rumor, but the evidence doesn't appear to support that idea. The official report states that the batteries were packed following the appropriate procedures for handling that type of hazardous material, and they passed at least two inspections—at the freight forwarder in Penang and before they were loaded aboard the plane."

"Yes, that's the conclusion of the two men, but one said something interesting. He said he worked as a forklift operator in the warehouse at Kuala Lumpur Airport and had loaded many lithium-ion battery shipments onto Malaysia Airlines planes bound for Beijing, but this shipment looked different. The previous battery shipments were just rectangular shipping containers containing the batteries. In addition to the standard battery shipping containers, this shipment included two large wooden crates, all bound together with that plastic wrap. The man thought it odd that two wooden crates, which are combustible, would be wrapped together with the metal battery containers, and he expected that those two items would have been separated."

"What'd he do about it? Did he report it to anyone?"

"No, he said it wasn't any of his business, but he mentioned it to his friend because he just thought it odd, that's all."

The couple finished their meal without much additional conversation. Jake's mind was in overdrive as he analyzed everything Siti had told him and what it might mean to the investigation.

"Sorry for not being very good company this evening, but I'm working for the Associated Press on this missing plane thing, and, so far, all I've got are a bunch of disconnected dots. We'll have to do this again sometime when I don't have deadlines."

Siti smiled. "Don't worry about it, Jake. Give me a call anytime. In the meantime, I'll enjoy my new designer bag."

<hr/>

Jacobs knew about the search activity underway in the Indian Ocean west of Perth. *That search effort is massive*, he thought. As many as forty-one ships and aircraft from eight countries had taken part in the search. Jacobs sat in his Kuala Lumpur hotel room and wrote notes from his meetings with Minh and Siti in his journal. When he finished, he grabbed his cell phone and called Ralph Henderson. Jake's call to Henderson went directly to Henderson's voicemail. "Hi, Ralph, listen, I've run some things to the ground here—got some interesting input from a couple of sources—but nothing yet worth printing. However, since the focus of the investigation has shifted to the southern Indian Ocean, I'm going to take a trip to Perth and see if I can connect some of the dots. I'll be in touch. Bye." Early that evening, Jacobs booked a seat on the first available flight to Perth, Australia.

After dinner, he returned to his hotel room, packed his bag for his flight to Perth the following day, and was looking forward to turning in early when his cell phone rang. It was his police contact, Minh.

"Good evening, Minh. What's up?"

"Mr. Jake, I remembered something else you might be interested in knowing. Our counterterrorism unit got an anonymous tip that a Penang freight forwarder who brings a lot of business to Malaysia Airlines' cargo division, MASkargo, might know something about a link between a piece of cargo and the disappearance of the airliner. The man, at first, was uncooperative, but our men have a way of convincing people to talk. They almost beat the man to death, but he finally told them what he knew."

"And what exactly did he tell them?"

"He said that he was contacted by a man from the Hang Shen Import-Export Company named David Lee. He said Mr. Lee wanted some equipment his company shipped to Penang from Karachi to be bundled with a shipment of lithium-ion batteries—but before bundling the equipment and batteries, he wanted the equipment laid out on tables for inspection."

"That seems odd. Did he say what type of equipment it was?"

"All he knew was that the boxes were labeled 'mining equipment.' He went on to tell the police that he'd seen a lot of mining equipment, but this stuff looked nothing like anything he'd seen before. What happened next was even stranger."

"How so?"

"After the man unpacked and laid the equipment out on tables, Mr. Lee brought in four Chinese men who inspected the equipment and used computers to test some of the pieces that looked like computers themselves. When the men finished their inspections, the freight forwarder repacked the equipment in their wooden crates and identified them on the cargo manifest as part of the battery shipment."

"So those boxes of equipment—or whatever they were—got through Malaysian customs as part of the shipment of batteries, right?"

"That's right, and that's why it was never reported to the investigators. I'm sure bribes were involved, and it shows corruption in our customs service operations—a fact our government would consider an embarrassment."

"Thanks again, Minh. I owe you one. Keep me in the loop if you hear anything else." After hanging up, Jacobs laid the phone on the nightstand and sat on the edge of the bed as he pondered this information. *You would think I'd get some answers as I get more information, but that isn't happening. Instead, I keep getting more questions. Dang.*

PART 7

The Story Exposed

CHAPTER TWENTY

Located in southwest Australia, Perth was the capital and largest city in the state of Western Australia. With an excellent harbor and access to the Indian Ocean, Perth enjoyed a bustling maritime presence. Located a few miles south of Perth Center, Fremantle Harbor was Western Australia's largest and busiest general cargo port. The inner harbor handled many sea containers, vehicle and livestock exports, cruise ships, and naval visits. An hour's drive south of Fremantle was the Stirling Naval Base, the epicenter of the massive air and sea search for the missing Malaysian jet. Jake knew he would only get the official news from the Base Public Affairs office, which was a reasonable place to start, but he expected his back-channel approach would be more productive. Based on his experience investigating the aftermath of natural disasters, political corruption, and drug trafficking, he knew people liked to talk about what they did, especially when they believed they were doing something important. He also knew buying a few drinks helped stimulate their minds and loosen their lips.

Jake decided to stay at the Crown Towers and use the hotel for his base of operations. It was a short six-mile cab ride from Perth's airport. Located on the Swan River's south side, the hotel was also a short ride to nearby Fremantle Harbor and an hour's ride to the Stirling Naval Base. Only a short walk from his hotel, the Crown Casino would also allow Jake to indulge another passion of his—blackjack.

The next day, after getting a good night's sleep, he busied himself as he spread the word that he was in town and was looking for information, and most importantly, was willing to pay for it. He spent the day visiting bars, restaurants with bars, and the casino talking to bartenders, waitresses, and receptionists. He even managed to win one hundred dollars at the blackjack table during a meal break. He did not think he had a gambling problem, but he reminded himself, got to stay focused, but all work and no play makes Jake a dull boy, right? That thought brought a smile to his face as he got into his rented car and headed back to the hotel. Tomorrow, he would replenish his business card supply and expand his search area to the south toward Stirling Naval Base.

As Jacobs motored his way south to Stirling early the next morning, he could not help but marvel at this part of Australia's geographical diversity. The rocky coast gave way to a rolling countryside dotted with pastures and vineyards; further inland unfolded a desert-like landscape sparse with life yet rich with Australia's vast mining of mineral resources. In the Southern Hemisphere, it was early fall, temperatures were mild, and Jacobs enjoyed his hour ride to Stirling. He knew he could only talk with someone in the Public Affairs office on base, but that was not his primary objective. Eventually, he would speak to them, but he wanted to explore the back channels and then compare the "off the record" information with official accounts.

———◉———

Jacobs sat at the Crown Towers bar and felt a bit down. He canvassed the local bars and clubs by the Stirling Naval Base during the past week. He did not uncover anything newsworthy—just a regurgitation of the authorities' standard stuff spoon-feeding the public. He had expected to meet navy personnel serving on the search and rescue ships and hoped they would have inside information that they would be willing to share about the ongoing operations. Instead, he learned that most military personnel spent their off time on base at the enlisted and officers' clubs. If they had a weekend off, they would drive or take the bus to Perth rather than frequent the honky-tonk bars outside the gates. *So I'm right back where I started*, he thought, as he swirled the ice cubes in his almost-empty glass of scotch. He decided to cheer himself up and play a little blackjack. By now, the ice in his glass had melted entirely, so he chugged the remaining diluted contents and started to get up when an older man sat down next to him and began speaking to him with a thick Australian accent.

"Hi, my name is McEvoy; friends call me Mac. Are you that reporter bloke?" The man's sudden appearance startled Jacobs, but he quickly recovered and shook the man's outstretched hand.

"Ah, yes, my name is Noah Jacobs, and my friends call me Jake—nice to meet you." Jacobs studied the man for a second. Obviously Australian, judging by his accent and in his mid-fifties. And judging by his weathered face, he works outdoors a lot.

"You're not from around here, are ya, Jake?"

"No, sir, I'm American. I'm a freelance investigative journalist trying to get information for a story I'm doing about that missing Malaysian airliner."

"Yeah, that's what I heard, and you're willing to pay for that information, ain't ya?" Before Jacobs could answer, the bartender walked over and stood in front of the two men and asked, "Can I get you something?"

McEvoy responded first. "Whiskey for me and whatever my friend here would like." Jacobs ordered another scotch and did not know why, but something about this man intrigued him. So he decided to play along and find out where this conversation was going.

"So, Mr. McEvoy, what's—"

The man interrupted. "Mac, call me Mac."

"Okay, Mac, what's on your mind? Do you know something about that missing plane?"

The old man lifted his drink to his lips and smiled before taking a sip. "Yeah, I do, but nobody believes me or any of my crew. They think I'm just an old drunk with an overactive imagination—been at sea too long, they say—fried my brain in the sun, they say, but I know what I saw, and I know what I know." He stopped talking and chugged the contents of the glass, then ordered another.

"Okay, Mac, I'm all ears. What'd you see?"

"Well, I captain a large fishing trawler for this big fishing outfit here in Perth. Two weeks ago, we had our storage wells full, and me and my mates were on our way back to Perth. We were at least a thousand miles out when this big plane flew overhead. It had two engines under the wings, and it looked like the pictures of that missing plane you see in the papers and on the idiot box."

"Idiot box?"

"Yeah, sorry. I know you Yanks have a hard time understanding Aussie English, but that's what we call a television. So, as I was saying, this big airplane flew right over us. I never saw a plane over those parts—further north, yeah—but never that far down south. The plane looked to be pretty low and wasn't going all that fast either. I swear, it looked to me like it was coming down—like it was going to land. We watched it until it disappeared into overcast clouds just south of us. A storm was heading our way, so my men were on deck securing the gear when one of them shouted, 'Hey, look, there!' I looked in the direction he was pointing and saw a person hanging under a parachute falling pretty fast. The chute looked to be tangled. We couldn't do anything but watch. When that person hanging under that chute hit the water, you just knew it hurt. I steered our ship in her direction as fast as I could."

"Wait, you said 'her,' as in a female?"

"Yeah, the poor sheila hit the water hard. It was a good thing she had a life vest on 'cause it kept her afloat until we could fish her out. My boys carried her to sickbay, and our doc went to work. She was barely alive. Both legs were broken, she was unconscious, and had a bad concussion."

"Did she have any identification?"

"No, nothing. The funny thing about that, though, the girl was wearing one of those military-type flying suits. You know, the type with all those zippered pockets. Well, the Velcro where they wear a name tag was empty. I don't know. Maybe it fell off when she hit the water. I know that it wasn't a coincidence that this sheila dropped in the water right after that airplane flew over us. She bailed out—that's what I think—that's the only explanation."

"Bailed out? Did you see any other parachutes?"

"Nope, just her. No one else, which makes you wonder—why was one female flying that big plane? Must have put it on autopilot or something—and jumped out. I mean, it looked to be flying fine—no smoke or weird noises—nothing. Doesn't make any sense."

The old fisherman's story captivated Jacobs. The conversation went silent for a moment as Jacobs sat with his elbow propped on the bar and his hand rubbing his chin. "Hmm, it does make sense if you're trying to make an airplane disappear," he mumbled.

"Whadya say, mate? My hearing ain't so good no more."

"No, nothing important—what time of day did all this happen?"

Mac rubbed his chin a couple of times and stared at the ceiling. "Let's see—it was early afternoon, right after chow. I'd say about fourteen hundred; that's two o'clock for you civilians. Yeah, about two."

"I take it you brought her back here to Perth, right?" Mac nodded. "Did she regain consciousness? It must have taken you three or four days to get back here, right?" Mac nodded again.

"Four days and three hours to be exact, and, no, she never regained full consciousness. Near the end, she'd drift in and out and would mumble some gibberish and, oh yeah, she said the same name more than once—'Walker.' The only other words I could make out were CIA and something about an island and a 'package.' The rest sounded like airplane stuff, like she was reading a checklist or something. I don't know squat about airplanes, so it was all Greek to me. She was in pretty bad shape, so maybe scenes from a movie she watched recently were playing over in her head—I don't know.

"When we got close to Perth, I radioed ahead, and an ambulance met us at the dock. I asked where they would take her, and the attendant said to the Royal Perth Hospital. It's kind of strange what happened next."

"How so?"

"Well, I called over to the hospital a couple of times, you know, curious to find out if she was getting better and was told both times, she's still unconscious and no change. So a week later, when I had some time off, I went to the hospital to visit. The desk nurse said she couldn't have any visitors except for family. I explained that I was the one who fished her out of the ocean and wanted to pay my respects, but the nurse apologized. 'Hospital policy,' she said— 'patient privacy,' she said. So I left, and that was the end of that— never went back."

"You reported all this to the police, right?"

"Yep, and the Coast Guard too. I also told them I thought the airplane she bailed out of was that missing jet."

"And what'd they say about that?"

"Said I was crazy. Said it was the wrong part of the ocean—said the missing airliner would have run out of fuel six hours earlier and much further north. So now, I just keep my mouth shut and keep my opinions to myself, that is, unless someone like you comes along asking questions."

"One last question. Do you have any idea of her nationality or race? Was she white or Asian—did she have an accent?"

"She was white, and if I had to guess, I'd say she was Australian. Even though she only mumbled a few words, it sure sounded to me like she was one of us."

Jake had some thinking to do. He stood, thanked the old fisherman, and asked, "Can I get you another one?" The older man nodded. Jake slapped a one-hundred-dollar bill down on the bar, winked at the old man, and said to the bartender, "Keep 'em coming for my friend."

Jacobs decided to forget about blackjack for the moment and went back to his hotel room. He wanted to capture the details of his conversation with McEvoy while still fresh in his mind and give some thought regarding what he knew and, more importantly, what he did not know. While he was tapping the keyboard on his laptop, he was also thinking about a woman suffering from delirium, mumbling about flying an airplane, an island, a package, the CIA, and someone named Walker. *Damn, it sounds like the plot of some spy movie.* That thought triggered another thought, and Jake grabbed his cell phone off the nightstand next to the bed and called one of his contacts in Kuala Lumpur.

"Hi, Siti, this is Jake. How are you doing?"

"I'm okay, Mr. Jake. What can I help you with this time?"

"Listen, I'm in Perth tracking down some leads, and I need your help again. Do you have access to the passenger manifest and the seating chart for MH370?"

"I don't have it, but I can get it. What exactly are you trying to find out?"

"As a starter, I'd like to find out how many Australian and American couples were on board, where they were sitting, and if anyone onboard was named Walker."

"Okay, Mr. Jake. I should be able to get that information. The names and nationalities of the passengers have already been released. I'll get the seating chart and match it up with the names. It'll take me about a day to pull it together, okay, then I'll email it to you?"

"That's great. Sounds like a plan. Thanks."

"Oh, Mr. Jake, just so you know. I saw a nice pair of shoes in the store to go with my new bag. Bye."

Note to self—don't ever negotiate with a woman. I think tomorrow I'll pay a visit to the Royal Perth Hospital, but now—some blackjack!

Langley, Virginia

On the other side of the world, the sun had just peeked above the eastern horizon. Walker opened one eye, and a quick glance at his alarm clock told him he had awakened fifteen minutes before the alarm. *Damn, I hate when that happens, especially when I'm still tired.* He dragged his weary body from the bed and went through his mind-numbing and monotonous routine of getting himself ready for work. He still had not heard any news of his partner's fate, and he had resigned himself to the fact she was gone. *No sense torturing myself over it*, he thought. *Shit like that happens in this business. I've got to move on.*

He made a stop at Starbucks this morning and hoped an extra-large shot of caffeine would shake the cobwebs from his head. Then he continued to the headquarters building and half-walked, half-shuffled his way to his cubicle on the third floor and then buried himself in some intelligence reports. He heard heavy footsteps in the hallway that were approaching his cubical when a familiar voice called his name. "Walker, in my office, now!" Josh Edwards never slowed his pace as he passed Walker's cube, which meant he expected Walker to be in his office at the end of the hallway one step behind him. Walker knew the drill. This meeting was something important—in truth—something *more* than important.

"Sit down, Jack. I've got some important news for you." Walker pulled one of Edwards's office chairs closer to the desk and sat on the edge of its seat, his eyes laser-focused on his boss. He felt every muscle in his body tense, and he braced himself for the worst.

"We've just been notified—she's alive." Those two words caused Walker to feel an electric shock surge through his body. He leaned forward, not wanting to miss a single word.

"A fishing boat pulled her out of the water after she bailed out. That's the good news." As soon as those four words came out of Edwards's mouth, Walker knew the worst was yet to come. In a second, his mind raced through the most terrible outcomes imaginable—paralysis, vegetative state, and amputation. His short-lived elation turned painful as if someone punched him in the gut when Edwards continued. "Both her legs are reported broken; she has a severe concussion and is in a coma. Her parachutes did not open fully, and she hit the water hard. She'd probably be dead if that fishing boat hadn't been only a couple of hundred yards away. Since she didn't carry any ID, it took a while to identify her through DNA. That's why the delay. The docs think she has a good chance of pulling through once her brain swelling goes down. Her people have her under guard in a Perth hospital intensive care unit. They'll let us know when there's any change in her condition. That's all I got. Any questions?"

Walker sat silently on the edge of his seat for a moment, with his eyes fixed in a blank stare. "No . . . No questions." He left Edwards's office feeling both happy and sad. After taking a few steps down the hallway, his pace quickened, and he cracked a small smile. *You crazy lady*, he thought, *I knew you'd make it, and I know you're going to be just fine.*

CHAPTER TWENTY ONE

Ever since Jacobs agreed to investigate the back-channel stories surrounding the disappearance of MH370, he had been sending snippets of information to his AP editor. Nothing he sent, so far, had excited his editor until he emailed him a story titled, **Did the CIA Hijack MH370?**

He described the old fisherman's account of rescuing a half-dead woman from the middle of the south Indian Ocean within minutes of a large twin-engine jet flying overhead. In his story, Jacobs emphasized the semiconscious woman's words—"Walker," "CIA," and "package." Was the fisherman's story evidence that pointed to a hijacking? Not any hijacking, either, but one orchestrated by the CIA, America's supersecret spy agency? Jacobs asked his editor to sit on the story for a while. He knew if the public were to take him seriously, he needed facts linking together all the pieces of this puzzle. He decided his next move would be to go to Royal Perth Hospital and find out, firsthand, everything he could about their mysterious patient.

Royal Perth Hospital, located on the northeast edge of the central business district, was a short cab ride from Jacobs's hotel. It enjoyed an excellent reputation as a teaching hospital, major adult trauma center, and the first choice to perform complex surgeries. So it was no coincidence that "the woman from the sea," as Stark became known, was brought there. To make her well again would be a challenge for the hospital's medical staff.

Jacobs's timing could not have been better: DNA analysis had confirmed Stark's identity just an hour earlier. She was moved to a private room in the intensive care unit a day earlier, but she was still in a drug-induced coma. Jacobs stopped in the hospital gift shop and bought a lovely bouquet in a cut-glass vase. Then he walked to the information counter and asked the receptionist if he could visit the "woman from the sea."

"I'm sorry, but Ms. Stark isn't well enough to have visitors unless you're family." The receptionist's reply stunned Jacobs. The only reason for his visit was to try to find out her identity for his follow-up research.

"You—you know her name?" he stammered.

"Why, yes, that information came to us just an hour ago. A. Stark. I'm sorry. Flowers aren't allowed into the ICU, but let me give them to the nursing staff to enjoy. I'm sure Ms. Stark will appreciate your thoughtfulness when she recovers. Who shall I say brought them?"

"Just tell her a concerned citizen wishes her well and a speedy recovery," Jacobs said as he nodded and smiled at the young receptionist. As he turned to walk back to the elevator, he noticed a tall, muscular man with a shaved head standing at the entrance to one of the rooms. *Maybe that's her room. I'd bet my last dollar that guy's a cop.* He pushed the elevator "down" button, and as he waited for the door to open, he glanced over his right shoulder one last time. *Yep, definitely a cop. Somebody thinks Ms. Stark needs protection. I wonder if that somebody is the CIA?* He now had a name and much work to do.

Returning to his hotel room, Jacobs lost no time initiating an internet search on "A. Stark." One link on the second page of the search results caught his eye. It was a year-old news article in the nationally distributed daily newspaper, *The Australian,* titled "Women in Aviation." With a photograph of each woman, the article acknowledged three Australian women for their achievements in aviation and their contributions to the field. Jacobs perused the article until one name—*Addison Stark*—caught his attention. The article described how, at an early age, Stark had developed a love for aviation. She fought and successfully overcame stereotypical bias in the male-dominated aviation industry to become a Royal Australian

Air Force pilot, intelligence officer, government analyst, and later, a commercial pilot for Qantas. Toward the end of the article, the interviewer asked her about her hobbies. She responded, *My favorite hobby is skydiving.*

Jacobs sat back in his chair, took a deep breath, and let out a long exhale. "Wow," he mumbled. "She sounds like one badass lady. Kinda like someone who would bail out of a hijacked airliner. Now I have to find out if this Addison Stark was a passenger, and for that, I need that manifest information from Siti."

Later that day, Jacobs received Siti's email that included the passenger manifest and seat assignments and a not-so-subtle reminder about a pair of shoes on which she had her eye. He smiled, shook his head, and opened the email's attachment. A glance at the passenger list confirmed there was neither a Walker nor a Stark on the list. Then he looked for male and female passengers sitting together. He discounted the Chinese and other Asian couples and found three non-Asian couples—two Australian couples in the economy section and one American couple in business class. *Let's see. The Australian couples are elderly—hardly hijacking candidates. The American couple, on the other hand—Jack Wilson and Susan Villa—is young enough and close enough to the cockpit to be suspect.*

A thought flashed in Jacob's mind. *There are dozens of security cameras at Kuala Lumpur Airport, and the American couple must have passed a bunch of them from the curbside to the departure gate area. I've got to call Minh.* He put the passenger list to one side, picked up his cell phone, and called his Royal Malaysian Police contact. After three rings, Minh answered. "Hi, Minh, this is Jake. Got a minute?"

"Yes, Mr. Jake, what can I do for you this morning?"

"I was wondering, did you guys look at the airport's security camera footage taken of passengers passing through the security checkpoint and as they walked toward MH370's departure gate?"

"Yes, we did. We work closely with the airport security people. The Transport Ministry upgraded the airport's closed-circuit TV network about two years ago and included automatic facial recognition. The airport police mainly use that to screen passengers on Interpol's no-fly list."

"Do you still have a copy of those files?"

"Yes, we have them in our evidence room, and we'll keep them as long as this investigation is open. We also sent a copy to the accident investigation team. Why do you ask?"

"I'm going to email you a photograph. Can you run your facial rec software and see if it matches any of the passengers heading in the direction of the departure gate?"

"Yeah, I can do that, but it'll take me some time since I'm not working that case anymore. Next week, I begin working the night shift, and there'll be fewer people around. I can do it then."

"Thanks, Minh—photo's on the way."

After he emailed Addison Stark's photograph to Minh, Jacobs put his phone down. *Now, back to the passenger manifest. According to their passports, they're both from Denver, Colorado.* Jacobs spent the next two hours searching the internet for information about the two Americans. His searches returned many hits because both names were common. Still, nothing significant showed up when he tried to narrow his searches by including geographic locations and interests such as traveling, flying, and so forth. *I don't have any contacts in Denver, but I do know someone in New Jersey . . .*

Jacobs had plenty of time to think about his story. He had begun organizing his notes as he sat in his economy window seat on the Emirates Airlines flight to JFK International Airport in New York City. He would spend twenty-eight hours en route, including a stop in Dubai, before reaching his destination. After nonstop typing on his laptop for an hour, he sat back and stared at the ceiling for a minute, thinking. *I have a name, a picture, and an address. By the time I finish this trip, I hope to have a story connecting the dots. So far, every time I get more information, it takes me off in a different direction. Maybe this time, I'll get some answers instead of more questions.*

A two-hour Uber ride from JFK to the small western New Jersey town of Bell Mills delivered Jacobs to his boyhood home, still occupied by his older brother. The driver followed the GPS queues from the first state highway exit that wound its way onto a sleepy country road and then onto Main Street. The ride caused Jake to feel nostalgic, and when they drove down Main Street, those feelings were amplified by his imagination. In his mind's eye, he saw the Christmas decorations strung from light pole to light pole across the street, the high school marching band, parade floats celebrating the Fourth of July, and, of course, the fireworks over the Delaware River. *A simpler time*, he thought.

Over the years, Jake would show up from nowhere with no advance notice, to his parents' and brother's chagrin. They were all gone now except his older brother Mike who bought the family home from his parents' estate. Mike retired from a career in local law enforcement and was content to stay put in the familiar surroundings of the only home he ever knew. The two brothers were a year apart in age and were inseparable growing up. Mike got into more than one fight when the school bullies would pick on his young brother.

Jake meandered up the driveway, rang the front doorbell, and waited. Mike opened the door, and before the two brothers exchanged any words, Mike gave his little brother a bone-crushing bear hug and a sharp slap on the back. "Well, look who the cat dragged in! How the hell are you, little brother? Come on in."

The front door opened into a hallway that opened into the living room. Looking around and thinking, Jake walked through the hallway in silence. The stairs to the upstairs bedrooms were on his right, and family pictures hung on the wall to his left. As he stepped into the living room, a sense of melancholy washed over him. Instead of roaming worldwide, he wished he had spent more time here during his adult years.

His head swiveled as he spoke. "The old place looks good, Mike. I think Mom would be happy with how you've kept it."

Ten years ago, both their parents were killed by a drunk driver on a nearby two-lane country road. Still a police officer at the time, Mike responded to the accident scene and would later confess that it was the worst night of his life. On assignment in Panama, Jake could not get home for the funeral, and he has regretted that fact ever since. Tragic and unfortunate experiences often drove family members apart, but for these brothers, it had the effect of bringing them even closer together.

"Yeah, thanks; I try to keep up with it. I have a lady friend who helps me pick things out; otherwise, it would probably look like a man cave. Want a beer?" Without waiting for an answer, Mike walked into the kitchen, grabbed two cold ones from the fridge, and handed one to Jake. "Have a seat, bro, and let's talk. I know you have this way of popping in for visits from time to time, but I also know there's usually an ulterior motive. So what's it this time? You need money, or no, you need a place to hide out from the law—what?"

Jake smiled and then took a sip of beer. "No, nothing like that. I'm doing fine. I just came back from Australia where I was doing some research for a story I'm writing." Mike nodded and knew Jake led an interesting life; he was always fascinated by Jake's stories. "The reason I came here was to kill two birds with one stone. It's been a while since our last visit, and I was feeling guilty, but I also need some cop help."

"I knew it. There always has to be a catch, but that's okay. I'm always glad to see you even though you want something. How can I help?"

Jake explained for the next half hour how he was trying to solve the mystery of the disappearance of the Malaysian airliner by using what he called "clandestine techniques." When Mike gave him a puzzled look, Jake clarified. "You know, the back-channel approach . . . uh, bribery." Mike smiled and nodded his head. Jake took a piece of paper from his shirt pocket and handed it to Mike. "Can you find out through police records if a Jack Wilson and a Susan Villa live at this address? And if they were ever issued Colorado driver's licenses? Their names are on the passenger manifest for the missing flight, their address is from their passports, but there's nothing else out there in public records about them. I used social media and Google—nothing."

"Shouldn't be a problem. My friends on the force will let me do a 'back-channel' search of DMV records, and I'm sure a couple of phone calls to the Denver police can check out their address. What's so important about these two characters, anyway?"

Jake explained, "I suspect the woman injured in a parachuting accident and fished from the Indian Ocean and Susan Villa might be the same person. If they are the same person, then why the false identity, and why did she bail out of that jet? So far, all I have are a lot of questions. The more I look into this disappearance, instead of getting answers, I keep getting more questions."

"I'll go down to headquarters tomorrow morning and try to get you some answers. In the meantime, you know the way to the guest room. Thanks to my friend, Mary, there're clean sheets on the bed. So make yourself at home, and I'll start us some dinner."

Two hours later, after finishing dinner, Jake pushed his chair back from the table. "That had to be the best meal I've eaten in a long time, and I've eaten in some real fine restaurants over the years, but your chicken savoy tops all of them."

Mike walked over and squeezed his brother's shoulder and thanked him for the compliment. Then the two brothers reminisced for two more hours until Jake said, "I'm going to turn in—been a long day—we'll continue, first thing in the morning."

Jake woke to the smell of freshly brewed coffee and fried bacon. He sat up in bed, rubbed his eyes, and glanced at the clock. "Oh my God!" He mumbled, "It's ten o'clock. I guess that trip took more out of me than I thought, or else I'm getting old—probably a little of both." He dressed, hurried down the stairs, entered the kitchen, and saw his brother standing over the stove as he flipped a half dozen pieces of crispy bacon.

"Have a seat, Sleeping Beauty. I didn't want to wake you—figured you were tired from your trip, but I got hungry waiting, so I figured I'd start without you."

Facing each other, the two men sat at the table, and Jake began devouring his breakfast as his brother watched. Then between mouthfuls, Jake looked up and saw his brother staring at him.

"What?" he mumbled with his mouth full of food.

"Oh, nothing. I was just thinking. We've shared many a meal at this table over the years, just feeling sorry for myself. I've missed you, bro."

"I've missed you too. I guess I've just been too busy to think about it, but you know what? Let's make each other a promise to change that. After all, we're the only family we got."

Mike smiled, stuffed a large piece of bacon in his mouth, and added, "And before you leave, teach me how to do that Facebook thing so I can send stuff from here." Mike finished his breakfast, grabbed his car keys, and headed for the door. "Time to do you that favor. Make yourself at home. I'll probably be a couple of hours."

Jake finished his breakfast, tidied up the kitchen, and decided to kill some time and take a walk. Midspring in Western New Jersey put nature's beauty on full display. Green grass, blooming trees, and flowers stood in stark contrast to the urban, industrial portrait of the eastern part of the state.

Jake left the house, and in ten minutes, he reached the western edge of town, where the land gently sloped to meet the Delaware River. He walked to the road from the riverbank that led back to town. Within a block of his house, he could see his brother's car in the driveway. He quickened his pace and practically jogged the last hundred yards. He was anxious to hear what Mike had discovered.

In the Jacobs's family, the kitchen tended to be where family members gathered to discuss things. That old habit continued as the two brothers sat at the kitchen table and faced each other. "I've got good news and bad news—"

"You know, whenever someone starts a conversation that way, there's usually more bad news than good news, so give me the good news first," Jake interrupted.

"You're right," Mike continued. "So, here's the good news. The address you gave me does exist. It's a condo in the Cherry Creek section of Denver, but it's not privately owned. It's owned by Metro Urban Services, Inc., which conducts business with a post office box. I did some more checking and found out it's a real estate leasing company specializing in short-term leases. I called their phone number several times, and each time it went right to voicemail."

"If that's the good news, I can hardly wait to hear the bad news Jake said with a sarcastic tone."

"Don't be a smartass—it seems your Jack Wilson and Susan Villa don't exist. At least, they're not in any database I could access. They're not in the FBI criminal database, and they're not in Colorado's DMV database, and—here's the kicker—no U.S. passports have been issued to anyone by those names with a Colorado address. You're chasing ghosts, bro."

"Shit, I hate when that happens—no answers, just more questions—again!"

"If you want my professional opinion, this kind of thing happens when someone wants to create false identities that appear legitimate. This has all the hallmarks of one of our federal agencies, like the FBI, CIA, Homeland Security, or maybe even some foreign intelligence agency behind this. Today, it happens mostly to deal with counterterrorism and drug trafficking, but those are the guys with access to the resources that can make it happen. So if I'm right, little brother, you better be careful how hard you kick this hornet's nest because its sting could be fatal."

"I'll be fine, Mike. I appreciate your concern, and I promise I'll be careful 'cause I fully intend to keep my promise to you about getting together more often." Both men smiled, and Jake continued. "I've got one more card up my sleeve, but that means going back to Malaysia. I just wanted to wait to hear your news before I booked the flight."

Jake was able to get a last-minute seat on an Emirates flight to Kuala Lumpur the following evening. The brothers sat on the small front porch and waited for Jake's ride, taking advantage of the spring warmth. Neither man spoke, but thoughts flooded their minds. Mike wondered when he would see his brother again and worried about his safety. Jake's mind wrestled with trying to fit the pieces of his mystery puzzle together. Finally, the Uber driver pulled into the driveway, and the brothers knew their time together had ended. They stood, shared one more hug, and then Jake turned and started to walk away.

"Hey, little brother, be careful and don't wait so long to come back for a visit."

Jake half-turned, smiled, and waved. "I promise."

Jake did not have time to do much thinking on his Uber ride to JFK because his driver happened to be an immigrant from Indonesia with the gift of gab. As soon as he heard Jake was going to the neighboring country of Malaysia, he would not shut up. Without Jake asking, the driver gave him advice about restaurants, places to stay, and sights to see. Jake's unwillingness to engage in conversation with the man did not discourage him, and he continued to talk for the duration of the two-hour ride. The driver delivered him to the terminal three hours before departure, so Jake had time to decompress and reflect on his visit as he waited in the Emirates lounge.

His visit was bittersweet.

On the one hand, he reconnected with his brother and intended to keep his promise and build a better relationship, but on the other hand, he left with more questions than answers—again. His brother's warning also caused him some concern. *My brother is not the dramatic type, so I need to watch my back.*

Jake's flight to Kuala Lumpur mirrored his flight from Perth to JFK—about the same duration that included a stop in Dubai. He sat in an economy class center seat since booking a flight at the last minute meant having to take what was available. *A center seat is not my first choice*, he thought, *but beggars can't be choosers.* Twenty-four hours later, the big jet touched down at Kuala Lumpur Airport. Jake decided to forego the hustle and bustle of a big city hotel and, instead, chose to stay in a quaint residential bed and breakfast. When he got settled in his room, he took out his day planner and decided to wait until the morning to contact Minh. *I hope Minh's had some success with their facial recognition software to verify that Addison Stark got on that missing airplane.*

Hopeful that the facial recognition spotted her, Jake called Minh the following day, but the phone call proved disappointing. "I'm sorry, Mr. Jake, but I can't help you. We don't have the airport video any longer. My superiors returned it to the Transport Ministry after they decided to conclude our investigation. My department's official determination was that there wasn't anything criminal about the jet's disappearance." Jake sat on the edge of the bed, rubbed his forehead as he listened to Minh's explanation, and hoped he would hear that conversation saving . . . "but."

Minh continued, "But I think I still may be able to help you. I can contact the Minister of Transport's (MOT) office and let them know there is someone with new information that would like to talk to the accident investigators. You can ask them to review the security camera video using their facial recognition software."

"Thanks, Minh, you're a lifesaver. So, yes, please set up that meeting, and thanks, again."

As part of the accident investigation team, Ana Miles and Brian Sloan now in Kuala Lumpur, worked in the office space provided to them and the other investigators by the Malaysian Ministry of

Transport. Collectively, the investigators had spent thousands of man-hours reviewing and analyzing every detail imaginable regarding the disappearance of MH370. Every new day brought new challenges, and as Ana and Brian drank cups of coffee in a small cafeteria, they reflected on that problem.

Finally, Brian broke the ice. "You know, everything we've looked at so far, and all the people we've interviewed, are beginning to point to one conclusion: pilot suicide."

"I agree. We know that, but the government's official position is denial when it comes to pointing a dirty finger at one of their own. But let me change the subject—will you be joining me this morning when that journalist shows up? I don't like talking to journalists, but he said he has some information he wants to share with us. I thought that was an interesting switch in roles. Usually, those guys are trying to *get* information, so I agreed to talk to him with the understanding that I'd be in the 'receiving' mode and not the 'giving' mode."

"Yeah, I'll join you. We can always walk away if the conversation goes south."

Jacobs left his bed and breakfast accommodations at eight o'clock in the morning, allowing himself an hour to make the twenty-five-mile trip to the ministry's headquarters in Kementerian Pengangkutan. The town had a modern look, and near the city center, he found his destination—No. 26 Tun Hussein Street. Its location on a tree-lined street offered a serene setting for the modern glass and concrete, ten-story building. The taxicab dropped Jacobs off at the main entrance and he followed the signs leading visitors to the main lobby. Once there, the receptionist greeted him with a smile.

"Hi. My name is Noah Jacobs, here to see Ms. Miles." She lifted her phone and made a call. After confirming his appointment, she smiled again. "Ms. Miles is expecting you. Please, follow me." She led Jacobs down a long hallway and, halfway down, stopped and opened the door of a large conference room.

"Please make yourself comfortable. Ms. Miles will be here in a moment. Would you like some coffee or perhaps tea?"

"Yes, coffee, black. Thanks."

Ana Miles and Brian Sloan arrived simultaneously with Jacobs's coffee. Miles made the introductions. "This is my colleague, Brian Sloan. He's an accident investigator for the American NTSB, and I'm an investigator for the Australian Transport Safety Bureau. We understand you have some information of interest regarding the disappearance of MH370."

"Thank you for meeting with me. I'm sure you're very busy, so I won't take up a lot of your time. Yes, I've been investigating the disappearance and have uncovered details that I haven't seen reported in the periodic updates you guys send out.

"First, do you know about a woman fished out of the southern Indian Ocean shortly after a large twin-engine plane passed overhead heading south? And were you informed of the three words she mumbled as the fishing trawler made its way back to Perth?" Jacobs took a sip of coffee and watched as Miles and Sloan exchanged glances.

"Mr. Jacobs, since I work for the Australian government, I receive daily updates regarding the surface and air search going on as we speak. Brian and I have been acutely involved with the manufacturer's analysis of the Inmarsat satellite data. We believe that data has given us valid information to support our decisions regarding the most likely area to search. That woman was fished out of the ocean over five hundred miles from the area we believe MH370 ran out of fuel. My director received information from the RAAF that the woman in question bailed out of an F-18, which experienced mechanical difficulties."

"With all due respect, ma'am, there's a big difference between the size and shape of an F-18 and a twin-engine commercial airliner. The fisherman was pretty adamant about his description of the aircraft, and he also said it looked like it was descending."

Miles explained, in general terms, how the satellite data analysis was used to determine the search area. "The problem with the fisherman's story," Miles continued, "is that it doesn't jive with the satellite data regarding three-seventy's position and time of day when the 'handshakes' took place. Besides, three-seventy would have run out of fuel hours before it reached the location where they rescued that woman." After listening to Miles's explanation, Jacobs took a final sip of coffee and decided to change the subject.

"Okay, here's what I think. I don't disagree with anything you said, but I'd like to show you something." He opened his briefcase and removed a folded map.

"I did some research myself," he said as he unfolded the map and laid it flat on the large oak conference room table. Miles and Sloan leaned forward and recognized the geographic area of the Indian Ocean stretching from the east coast of Africa to the west coast of Australia and from India in the north to Antarctica in the south. "See this line? I drew it starting at the lat-long coordinates the fisherman said they were at when they picked up the woman, all the way north to the coordinates where the military radars lost three-seventy."

"So, what's your point?" Sloan asked with an annoyed tone in his voice.

Jacobs overlooked the inference and continued. "See this speck of land? That's Diego Garcia, just barely fifty miles west of the line I drew. Also, remember the rescued woman mumbled three words over and over—'Walker,' 'CIA,' and 'package.' I did some snooping and found out the name of the woman is Addison Stark. She's been written up in the Australian's 'Who's Who in Aviation,' and her biography includes the fact that she piloted transports in the RAAF, not F-18s."

"But there's no Stark, or Walker, for that matter, on the passenger manifest."

"Exactly, but what if they used an alias and false documents? Out of all the passengers, three Western couples were on that aircraft. Two elderly couples were Australian, and one younger couple was American—except the American couple, Jack Wilson and Susan Villa, don't exist—"

"Wait a minute," Miles interrupted, "what do you mean they don't exist?" Jacobs explained how their home address and identities were fake based on his brother's search of various databases. "So here's what I think," Jacobs continued. "Wilson and Villa, or whatever their names are, were intelligence agents who hijacked the plane to Diego Garcia to remove a special package. They refueled the plane and flew it deep into the southern Indian Ocean to dispose of it."

"That seems like a lot of trouble to go through," countered Ana. "That's a big ocean. They could have dumped it anywhere, and what about the satellite data?"

"Computers can be hacked or spoofed to make false output. So if the location and time of the handshakes were false, and you based your search area on that false data, then you're searching in the wrong area."

Ana shifted in her chair and replied, "I still say, why go through all that trouble? Why not just ditch it anywhere?"

"First of all, the handshakes would have revealed the actual location. Second, another source of mine mentioned that the police investigation looked into the pilot's activity on his home flight simulator. His simulator destination corresponds to the course you calculated from the satellite data. My source speculated that the pilot was planning a suicide mission. I think two separate events coincided that night, and the agent-hijackers used the pilot's suicide attempt to cover up their hijack mission. That package must have been something very special to cause the U.S. and Australian intelligence agencies to go through so much trouble to cover it up."

As Jacobs spoke, Miles and Sloan exchanged glances from time to time and nervously shifted their bodies. Their body language changed, and he suspected he hit a nerve when he mentioned "pilot suicide."

He decided to press his luck. "Have you guys come to any conclusion about suicide?"

Miles shot back, "We're not authorized to comment on the specifics of the investigation, and we do not speculate. Whatever information we get, whether from interviews or data analysis, we consider it and pass it up the chain to the Malaysian Transport minister. After that, the official accident report will come out of his office." Miles decided to stop the interview at this point. "Thank you for bringing this information to our attention. If you'll excuse us, we have a lot of work to do."

"Sure, no problem, but before I go, I'd like to leave this with you. It's a photograph of Addison Stark. A little birdie told me that you have a copy of the airport security camera video from the night of the accident. You might want to use your facial recognition software to see if you can spot this woman in the crowd, especially in the vicinity of MH370, or better yet, boarding MH370. You two have a good day now."

The three parted company. Miles and Sloan waited for the elevator, and Jacobs walked toward the building exit. He smiled slightly as he pushed open the double glass doors and thought, *I'd love to be a fly on the wall and hear the conversation those two are having right now.*

Later that day, as Miles walked to the cafeteria, she passed Sloan's cubicle and saw him hunched over his computer keyboard. "Excuse me, Brian, what are you doing?"

"Oh, hi, Ana. While you were busy working with those Boeing and Inmarsat engineers, I thought I'd check out the airport security camera video. I'm curious to know if our journalist friend is onto something or just full of crap. I finished loading everything, including the photograph of Addison Stark, and I'm just about ready to run the facial rec. Wanna watch?"

"Sure do. Go . . ."

"Before I start, let me tell you how this will work. I've got the videos sequenced, starting with the cameras monitoring the passenger arrival area at the curb outside the terminal. Then there's a video in the terminal area before the security checkpoints. After the checkpoints, three camera locations record along the concourse route to three-seventy's gate and gate waiting areas. Ready?" Miles nodded, and Sloan pressed the ENTER key on his keyboard. The video progressed, faces flashed on and off in the upper right corner of the screen, the software searching for a match. The security checkpoint camera focused on people approaching the two security guards, who check identification and boarding passes. A woman wearing a broad-brimmed hat happened to look up—the image on the screen froze—and the word "MATCH" appeared on the screen.

"Damn, he's right. Look. It's the same woman they fished out of the ocean—Addison Stark!" Miles leaned closer to the monitor and told Brian to continue. "Let's see how many times she shows up after security."

Brian pressed the ENTER key a second time, and the process continued. It stopped again when the second camera along the concourse caught a three-quarter view of a face under a broad-brimmed hat. "There she is again. She's heading in the right direction. She's halfway down the concourse, and three-seventy's gate is at the end." Sloan started the recognition process a third time, and the footage ended with no more hits. "Damn it, wouldn't you know it. Talk about close but no cigar."

Ana smiled and patted Brian on the shoulder. "I love your American slang. Not sure what that means, but she boarded a flight to somewhere that evening. The only problem is—there were, maybe, twelve gates with departing flights past where we last saw her. So how did she end up in the middle of the Indian Ocean less than twenty-four hours later, regardless of *what* flight she boarded? Listen, I was on my way to the cafeteria to get something to eat. Want to take a break and join me?"

"No, you go ahead. I want to pull the security video for those other gates and see if I get any hits. Stop by on your way back. Hopefully, I'll know something, one way or the other."

Thirty minutes later, as Miles headed back to her office, she stopped by Sloan's cubicle and held two cups of coffee in her hands.

She placed one next to Sloan's keyboard and sat down on the chair next to his desk. "Here you go, and you probably need a jolt of this."

"Yeah, thanks. I wish there were a remedy for frustration. I ran the security camera video for all the departing gates on that concourse, but no hits. Maybe she was deliberately trying to hide her face from the cameras by wearing a wide-brimmed hat because she was up to something that would eventually cause people to look for her. I don't know, or maybe there's a logical explanation for this that we're just missing."

Miles leaned back in her chair and stared at the far wall for a short moment before she responded.

"I was just thinking. As investigators, we must focus on the facts and draw conclusions based on those facts. We can't let ourselves speculate unless it opens a new path to investigate, so here's what I suggest. That journalist reported that the woman the fisherman picked up mentioned a man's name—Walker—and the CIA. He also mentioned that he thought the woman, Addison Stark, worked for the Australian Secret Intelligence Service, so let's shake those trees and see what falls out. We'll send official inquiries up through our respective chains of command to the directors of the CIA and the ASIS and ask if they had an operation going on that involved MH370. I think I know the answer, but all we can do is ask."

"Yep, I'm with you on that. Let's start writing this up. Maybe by the time we finish our report, they will have found the wreckage."

Ana rubbed her forehead. "As far as I'm concerned, the facts point to pilot suicide for our report. The plane may have been hijacked—we may be looking in the wrong part of the ocean—but all of that scenario is pure speculation. So let's write this up, present the facts we believe support our probable cause of pilot suicide, and let the chips fall where they may."

Two weeks later, Miles and Sloan got their answers. The American and the Australian spy agencies both responded with an emphatic NO. Miles and Sloan expected negative responses, but what bothered them was how the agencies framed the answer. Both agencies issued a suggestion of pilot suicide as the cause of the disappearance. "Further investigation into this allegation will have a negative impact on national security. If you persist, you do so at your own peril."

"I guess that's that, but I don't like being threatened."

"Yeah, neither do I," Sloan added. "Just as well, though. There's not much left for us to do except finish our final report and submit it to the Malaysians."

<hr>

Sitting at his laptop, Noah Jacobs typed CONTROL-SAVE on the finishing touches of his final draft of his lengthy article for the Associated Press. They were expecting the story as an inspired explanation of the disappearance of MH370 and the untimely coincidence of the "package" and subsequent CIA and ASIS chase versus the distorted thinking of a very troubled pilot. Noah, restating now what he thought he knew, thought to himself, *You could not have written a fictional novel and made up a better story.*

Taking a deep breath and a long exhale, he reflected on the unsuspecting passengers and crew who had never made it to their destinations that morning. *He should call Hope Lee.* He and Hope had talked several times since they had first met at her news conference a month ago in KL. But now, Noah had a story to share. While she would not necessarily like the ending, she might well appreciate the heads-up on his new revelations and his investigation's facts.

Hope Lee answered on the third ring. "Oh, hi, Noah, nice of you to call. Yes, I have time to talk about MH370. . . ."

"Hope, I just finished writing my story for the Associated Press. It could be published soon, so I wanted to give you a heads-up to ready yourself for this next news cycle." Hope had recently reflected on the expansion of information she had received after the news conference—and how many additional questions had arisen now.

The reports on Malaysian agencies and their embarrassing performances were deflected according to each department's political power structure. Being the politically weakest department, the Ministry of Transport Air Traffic division took the biggest fault-finding hit for its misconduct, followed by the performance from Malaysian Airlines and its misuse of its flight following system. Simultaneously, the RMAF skated sideways on their lack of attention to intercept a rogue aircraft, one that they had later deemed "friendly" with no hard evidence. This was likely a distinct cover-up for the very likely fact the air force was sleeping that night, and it never saw MH370 in real-time but manufactured their response, days later, after reviewing the radar videotapes.

Hope also recalled the delays and time lost before beginning the search and rescue operations, first in the South China Sea and later, the Malacca Straits and the Andaman Sea. The fog of confusion surrounding these events quickly caused the public to forget the mistakes made and reported the day before. As the search and rescue drama played out on the nightly news—whenever a new piece of metal, or oil slick, or the discovery of the infamous satellite 7th arc, moving the search squarely in the south Indian Ocean—all this was a distraction from the investigation of what happened during the flight of MH370.

Noah spent the next fifteen minutes describing his investigation efforts to Hope, describing well-placed sources, having luck finding a fisherman with a "whopping story," uncovering likely American CIA and Chinese involvement and the possible coincidental airborne battle royal between the "package" chasers and a deranged pilot's suicide attempt.

Hope was stunned by the idea of pilot suicide, one that Noah could not fully corroborate. She had heard stories of Captain Zara's family trouble and knew of his simulator, but not in the details and nuances that Noah had uncovered. She was speechless at the accounts of possible international involvement of the CIA and ASIS chasing a secret "package" destined for China and possibly diverted to Diego Garcia. And his nearly perfect evidence trail of an Australian girl named Addison Stark being spotted at the KL airport that night and then being picked up in the southern Indian Ocean only hours later by fishermen as a transport plane flies overhead.

As Noah came to the end of his story, both became silent. Then after a few moments, Hope responded first. "This is quite a fantastic revelation on what may have happened on board the aircraft that night and subsequently in the Indian Ocean. With the aircraft parts that have now begun to wash ashore in Western Africa, I now know that Mom and the others are gone! It has been a hard pill to swallow for all the MH370 families. Thank you for sharing all this with me."

Noah, almost in tears, spoke softly and said, "Hope, I'm so sorry for your loss. May your mother rest in peace."

EPILOGUE

Double agent David Lee sat on his condo's balcony overlooking Mission Bay, north of San Diego. The late-afternoon sun warmed his body, easing the painful effects of his arthritis. He and his wife still mourned their son's death at the hands of Chinese soldiers in Tiananmen Square those many years ago, but at the same time, he felt thankful and happy for having had an opportunity to get his revenge. In Karachi, his CIA handler had received word that both the Chinese State Security and the Malaysian police suspected he had some involvement in the disappearance of MH370 and wanted to "talk" with him. So on a rainy Saturday morning four weeks after three-seventy's disappearance, an American extraction team whisked Lee and his wife from Pakistan only hours before Chinese and Malaysian authorities, accompanied by Pakistani security forces, arrived at his apartment's front door.

Lee reclined in his chair, and a small smile parted his lips. He considered himself a lucky man. When asked by the U.S. State Department authorities where he would like to live, Lee chose Southern California. After the Tiananmen Square massacre, one of Lee's uncles and family immigrated to the United States and settled in San Diego. Not only did the U.S. government bring Lee to America, give him a nice place to live, establish a new identity for him, but they also gave him the ten-million-dollar reward for his role in the successful mission to "retrieve the package."

It can't bring my son back, he thought, but it will help my cousin's three children get a good education.

Noah Jacobs sent a final copy of his story to his editor and told him he had finished his investigation and could release the story. When the *Star* published the report titled, *"Did the CIA Hijack MH370?"* it was immediately met with a firestorm of condemnation and denials from the Malaysian and the U.S. government. Local authorities discounted the story as nothing more than another conspiracy theory. After the Associated Press published his story, Jacobs enjoyed an intense but brief fifteen minutes of fame. He agreed to an interview with CNN, during which he laid out his case and his supporting rationale.

"I know my story lacks hard proof, but what makes up for that is the plethora of unexplained circumstantial evidence. For example, the woman fished out of the ocean after apparently parachuting from a commercial transport plane and her disappearance from the Perth hospital without an explanation. I believe there's strong evidence that one or more sovereign nations played a part in the disappearance of MH370."

The interviewer commented, *"But the Malaysian Transport minister said there was no conclusive evidence of foul play. So you don't believe him?"*

"No, I don't. I believe their investigation was a whitewash to make the Malaysian government look good. They repress anything that casts a bad light on themselves, especially regarding their incompetence shown immediately following the airplane's disappearance."

"Oh, how so?"

Jacobs inhaled a deep breath and explained that the Malaysian Area Control Center wasted four precious hours after receiving MH370's last transmission to declare the plane was missing. During that time, the Royal Malaysian Air Force never scrambled fighters to intercept and visually verify who was flying the plane. *"If that's not incompetence, I don't know what is."*

The furor lasted a week, and the Transport minister dug in his heels. He was adamant about the integrity of their reporting agencies and vocalized nothing would change his mind. He ordered Jacobs arrested, which he was, and Noah remained in jail for one week. The Malaysians wanted him to retract his story, but he refused. In the West, that situation would be called a "Mexican Standoff," and the Malaysians were the first to blink. Not wanting any more bad publicity, the Malaysian court ordered him released and expelled from the country. The public began to lose interest in the constant bickering, and the story soon became old news. Jacobs's story did catch the eye of the foreign news editor at the *New York Times*, who sent him an email and inquired if he would be interested in working for the *Times* in their foreign news division. His base of operations would be New York City. The *Times*'s offer brought a smile to his face. *Yes, I think I'll take them up on their offer. It would be great to work for them, and I'll be able to keep my promise to my brother. That's a win-win.*

Along the western coast, the Australian government erected a memorial to the victims of the missing flight. Symbolizing the passengers' religions, a large white-marble cross, a Star of David, and a Crescent Moon and Star stood in front of a semicircle of fourteen national flags representing the passengers' home nations. The inscription on a monument in the middle read: *"In Memory of 239 Lost Souls of MH370."* Local residents wondered why the government selected such a remote location and why the construction activity took place mostly at night and required several pieces of heavy earth-moving equipment—almost as if they were burying something. When curious citizens asked the local officials about this, all they got in response was a shrug and an "I don't know."

A man and woman walked arm-in-arm on a secluded beach twenty miles north of Perth. The late-afternoon sun had begun to set over the Indian Ocean as they spread their blanket on the sun-warmed white sand in front of a large boulder. They sat against the warm stone and faced the setting sun as it peeked between puffy white clouds. Addison leaned on Jack's shoulder and said, "I never tire of watching sunsets."

"Yeah, and I never tire of watching them with you." They relaxed, momentarily detached from reality, enjoying nature's beauty. Neither one realized, at the time, how deeply their experiences aboard MH370 affected them. Upon returning to their respective countries after completing their mission, they felt a strong and growing bond. They kept in touch, visited each other, and the bond continued to grow. Jack decided to take early retirement, and Addison left government service and returned to flying for Qantas. They began a new life together, but they both knew they would always be inextricably connected to the MH370 mystery. Addison thought, *I think I finally found someone who gets me.*

Notes on MH370 . . .

FROM A. A. ZICARD—MAY, 2022

I had worked in S.E. Asia since 2006. As an independent contractor for Boeing Flight Training Centers, I was teaching B777 pilots from various airlines in Korea, India, Turkey, Singapore, Hong Kong, and Taiwan. When the news of Malaysian Airlines MH370 first hit the streets, the disappearance of the B777 that March 2014 morning shocked world travelers. With spectacular worldwide headlines, the daily story took its toll on the aviation community: two hundred thirty-nine passengers and crew onboard disappeared into oblivion. On four continents, the families of those missing passengers were devastated.

From the beginning of this international spectacle, a media frenzy began. It was fueled by a lack of information but also included many dazzling theories. Media outlets competed for ratings. CNN news in America ran over four hundred reports and special programs for its audiences that next year, raising ratings. Sensational headlines were ever-present in the various daily "rags" of the world. AirlineRatings. com reported that over one hundred nonfiction books had been written on the subject. While some of these books are not substantial, quite a few serious writers have given their opinions on the events of that ubiquitous day.

Do you think it is easy to disappear in today's world? Consider the vanishing of half a million pounds of steel and aluminum, that was purposely built to be continuously available and electronically connected. In this modern era with twenty-four-hour radar, infrared mapping, and satellite surveillance covering most of the earth's surface, such a disappearance begs the question—how can a sophisticated machine, such as a B777 jumbo jet with its redundant communication systems and modern instruments, vanish without a trace? A common feeling of disbelief weaving through this disappearance story was the glaring lack of evidence - no crash site, little actual wreckage, no bodies or eyewitnesses, and the uncommon lack of communications from the pilots not reporting what was happening.

In July 2016, a large piece of the airplane wreckage (wing fla-peron) was washed ashore and retrieved on Reunion Island in the Indian Ocean. In later months, other wreckage components appeared on the African beaches of the west Indian Ocean. The discovery of parts from MH370 (confirmed by manufacturing serial numbers) initially buoyed hopes that additional clues would be found to help investigators pinpoint the crash location and reasons for the disap-pearance. But that did not happen. Instead, the story became strang-er, with more unanswered questions.

Not finding MH370's crash site or the cockpit or its black boxes has confounded the entire aviation community. The lack of specific information is exasperating. The abundance of possibilities and fol-low-on conspiracy theories is enormous, leaving the traveling public in a holding pattern year after year. The official Malaysian MH370 accident report (July 2018) states, "... *the investigation was unable to identify any plausible aircraft or systems failure mode that would lead to [1] the observed systems deactivation, [2] diversion from the filed flight plan route and [3] the subsequent flight path taken by the aircraft* ... **The possibility of intervention by a third party cannot be excluded either.**"

For MH370, known events collided with other outside circum-stances—mistakes from air traffic control, malfeasance in the airline operations department, lack of transparency from government agen-cies—all leading to confusion, chaos, panic, and terror for the pas-sengers, crew, families, the airlines, and bordering countries.

In this writing effort, you will find protagonists, antagonists, rogue criminals, and spies alike: along with those embarrassing events, mis-takes, misconduct, and cover-ups that are portrayed and dramatized. Was this international terrorism gone awry, a hostile takeover, or a pilot suicide that became a global fiasco for those involved?

As the surface and underwater searches have ended without

significant new information, one must wonder if, after eight years, finding the wreckage will help explain the mystery. Most likely, the plane location is deep underwater. Is MH370 in a million pieces or largely intact? Did she enter the water with flaps up, or did someone extend the flaps? Who, if anyone, was in the cockpit, strapped in a seat—the captain, first officer, or an unauthorized stranger? Can the flight data recorder and voice recorder be recovered? Are they readable? Will the transponder switch on the center console be in "standby" mode, explaining the disappearance from ATC radar scopes? Are all the oxygen masks out, hanging from the compartments overhead?

Yes, we can possibly garner additional information about what happened during the flight, but none of that will likely explain the "why" or "who" of what happened. This is the problem of our human mind acting out: The more facts we have, the more questions we can think of.

For more on the MH370 story with current news and updates, you can visit:

www.MH370-MysteryFlight.com

ACKNOWLEDGMENTS

June 2022

Here is a special toast to my lovely wife of forty-two years, Valerie, who was often found patiently watching me through the window panes of the doors to my office, and wondering whether I would ever rejoin society again. Yes, I am returning. We will be traveling together again this summer to New York City and Florence, Italy. My sons, daughter, and grandchildren did not hear from 'Pop Pop' much either, and I appreciate their love and patience with me.

Among my dear friends, fellow pilots, and fraternity brothers, I wish to acknowledge them for their support and encouragement; especially Bruce Rudolph, Tom and Barbara Fanta, Frank P., Pat Durbin, and Tom Miller, who were particularly helpful in their support and review of my writing drafts while suggesting valuable improvements. I love you all!

About the Authors
FROM A.A. ZICARD -- JUNE 2022

Since the late sixties, Jim Holling and I were friends, meeting as students and then as fraternity brothers at Parks Air College, St. Louis University. After graduation, we drifted apart, with only sporadic meetings at fraternity reunions. Jim became the consummate husband, father of two, aeronautical engineer, National Guard veteran, Civil Service safety manager, and a splendid mystery-thriller author. Art appreciated a thirty-seven year career with United Airlines, flying the various Boeing airliners as pilot, instructor and check airman, and marrying a beautiful flight attendant, together raising a family of four in Colorado.

Starting in the fall of 2019, Jim and I came together again to effect a fictional collaboration inspired by the events of the airline-based MH370 story. By then, Jim had three other fiction techno-thrillers to his credit. In the beginning, we thought that we could simply follow the known facts of MH370, sprinkle it with a liberal amount of fictional creativity, and the book would come together. Not so. The publicly known facts were fewer and farther between, and theories and speculation have long since taken over. With the public release of the accident report in 2018, the lack of information, missing data, and the remaining questions became the more significant story than the fewer reported facts. For example, "Who was flying the aircraft when the jet veered off course, and why was there no communication from the cockpit, with its numerous communication backups, as the airplane flew onward for six more hours?"

Given the international interest in this mystery fight, Jim and I proceeded with crafting the story. We rationalized that the public had not only an interest in the sensational and bizarre but also had a natural, healthy, shared curiosity for this story as a frequent member of the traveling public. In rendering the story, we attempted to simplify and explain many of aviation's fundamental elements regarding safety procedures, pilot duties and responsibilities, airline operations, and international traffic protocols. Sound boring? It is Not!. The dramatization is visceral and heart-pounding, while remaining easily relatable for the everyday passenger.

In the fall of 2020, with much of the initial storyline complete, Jim Holling got sick with COVID-19 and pneumonia and later died in the hospital in December that year. It was a personal tragedy for his family, and it was a sucker punch for me, losing my partner and good friend. Our book would not have happened without his experience in starting this project and teaching me the ropes. Thus, I have included a heartfelt dedication to Jim at the beginning of this book.

While the MH370 aircraft crash site has never been found, and its factual ending possibly forever in doubt, our book hopes to raise awareness and compassion from world readers desiring the facts, with trueful analysis, and corrections to the aviation industry as needed for the betterment of all.

We hope you will find it to be an excellent aviation read. Here's hoping you enjoy your flight!

For more information about the MH370 story and updates, or authors A. A. Zicard, J. E. Holling, see:

www.MH370-MysteryFlight.com

https://jimtheauthor.wordpress.com

For author information and speaking event details, please contact:

aazicard@gmail.com

Word of mouth is critical to an author's long-term success. If you purchased this book and appreciated it, please leave a review on the Amazon author's sales page. Thank You.

J. E. HOLLING BOOKS

The selections below of J. E. Holling's espionage-techno-thrillers are available in paperback and eBooks at Amazon.com:

https://www.amazon.com/-/e/B06XCX6MVQ.

www.jimtheauthor.wordpress.com

The Falcon's Revenge is J. E. Holling's debut novel. The aviation theme of his novel is not a surprise considering Hollings's background. He's held positions in engineering, program management, aviation safety, and the military. His first fiction novel draws on these lifelong interests and experiences. His second fiction novel, *An Evil Among Us*, is the sequel to *The Falcon's Revenge* and continues to explore current topics concerning weak borders and terrorism. Technical writing was always a big part of Holling's work. Now, he turns those long-honed skills to the task of telling a compelling story . . . a story that could be tomorrow's headline. Mr. and Mrs. Holling are now deceased, survived by two grown children.

What has a war orphan, a terrorist organization, and an F-16 fighter jet got in common? The answer is the motive, method, and means for revenge. Prior to the start of Operation Enduring Freedom, a young Afghan boy's parents and younger brother were accidently killed, and his sister was critically injured by American commandos. The seed of motivation is planted. A terrorist organization called the Warrior Brotherhood provides the method by nurturing that seed to adulthood and indoctrinating the young man with radical religious and political beliefs. When he's an adult, he learns to fly and joins the fledgling Afghan Air Force. The third leg of the triad is complete. He is sent to the United States to learn how to fly the F-16, a.k.a. The Fighting Falcon. He finally has the means, and soon, the opportunity, to exact his revenge. One of the Warrior Brotherhood's international terror cells ships weapons and a stealth drone to Mexico from their secret base in the Cape Verde Islands and smuggles the cache into the U.S. Dubbed Operation Falcon by the terrorists, its goal is to secretly arm an F-16 and attack a large public gathering at an airshow celebrating Military Appreciation Day. The airshow VIP list includes the president of the United States, government officials, and defense contractor CEOs. A recently retired FBI agent, now private detective, Eric Tyson, discovers and tries to stop the terrorists from carrying out their plan. Betrayal and deception play out on the ground and in the sky of the American Southwest. Time is running out . . .

An *Evil Among Us* is the sequel to *The Falcon's Revenge*. In the sequel, the Warrior Brotherhood plans a second assault on America. This time, they team up with a North Korean nuclear physicist-turned-assassin. Together, they develop a modern weapon and deploy it on a high-altitude airship with the goal of bringing America to her knees. Eric Tyson, the FBI consultant and private investigator, returns to confront his old nemeses. After he thwarts an attempt on his uncle's life, Tyson becomes suspicious and investigates what seems to be a series of unconnected events. Following his gut instincts, he finds the connection and tries to stop the attack. Intrigue, blind corners, and dead ends fill Tyson's investigative journey. Before it ends, it will wind through three continents and affect millions of people. Will old-fashioned police work and obsolete technology foil the terrorists' modern-day plot? Can the forces of good prevail and stop an evil among us?

CPSIA information can be obtained
at www.ICGtesting.com
Printed in the USA
LVHW101648060922
727695LV00002B/195

9 781977 250582